The Deeps Beneath Castle Houska

Written by Erik Lange

Cover art by Erik Frankhouse

First Printing, 2019

First edition

ISBN 978-1-7324326-3-5

This book is dedicated to my wife Julie.
From a fortunate husband.

Synopsis

Thomas Davies' service to the ruthless and enigmatic Karl Lark continues. After almost six months of supernatural strangeness, all the while committing a breathtaking array of crimes, he knows more is coming. And the wait is not long...

A secretive corporation engages Mr. Lark to track down children kidnapped from its Bright Child Genetic Initiative, bringing Thomas into contact with undreamed of horror. All while continuing to support his employer's insatiable desire for ancient artifacts.

Between searching for genetically engineered children and dealing with ancient intelligences left on Earth long ago, Thomas is just trying to survive.

Ultimately this leads to a castle, built over 750 years ago. Its purpose is not to keep things out however, but to keep them in...

Chapter 1

"Tell me again Mike, why are we driving into the Black Forest in the middle of the night?" I say this while looking at the only other person in the car. Mike is smiling while enthusiastically driving our Volkswagen rental down a narrow German road.

Looking at him, it occurs to me for the thousandth time Mike is a handsome guy. At just under six feet tall, chiseled good looks, and military style short cropped black hair, and more than ten years younger than me. Lucky bastard.

"There are traces in this area of the Abomination we are tracking. Looking around with the Oculus I found an old, like hundreds of years old, abandoned mine. At least I am pretty sure it is a mine. It is a hole in the ground that serves no other purpose. There is a good chance that is where we will find it, so I informed Illych and he said to check it out. Cheer up Thomas; this can't be as bad as the Ukraine."

If Mike says the Oculus shows signs of the Abomination then it is probably here.

"Let's not talk about the Ukraine. The rush to get the Magi Balthazar home, being taken prisoner by a rogue Ukrainian military element, followed by a horde of Bound Humans, Abominations, and Lesser Created violently assaulting the compound we were being held in. We barely escaped alive and now we are tasked to go back and hunt down the strays." This particular Abomination has been attacking lone hikers and motorists on its way to this mine.

"We have been one step behind this thing all the way from Slovakia," Mike confirmed.

Is its goal to go to ground? Literally underground, trying to hide or lick its wounds? The why does not matter. Having seen what these things do to innocent people, hunting them is no longer a chore.

Turning to look out the passenger window I can see the trees on either side of the road arch overhead, creating a canopy that prevents starlight from shining down on us. Combined with the moonless night, it is pitch black outside. We could be driving in an unlit tunnel and be unable to tell the difference.

"Why the dead of night, Mike? This place is spooky enough in the day."

"After Hoia forest and the tunnels under Ellora you are still afraid of the dark?" From the tone in his voice I can tell he is enjoying my discomfort.

"Before Karl Lark brought me on board I was afraid of the dark. Now that I know what is out there it is not fear that I feel, it is terror."

Mike chuckles, "Thomas, this is recon only. If we run into anything we will leave. Anything hostile will show up on the Oculus way before we will be in any danger."

Shaking my head I consider his point of view. A former US Army Ranger, he has been with Mr. Lark for more than two years. Only in his late 20's Mike still has youthful exuberance and confidence in his indestructibility. I, being in my early forties feel none of that. Confidence makes sense from his point of view.

We drive in silence for another twenty minutes. I pass the time thinking how comfortable it was at the hotel we just left. Since our foray into the Black Forest is in the middle of the night, we prepared early and went to the nearest pub. Germans are a friendly bunch despite their poor PR. The beer was excellent and I got to watch several attractive German women compete for Mike's attention.

To be young and handsome has its perks. Not that I am an ugly duckling, similar in height to Mike with more average features. After almost six months working for Mr. Lark and the required physical training, my physique is better than average. On my own I could have found a date no problem, but when standing next to Mike….

Arriving at our destination ends my daydreaming. Mike pulls the car off the road and closes his eyes to operate the Oculus. After a few minutes in a shallow trance his eyes open and blink while he shakes his head. "There is no one or no-thing nearby."

Nodding in understanding, I debark from the vehicle. It is now one in the morning. Time to stop playing games and put our game faces on.

There is something primeval about a forest in the dead of night. Looking out into the black I know there is nothing even remotely dangerous within ten or more miles of where I am standing. Mike would have already seen it with the Oculus. The pitch black of the forest around me strangles my confidence regardless.

We silently exit the vehicle and begin pulling our gear from the trunk. If someone drives up on us right now they will find two grown men, alone in the dark, stripping down to being almost nude.

This is followed by dressing in black tactical gear. We carry a lot of custom gadgets, the foremost of which is the ComDat, a radio-like device with unlimited range that cannot be intercepted or jammed. I could in a submarine deep beneath the ocean on the other side of the world and my voice would come through crystal clear. And as far as I know, this tech is unique to our employer Mr. Lark's organization.

Installed in the helmet I am wearing are a number of microphones connected to a tiny computer. The sounds we hear are changed to protect our hearing from gunfire or help us detect soft noises like someone sneaking up on the wearer, very useful.

Between the night vision incorporated into our helmets, Oculus, augmented hearing, carapace body armor, and the guns we look the formidable pair to say the least.

Mike performs a communications check, "Illych, you copy?"

"Loud and clear."

"We are walking into the forest now."

"Understood, I will monitor."

This boring, businesslike military-speak comes through the ear pieces connected to my helmet loud and clear. Illych will sit and listen to us without comment for hours if necessary.

Mike turns and waves me to follow him across the line where the roadside ends and the forest abruptly begins. The good news: Germans are proactive in the care of their forests. The underbrush is minimal and our pace good. It is early winter making the temperature cool but not cold. Carrying this much gear is driving up my body heat and the low outside temperature is appreciated.

The night vision makes navigation pretty straightforward and Mike stops about every ten minutes to consult the Oculus.

With Mike surveilling our immediate surroundings it is ok to communicate. We could have been on different continents and the ComDat would relay our whispers.

"What kind of mine is it?"

"Abandoned."

Ha-ha, that did not help, "Is it a big hole in a hill or a hole in the ground?"

"I am not a geologist, it does not look like a natural cave and it goes down hundreds of feet with branches off the main tunnel. The entrance was filled in a long time ago from the look of it. It is hard to tell with the Oculus. I am not the expert with it like Mr. Lark is but I detected evidence of the Abomination we are tracking. The entrance to the mine is partially cleared, just enough for us to get in." Mike pauses, turns his helmet to face me, and finishes. "Now you know everything I do."

In our black tactical dress and full face helmets we are almost impossible to see in the dark night unless someone was very close and looking for us and Mike continues to assure me no one is nearby.

"I do not understand why we need to get so close. The Oculus has a range of twenty kilometers."

"Thomas, I already said I am not as good at this as Mr. Lark or Illych. We are getting this close because I have detected evidence of an Abomination but I cannot find the actual creature itself. We will keep getting closer until I have a solid identification. Now stop being a sissy about it."

"Fine I will stop asking."

"And I am not a sissy."

Making adjustments to our direction of travel based on what the Oculus is telling him, we travel at a good pace. Another ten minutes of stalking through the dark brings us to our destination. I expected a gaping hole in a hillside held open by creaking timbers or maybe something like the ring of stone around a well.

Instead what we find more resembles a man sized gopher hole.

The mine opening is filled with stone and earth probably from generations ago. There are no visible markers to show anything is here and the ground above the mine resembles the forest floor around it. Something dug a hole down to the entrance, scooping the earth out by hand, creating just enough room for a man to crawl in. Into a pitch black hole down into an abandoned mine...

"Thomas, you go first."

I look at Mike. He is not smiling. He is serious.

"I need to operate the Oculus as we go in and if something comes at us I need you to protect me."

Looking down at the hole I realize the dig is fresh and it is unlikely any safety codes were referenced during its creation. Shrugging, I hold my KRISS in front of me while activating the light under the carbines barrel, and begin crawling into the hole. Face down, I army crawl for more than ten feet through the tight hole causing my feelings of vulnerability and claustrophobia to combine in a most uncomfortable way. The earth is fresh, not muddy, a blessing of sorts. The gopher hole finally ends with me dragging myself free onto the crushed stone floor of the mine shaft proper.

Standing up, I find the mineshaft to be comfortably better than six feet tall. At this point the tunnel is still dug through earth, not stone, and a combination of stone and ancient wood beams support the ceiling and walls. In some places the dirt has broken though and heaped along the walls and on the floor.

Moving to the left side of the tunnel with my KRISS at the ready, I wait for Mike. A few minutes later he crawls into sight, stands up, and begins with the Oculus again. Most of the time when an Oculus is consulted it takes one or two minutes. Experience speeds up the process. The more detail needed, or the more complex the target, the longer the duration.

I look at my watch and determine Mike had been consulting his Oculus for almost five minutes. "Mike, are you ok?" I had to ask. He is new to operating the arcane device but this is ridiculous.

He closes his eyes and shakes his head. "This place does not make sense. I can find traces of the

Abomination, like it is here, but I cannot find the actual creature."

"Flip-trap?" I spoke it as I thought it.

"This would be the perfect spot for an extra-dimensional mouse trap,"

"No, I have seen flip-traps before and none are present." Mike is firm in his rebuttal.

Our whispered exchange ends with Mike indicating with a hand gesture we are moving deeper into the mine. The tunnel slopes downward at a steep angle and not much further along the dirt walls change to solid stone. Looking at the tool marks on the rock surfaces around us I suspect this mine was made before the invention of dynamite. It would have taken years and years to cut the tunnel we are walking through.

Coming upon the first branch, Mike consults the Oculus again. This time it is quick and he announces the side tunnels contain nothing of value.

Our footsteps are loud, echoing off of the rock surfaces and through the tunnels. The gravel and rocks we walk upon are an uneven and unpredictable surface producing noise with every step. It also does not show footprints making it impossible to know if anyone or anything has traveled this way recently. Mike is positive nothing is alive in the mine thus there is no need to be quiet. This is a good thing, because if anything is here, we are not going to surprise it.

After walking several hundred feet and ignoring a half-dozen side tunnels we find ourselves in the entryway to a larger chamber. Standing in the opening I paint the chamber with my light, finding it at least fifty feet across and almost that high. After scanning the walls and ceiling and the other tunnels leading away from the chamber I finally point the light at the floor.

There is blood, a lot of blood.

It covers the whole center of the chamber in splashes, sprays, and congealed pools. Where it dried it shows up as black on the grey stone. Some of the pools have not completely dried and retain their characteristic red color.

Mike speaks first, "This is where I am getting signs of the beast. Apparently I was picking up its blood. But where is its body?"

He closes his eyes to consult the Oculus and I take a few steps into the chamber to get a better look at the mess on the floor.

Mike yells out, "Thomas!" while lunging forward into the chamber. He grabs my shoulder pulling me back towards the entryway with such force I stumble back several steps and fall down on my backside.

Mike is now in front of me not more than a single step into the chamber and a great huge black form appears in the light from his KRISS. It is impossible to make out what it is or where it came from in the chaos of the shaking light. Mike yells out while firing off a long ragged burst from his weapon and then falls backward into the tunnel landing on top of me.

The only two light sources available are mounted on our carbines and they are obscured as we struggle to extract ourselves from an undignified situation. Our night vision compensates for the light level but the constant changing from bright to dim is washing out our ability to see.

Whatever just appeared is not the friendly neighborhood welcoming committee. I one-handedly point my KRISS into the chamber and fire off a long burst. Something in there lets out an impossibly loud feline roar I can feel as much as hear.

With no small amount of exertion I roll and extricate myself from Mike lying on top of me. Quickly jumping to my feet I turn to face the chamber and fire another long burst. There is no way to tell if I hit anything and no growl is heard in reply.

Briefly taking my eyes from the chamber I look down to see Mike curled up in a semi-fetal position. This is not good. With the KRISS in one hand pointed towards the chamber, I reach down with the other and grab Mike's collar. Leaning back I start dragging him up the way we came. Every few feet I fire another burst into the chamber. After several such bursts I pull the trigger and hear the click of an empty weapon and feel the icy clutches of fear. After a practiced reload I risk another look at Mike.

He is being too quiet with his arms wrapped around his chest like he is hugging himself. Everywhere I look on him is covered in fresh, wet, red blood. Whatever is back in the chamber slashed Mike's chest open while knocking him back into the tunnel on top of me.

The thing in the chamber lets out a low, guttural growl so powerful the loose stones on the ground shake. Without a thought I point the KRISS towards the chamber and let off another burst.

"Mike, can you walk?" I am terrified. That thing appeared out of nowhere and is almost the size of a horse. The gunfire seems to be keeping it at bay for now but based on past experience that will not last much longer.

"Yes, help me up." I feel relief hearing his whispered voice.

Gripping his offered hand I pull and he slowly stands with a groan. When Mike's arms fall away from his chest his injuries become visible. Four parallel slashes from collar bone to midway down his abdomen. Nothing is gushing blood or hanging out; this is good. He is pale and his face betrays how painful the injuries really are. My guess is the only reason the former Ranger is remaining upright is adrenaline and force of will.

Mike points his KRISS down the tunnel and fires off a burst. "Thomas, re-load your weapon before mine goes dry. Then reload mine while I will use the Oculus." I do as instructed and point my weapon down the corridor towards the chamber.

Mike's eyes close for a bit. When he opens them while coughing a humorous half-chuckle, "It is a gigantic cat, like a lion or tiger only much, much bigger."

It is a living thing and our weapons will be effective. That is what Mike is really saying.

"It is stalking back and forth in the chamber. I think the gunfire startled it."

We begin shuffling backwards while keeping our weapons at the ready. I start to ask Mike about our escape plan when the monster in the chamber roars. My earpiece protects my hearing but the roar is as much a physical force as a sound that I feel in my bones. This is the voice of an apex predator when it is angry and wants to kill something. We just made the Tyrannosaurus Rex of felines angry, this can't be good.

In spite of the deafening roar, the microphones in my helmet pick out the sound of disturbed stones on the floor. It is coming.

Mike's injuries do not stop him snapping his carbine to his shoulder and I follow suit. The military grade tactical lights on our weapons illuminate the tunnel the fifty feet to the chamber opening. A feline head almost two feet across with the features of a jungle cat surges into view. The low ceiling of the tunnel prevents pouncing or jumping, it is barely big enough for the cat's enormous body. In spite of the closed space, the thing is fast. We will never be able to outrun it.

With at most, a hand full of seconds before the things monstrous jaws end us, Mike and I open fire at the same exact instant. The KRISS is a supremely controllable weapon when fired on full auto, the reason we carry them. And each weapons magazine contains twenty five rounds of brass jacketed hollow points in 45ACP, a round specifically engineered to put a man down in one shot.

The giant cat fills the tunnel completely, and missing is almost impossible. We empty our weapons in less than two seconds and it is barely enough. The giant cat crumples and stops moving a mere five feet in front of us. The feline features of its giant head a ruin of bullet impacts.

We reflexively reload and Mike does not hesitate to empty another magazine into it. No sooner does his weapon click empty and he shudders, slumping against the wall, his KRISS falling from his grip. His need for immediate medical assistance now very obvious.

Through the ComDat Illych hears everything. Thankfully he is a combat veteran and knows better than to distract us. I need him now though.

"Illych, Mike is badly injured and there is no way I can get him out of this place. No one else is observing us. Do I have permission to translate out?"

"Affirmative," His terse reply reassuringly comes through loud and clear.

I reach into one of the many pockets in Mike's trousers and pull out a six inch long brass baton. Holding it with both hands I give it a twist, unscrewing one end from the other. Flipping one end I screw the pieces back together.

No sooner does the baton twist closed and the world around us goes instantly black. A fraction of a second later we find ourselves on a black stone floor in the middle of a circle of black stone pillars. The air is cold, below freezing, and it is twilight dark. We just translated from the mine tunnel to a place called the Compass. Illych is there, waiting just outside the stone circle with a stretcher on an electric cart. Leaving the cart, the former Green Beret runs towards us. He is a tall man and crosses the distance in fewer strides than it would take me.

Then the nausea hits.

Translating has a nasty side effect of bad nausea that lasts for about a minute. Mike cries out from it. I can only imagine what the pain of his wounds combined with side effects of translating is like.

As soon as the nausea ends Illych and I carry Mike to the stretcher, activate it, and start down the smooth stone road towards the Citadel at a jogging pace. The stone road from the Compass to the Citadel is perfectly straight and level and takes about thirty minutes to walk. At this rate we will make it in twenty. Although Mike looks terrible, his wounds are not immediately life threatening. We just need to get him back to the Citadel for the Doctor to patch him up.

As we quick-walk, Mike is silent and Illych and I discuss the events in the abandoned mine.

Illych speaks first, "I was listening the whole time. How did this cat thing get the drop on you? The Oculus should have seen it from miles away."

"Mike did not see anything with the Oculus. The big cat just appeared like it translated in. If Mike had not pulled me back into the tunnel I would probably be dead."

"I will report this to Mr. Lark after the Doctor patches up Mike."

The rest of the walk is in silence. The spaces between the Citadel and the Compass are populated by Lesser Created, ancient androids left here eons ago. Most ancient myths of Faeries, Goblins, and such are based on interactions with these strange creatures. They are not hostile per se, but exposure to them can have unintended consequences, such as time loss or death.

This means the walk from the Citadel to the Compass is not safe unless we travel in pairs and keep our wits about us. For the uninitiated individual such a walk would be fatal.

As we get closer to the Citadel I can see its massiveness, even in the gloom of this place. A great huge circular building a half-a-kilometer in diameter and at least ten stories tall rises up before us. Pitch black in color and only broken by a single gate with two huge double doors guarded by ancient Ushabti, Lesser Created Mr. Lark pressed into service as door guards.

The main gate doors open automatically when needed and as we draw close the doors open and the bright light from inside the Citadel temporarily blinds us. As soon as we are safely inside, the doors close behind us.

Wheeling Mike through the unnatural architecture inside the Citadel we arrive at the small square building the Doctor resides in. I am not fond of what will happen next. We transfer Mike to a gurney inside the waiting area. Illych grabs a small red stone off a shelf near an inner door and presses it into Mike's hands. Our wounded companion's eyes close into unconsciousness and Illych and I immediately stand back and away from the gurney.

Then the creepy part begins. A gangly green humanoid a little over four feet tall opens the inner door and walks out into the waiting room. It has huge solid black eyes showing our presence in their reflection. The Doctor silently pushes the gurney with Mike's unconscious form on it into the inner room, closing the door behind him.

Mike will be brought back out in about fifteen to twenty minutes on the same gurney completely healed. Waking up in the waiting room, healed, and fit for service. As long as you are still technically alive, not brain dead, when the red stone is put in your hand the Doctor can heal you. Even amputations are restored.

Illych and I stay long enough to watch Mike being pushed into the Doctor's work area. Then we leave to put away the gear and get our report to Mr. Lark.

Chapter 2

.

The next two days at the Citadel are uneventful. I spend my time at the library in study. Mr. Lark always makes sure I have a backlog of texts, tomes, and documents to review and comment on.

That is where I am, bent over a five-hundred year old tome with a jewelers loop in my eye when Illych, Mike, and Mr. Lark walk in. They sit in a circle of overstuffed chairs in the middle of the library and Mr. Lark waves me over to join them.

Mike and Illych are dressed as I am in black tactical. Mr. Lark however is doing the grey suit thing with his trademark cane and its oversized bronze sphere headpiece hiding an Oculus

Mr. Lark is an elderly man, if I had to guess he is in his late sixties, slightly below average height, a full head of all white hair combed straight back.

I join the three men in the circle of chairs.

Mr. Lark speaks first, "Keeping busy Thomas?"

I reply, "There is enough in this library to keep me busy for years Mr. Lark."

"Yes, I understand. For now though I will interrupt you. I want the four of us to discuss your recent experience in the Black Forest. Your report intrigued me so I took it upon myself to visit the abandoned mine. How something so large was missed by Mike is difficult for me to understand. He is not an expert with the Oculus but his skill is sufficient to see something the size of a grizzly bear from miles away. I considered that perhaps we have a training or technology issue."

Mike interjects, "I was focused on the Abomination we were tracking, that is probably why I missed it." Mike, like the other ex-military men at the Citadel takes pride in his skills. Missing something so obvious is a slight against his perceived competence.

"Mr. Daugherty, you missed nothing. Relax for a moment while I explain. The liger that almost consumed both you and Mr. Davies was not visible to the Oculus."

"Wait, what is a liger?" I had to ask.

"The giant feline in the abandoned mine is a natural living creature called a liger. It is the offspring of a male lion and female tiger. They grow to epic proportions. The largest ever recorded was over twelve-hundred pounds. The one you encountered was smaller, just over nine-hundred pounds. After determining what it was, I used the Ouiblet to translate its corpse somewhere else where it will never be found. Then I took the time to carefully analyze the entire chamber where it had appeared."

I found myself leaning forward on my chair in anticipation while Mr. Lark paused.

"You missed the liger because it was a trap and a unique one at that. When we rescued Balthazar from Hy-Brasil we transported him in a tesseract he called a Quixault that he provided. The liger was being kept in a very small Quixault, in stasis. When something enters the chamber the cat is ejected into it."

"Due to their fantastic size and metabolism, ligers consume significant amounts on a daily basis. The liger basically appears out of thin air and eats whatever caused it to appear. Then the Quixault eventually sucks the creature back into stasis until the next victim appears."

Illych spoke next, "Why? Was this thing guarding something?"

Mr. Lark smiles, "No, there was nothing of value anywhere in the mine. The liger I believe was there to take care of a cut-out, so to speak. Most likely the Abomination was mentally compelled to go to this mine when its mission is complete or it is unable to locate its masters. It dug its way into the mine and went to the chamber as it felt it should do. Then the liger appears and eats it. No more loose ends. "

Now I was beginning to understand. All those things chasing us across Europe had mostly disappeared. Once they had failed to stop Balthazar's return, the Adversary had disposed of the evidence. It was a ruthlessness that reminded me of Mr. Lark's policy regarding those who wish to leave his employment.

Mr. Lark continues, "This use of the Quixault is difficult to detect with the Oculus. I had to be within a few feet of the actual construct. In the future we will need to take into account such devices when entering unused or abandoned places."

All of us nod in agreement. It was just another hazard to toss on the pile of nightmare ways to die in service to Mr. Lark.

"Illych, next is your report."

We all turn to look at Illych.

"Held and Tank have been backtracking across our previous path in Europe. They have also been checking news releases. There has been a rash of bodies found, especially in Austria and Slovakia. The Adversary has been eliminating the people it kidnapped and bound into service to hunt us. I was reviewing the list and found something that resembles a grouping. At least half of those who disappeared and then were subsequently found were from numerous locations on our path."

"However, about half of the victims are grouped by a single association. A tour bus in the Czech Republic crashed, killing everyone on board. I have the passenger list. Several of the people claimed to have died in the bus crash have been found along our path. The local authorities covered it all up but we found out anyway."

This is interesting and I had to interrupt, "Where was the bus when it crashed?"

Illych looks at me and frowns, "Patience Thomas, I am getting to it. The bus was taking a tour group to a place called Castle Houska in the Czech Republic."

It is now Mr. Lark's turn to speak, "This has led me to send you back to the world Thomas. I will set you up in a hotel somewhere in the USA, your choice, so you have internet access. Get the materials you need and research this Castle Houska."

Electronics are forbidden in the Citadel. We can have simple stuff like an electric cart and flashlights but computers, phones, and internet connections are strictly forbidden. The Lesser Created can exert influence over them. Mr. Lark's enforcement of this policy is very strict.

"After you have completed your assessment we will meet again. Then plan on visiting this Castle Houska as a tourist, with either Mike or Held to accompany you. They can use an Oculus up close. Depending on what is found will determine next steps."

Mr. Lark made a point of looking at me directly, "Don't dawdle Thomas. Get what you need and then return to the Citadel. I want this moving forward as soon as possible."

He stood while I was still nodding, "I have to leave now. Illych will contact me when you have something to report." Mr. Lark, without so much as a handshake or a goodbye, walks out of the library. Probably on his way to the Compass to whatever he does when he is not here.

All the members of the team stay at the Citadel when not on a mission or on vacation. Mr. Lark however only visits briefly. What he does or where he goes when not here is a mystery to all of us.

After Mr. Lark is gone, Illych speaks, "Where are you going to setup in the world Thomas?"

"It does not matter, some random decent hotel with internet that I have not been to before."

"Understood, I will let Mr. Lark know. He will probably leave a dongle at the Compass within a few hours. You might want to start getting ready."

"Will do."

Mr. Lark must have been in a hurry because Illych is back in the library in less than an hour to tell me the dongle is waiting. I quickly pack and the two of us leave for the compass.

Keeping the Ouiblet a secret is a big deal to Mr. Lark. Teleportation will draw a lot of attention should anyone find out. So when setting up arrival points in the real world, it has to be a place where people are unlikely to be. Parks and abandoned buildings are popular and we do not use the same place twice.

The Ouiblet translates me to a park not far from a hotel in Texas. All I have to do is cross the street and check in. The phone in the room connects me to the nearest store from where a laptop is delivered to my room. That takes less than an hour and I am connected to the internet. Every time I need access to the internet a new laptop is purchased. When I am finished I abandon it. Mr. Lark has something close to an obsession about the internet, tracking, face recognition, etc.

Mr. Lark maintains fellowships with prominent libraries and knowledge repositories around the globe. They are expensive, internet accessible, and very useful.

Within hours I have pictures, maps, and the history of Castle Houska or Hrad Houska as it is referred to locally. My quick analysis tells me nothing about the castle makes sense. Nobody ever lived there and it is not in a strategic location. I make notes, print a bunch of copies out and leave. After checking out of the hotel I walk back across the street to the park I arrived in. While passing an empty park bench I casually place the laptop down for anyone to take. Fishing the dongle from my pocket and grasping it with both hands I make the motions so the Ouiblet can return me to the Compass.

Arriving in the cold and gloom that is the Compass I walk into one of the hexagonal steel vaults surrounding the stone circle and used the ComDat left for me to contact Illych. Travelling the wild spaces between the Citadel and the Compass is dangerous when alone so I must wait for a travel buddy to get to the Citadel.

Expecting Illych and one of the other men, like Mike, to come and get me, my surprise is genuine when Illych walks into sight with Mr. Lark beside him. Something is up. Mr. Lark is not coincidentally leaving just as I arrive.

The two men walking towards me continue straight into the Compass. Mr. Lark speaks first while waving me to join them, "Thomas, I hope your research expedition was successful. Unfortunately something has come up and we will need to wait until another day for your report."

He continues, "Please put the results of your endeavors in the vault with the ComDat. We are leaving."

This is confusing. Something important must be going on for this sudden change, "Right now?"

"Right now."

Chapter 3

Working for Mr. Lark is never dull and today is no exception. It started out getting ready for a visit to Castle Houska and instead, immediately after my return, we translate straight from the Compass back into the world.

Earlier today I arrived in Texas mid-day and returned after night had fallen. It is easy to figure out the approximate time from the position of the big bright thing in the sky. Unfortunately there is no night or day in the pocket dimension wherein the Citadel and Compass exist because there is no sun to rise or set. It is a real possibility to lose track of what time it is back in the world and the day or night come as a surprise every time we translate back to the world.

The translation from the Compass ends with us in a hotel suite. The windows all have their drapes pulled shut preventing me from looking outside. From what little I can see, it is night out. Extrapolating from my recent visit to Texas, most likely we are in North or South

America. The small room we are standing in is central to a suite in the middle of the open concept layout. Around us are overstuffed chairs and a sofa in a circle.

Illych and I stand still while enduring the post-translation nausea washing over us. Mr. Lark, who is unaffected by such mundane things, stands patiently waiting for us to recover. Then he waves us to take a seat.

Once seated he speaks, "An opportunity has come to my attention that will have a significant positive impact on my organizations operating fund. The search in Europe will be continued by the other team members. We three will be traveling to Argentina late tomorrow. There is a remote research facility in the Patagonia region that has lost valuable, possibly irreplaceable, research assets under unusual circumstances. The research sponsors are willing to pay a significant finder's fee to have them returned. No questions asked."

"I have decided to bring both of you. Illych, you and I have done similar work before and you know what to expect."

Illych nods in agreement.

"Thomas, I want to take this opportunity to instruct you on my expectations during the fact finding visit we are about to undertake. The client will be bringing us into their secret facility to give us background and allow for us to investigate their loss. This is a very sensitive situation. They will be showing us their dirty laundry, so to speak. We must demonstrate we can handle the confidentiality required for such an activity. Discretion in what we discuss between ourselves and the questions we may pose to the client is critical."

"As such you will observe only. Do not speak unless I give you express permission. There may be things you will see that offend your personal sensibilities."

He paused after saying this, leaned towards me while looking me straight in the eye. "I do not care how offended you may feel." His voice took on a sinister tone as he said this.

"You will keep your opinions and comments regarding your perception of the clients business and its moral implications to yourself. We are there to recover whatever they have lost."

"There will be no emotional heroics. My organization is not the resistance, you have not joined the rebel alliance, and we are not engaged in making the world a better place."

"Should you choose to ignore my instructions and prove to be a liability during this visit, Illych will quickly render you unconscious. Later, after our return to the Compass, I will translate you to the middle of the Pacific Ocean with a life preserver and for the remainder of your life you can consider your lack of vision."

I look at Illych. His face is blank but he nods, indicating he would do as described.

Mr. Lark's eyes were boring into me from scant feet away. He is not smiling. If I screw up during this visit I am pretty sure the Pacific Ocean thing will really happen. In my experience Mr. Lark's word is as reliable as the sun rising in the morning.

After a long pause Mr. Lark continues, "There is a suite for each of you in this hotel. Tomorrow morning there will be a delay in our movement to Patagonia. Thomas, you have an early appointment with a tailor in the morning. Other than that small detail, all of the equipment and personal items needed for the next few days are in your rooms."

"Illych, this is your room. Thomas, here is the key for your room. It is directly across the hall. I will be waiting in the lobby tomorrow at 7am."

With that said he stands up, fishes a dongle from a pocket and is gone.

I look at Illych, "What was that all about?"

Illych shrugs, "We do business with some shady characters. That pep talk was to get you in the right frame of mind. My guess is Mr. Lark is expecting that we will see some very messed up stuff over the next few days."

We say our good nights and retire to get a few hours of sleep, the clock beside my bed indicating it is already past the middle of the night.

I set the time on the alarm clock in the room and call the main desk for a wakeup call. After the talk Mr. Lark had just given me I really do not want to keep him waiting, even by accident. Looking at the hotel information in my room I discover this is Miami. At least I know where I am. In spite of the disturbing pep talk and the strange bed, I fall asleep instantly.

Promptly at 7am I am in the lobby, ready to meet the others. The lack of sleep is leaving me a little groggy in spite of the few hours I did get. As my companions show up I recall the tailor comment the night before. The first and second time I met Mr. Lark, he and the men accompanying him, were dressed in tailored grey suits, expensive tailored grey suits and apparently now it is my turn. The tailor is to take my measurements and have matching suits ready for tomorrow.

After the tailor Mr. Lark takes his leave. As he is leaving he hands the car rental keys to Illych, leaving us to our own devices for the rest of the day. The suits will be delivered to the hotel first thing tomorrow morning.

Now we have a car and time to burn in Miami. So we do what any reasonable visitor to Miami on a beautiful sunny day would do, find the beach and locate an outside coffee shop. The two of us sit down at a table with strategically placed chairs, watching the local wildlife.

It is a tough job but someone has to do it.

Illych is not in a particularly talkative mood but I am not letting him off that easily.

"What is the deal with the grey suits?"

Illych shakes his head from side to side, "Mr. Lark has quirks, Thomas, a lot of them. I made my peace with it years ago. I think the suits draw too much attention to us but he likes the look when we are operating in a formal capacity." Illych makes a quotes motion with his fingers while saying 'formal'.

The rest of our time is spent relaxing in the sun and watching the beach activities. Illych is not interested in answering any more questions and I soon grow weary of trying.

Hours pass before we return to the hotel and go our separate ways. Last night's lack of sleep combined with a couple of hours in the Miami sun has me sacking out instantly after a room service dinner.

The next day the suits arrive mid-morning and fit perfectly. Apparently they had been the only thing keeping us from leaving because no sooner am I dressed and looking smart and Mr. Lark shows up in the hotel lobby to collect us.

Illych drives. He and Mr. Lark are silent during the short ride. I take the hint to stay quiet and soon find our destination is a private airport. We are travelling on a chartered long haul executive jet. The flight to Patagonia is fairly long and Illych explains the pilots do not work for our potential client and not to talk to them regardless. Since they are in the cockpit behind a closed door for most of the trip, this will not be much of an issue.

Without delay we board and I find a comfortable chair, pull out a book and start reading. Illych is doing what most military men do during unexpected downtime, picking a comfortable chair, closing his eyes, and going to sleep. Mr. Lark sits apart from us, his eyes closed, while resting his hands on the brass sphere of the Oculus atop his cane.

I understand the flight is a necessary evil. Just showing up in a car in Patagonia would raise questions. Flights would be checked, border customs consulted, and questions asked. People would start to wonder how we just showed up, appearing out of nowhere with no record of us traveling by conventional means. Just translating in with the Ouiblet draws attention that is best avoided. Better to arrive in a way that does not raise suspicion or trigger questions difficult to answer.

Mr. Lark's Ouiblet is unique and the ability to instantly translate to anywhere in the world is an asset of incalculable value. It is also an inconvenience we must endure, starting half-way around the world from our destination just to protect plausible deniability.

After a few hours of quiet flight time Mr. Lark comes over to sit by Illych and myself.

"Thomas, we did not have time before we left to discuss your Castle Houska research. Please share the results of your efforts."

I do as instructed and relate the details of the castle's history. Even with giving the condensed version of my findings, the explanation takes almost half an hour.

I conclude with, "Based on what I have learned it is possible there is a reason behind the legends. There may be something underneath the castle that is being kept hidden. As is typical of similar situations there is no direct proof though."

Mr. Lark replies, "No proof you say? Why? How? Because there is no video tape of monsters crawling up out of the ground? Based on what you have described I am confident there is something of interest to me under the castle."

"You guess there is something there?"

"No Thomas, I know there is something there."

"I do not wish to test your patience but how can you know this?"

"The Greek's defined this thing called logic. You tell me a castle was built in the late 1300's over a span of 17 years. At that time in European history the local ruler would have cared less about the superstitious ramblings of the local peasants. The aristocracy would have only endured the expense of that castle if it was necessary. The castle is located in a place of no strategic value. The resources to construct it were considerable and from a practical standpoint, wasted."

Mr. Lark pauses and then continues. "The castle has never been occupied and does not have the normal requirements of a fortification, such as a cistern or well. Over a span of seven hundred plus years, in which hundreds of more useful structures in Europe have been destroyed in war or left to rot away, this useless structure has been maintained in good condition. Even with changes in ownership such as during World War Two and the socialism of the Soviet Union."

"No Thomas, logic proves there is more to Castle Houska than a legend and coincidence. You will go there after our return from Patagonia."

Mr. Lark then returns to his original seat leaving Illych and I alone again.

I look at Illych, "He has a way about him that is difficult to understand at times but his point is valid. So much about the castle points to it being a prison."

Illych nods, "And we are going to find out soon enough."

We sit quietly for a while listening to the faint roar of the jet engines. Then I decide to ask Illych something I had wanted to know for some time.

"Illych, you have been with Mr. Lark for more than eight years now haven't you?"

His passive expression remains unchanged during his reply, "Yes."

"Mike and Held have explained how they came to be with Mr. Lark and you know my story. Tank's reaction to the question makes me believe he will snap off my arms and legs before telling me. But you were by yourself with Mr. Lark for almost four years. How did you get into this?"

Illych looks at me and rolls his eyes. "You have caught me in the mood to talk, so yes, I will tell you how."

"I was in the US Army Green Berets doing a tour in Afghanistan. The military post we were on was shared with the Afghan Army. Turns out the Afghan soldiers have forms of entertainment people from the west would find horrifying, to say the least. Special Forces training will harden you to many thing but the screams of the victims kept me up most nights. The US officers in command told us to ignore it and not get involved. This is their culture and we had to accept it."

"One night one of the victims escaped into the open compound next to our barracks. He was being chased by an Afghan Army officer. One of the goals in training a Green Beret is to make an 'unbreakable' man. Unfortunately that night I broke. I walked up behind the officer. He did not even see me when I grabbed his head from behind and snapped his neck."

"I was promptly taken into custody for murder. There was a show trial for political purposes to make the Afghans happy. I was sentenced to twenty years solitary confinement in Ft. Leavenworth and reduced in rank."

"Two years into my sentence Mr. Lark translates into my cell in the middle of the night and offers me a deal. Exchange my prison sentence for permanent service to him."

Illych stops talking and there is silence in the plane for some time. I am aghast. That was one of the most horrible things I have ever heard. Illych is a good guy, tough but honorable. To be treated that way is awful. Killing the Afghani officer was probably a bit much but I was not there so who am I to judge.

Illych, apparently done talking, closes his eyes and in a few minutes the change in his breathing indicates he is asleep. I decide to follow his example and put a pillow under my head and close my eyes.

Illych nudges me awake after sleeping for hours and points out the window. We are circling our destination in preparation for landing.

The research facility has its own airstrip. From the air I see a circular central building surrounded by an elliptical outer building. From the air it almost looks like a giant eye. The outer elliptical building is huge, perhaps as much as a kilometer in diameter at the widest.

The landing strip has hangars and a terminal building. The terminal is in turn connected to the outer ring building. Everything looks modern, clean, and well maintained.

We land and after taxing to a stop, the stairway is lowered by the pilot and the three of us exit. Patiently standing outside is a man waiting for us. He is Caucasian, of average height, with dark hair, and lean build. His dark suit fits him well and his smile is practiced.

Mr. Lark takes the lead with Illych to his right, me to his left.

The man takes a few steps toward Mr. Lark and extends his right hand. "I am Dr. Paulo Hess, the director of this facility."

Mr. Lark takes his hand, shakes it once and releases it. "I am Mr. Lark."

"And your colleagues?" Dr. Hess says this while visibly appraising Illych and myself.

"Will remain anonymous. They are here because I value their opinion which they will share with me later."

"Understood, I trust you understand we do not invite visitors here from outside the program. This facility and everything you see here is never to be shared or publically revealed."

"This is known and does not require further discussion."

Wow, it was like watching two predators dancing. They want to work together but need to make sure the other knows the rules.

"Please follow me inside then."

We walked through the doors into the terminal. The building is modern and mostly done in white. The terminal halls are spacious and empty of other people. Dr. Hess walks at a good pace, leading us to the walkway connecting the terminal to the outer ring building.

"Mr. Lark, your organization was contacted because we have a number of people who have gone missing from this facility. Our own attempts to locate them have failed and due to the anonymous nature of our work we cannot pursue a search through more common channels."

By common channels I think he means law enforcement or anyone that might object to whatever is happening in this place. At least that is what I would guess.

Mr. Lark interrupts, "Dr. Hess, what is the nature of your work here? It will be relevant to how we pursue your missing people."

"This facility is dedicated to the Bright Child Genetic Initiative. The brightest minds from all over the world who wish their intelligence continued in their offspring work with us. Those children are then raised here."

"And they were kidnapped?"

"It is the only reasonable explanation for so many to disappear so quickly."

"How many children were taken?"

Not just children were taken. Over three-hundred and fifty children and adult staff have disappeared."

What? How can that many people just disappear? It is not like they would all fit on a bus.

Mr. Lark did not skip a beat, "When and where were they taken from?"

"We are walking there now. The central building I am sure you saw from the air, is the children's dormitory."

We walk through another set of doors that lead out into the space between the outer ring building and the inner circular dormitory building. The space between them is perhaps a hundred meters and features neatly trimmed grass with concrete walkways. There are no decorations or benches or anything else indicating the space is used for anything other than separating the two buildings.

I notice that while the side of the ring building facing outwards is solid windows to its six story height, the inside is without any windows. And where are the people? This is a huge facility and the only person we have seen is Dr. Hess.

The central building matches the ring building in height and only has external windows from the roof down to half its height. Looking at the construction of the buildings around us it is obvious this was not a dormitory for children, it is a prison and I am beginning to suspect Dr. Hess is telling us half-truths.

"The central building includes living spaces, male and female dormitories, and the classrooms for the children's education. We believe in a hands-on approach to learning so there are many labs and workshops to help enhance the children's learning experience in the lower levels."

Dr. Hess is proud of this place. You can hear it in his voice.

"The children and staff disappeared from this building. Their disappearance coincided with the disabling of the building's security systems. The security cameras went offline and we have no recordings of what happened."

"The outer support building did not experience any such loss of function. The disappearance happened very quickly, in a matter of minutes. By the time we knew what was happening and came to investigate, they were gone."

Mr. Lark is looking around very intently. "I need to inspect the entire building from top to bottom."

"I expected as much and I will walk you through the entire facility. There are three sub-basements and four upper floors. I suggest we begin at the bottom."

Whereas the outer ring building is almost clinical in its décor, the 'dormitory' is spacious and is in warmer colors. Complex and colorful art is mounted on the walls behind locked glass cases.

First we take an elevator to the lowest sub-basement. It is a mechanical space filled with piping and machinery for heating and cooling. While inspecting this lowest level, Dr. Hess shares that they brought in ground penetrating radar and found no tunnels or spaces outside the concrete foundation of the building.

The second subfloor is storage with wooden crates and furniture stacked throughout. Mr. Lark quietly walks the complete perimeter of this floor with his cane in hand. I know he is using the Oculus mounted on the cane to look deeply into our surroundings.

The sub-floor highest up has a break area for the staff and a small cafeteria. There is a medical room and a number of empty rooms. Either they are normally empty or their contents have been removed before our visit.

The windowless first and second floors are large, open laboratories. Benches with various test instruments are everywhere. Experiments in various stages of construction can be seen. There are hoses, cables and wires lying about the experiments. What they are or what they did is beyond my understanding. It is obvious these children were working on things I never saw in the schools I attended as a child.

The third floor is classrooms and a cafeteria. The classrooms were built for small class sizes of no more than twenty students. This floor has windows looking out into the sterile space between the buildings.

The final upper floor is the rooms for the students. Girls on one side, boys on the other, with a hall containing a chaperone's desk between. The rooms are small and tidy. Two children lived in each room and they look comfortable. I suspect the children did little more than sleep in them.

Mr. Lark says little during the inspection. Dr. Hess volunteers nothing and I think the understanding is that discussing why the children are really here and what they were doing is an off-limits topic.

The tour ends back on the first floor at the doors we had arrived through.

Dr. Hess stops us at the door, "Mr. Lark, do you have any other questions?"

"I need photos of everyone missing."

"I expected as much." Dr. Hess walks off to one side of the hall and reaches behind a desk near the entrance pulling out a binder which he hands to Mr. Lark.

Mr. Lark opens it. From where I am standing I see that each page displays the photo of a child. The photos are numbered full body shots. The binder contains no names, nor any other information. The children are not smiling in the photos.

"How many?"

"One-hundred and ninety-six staff and one-hundred and fifty-four children."

"The ages of the children?"

"They are divided between thirteen, fourteen, fifteen, and sixteen years of age."

"Is the contract exclusive?"

"Yes, all of our efforts have failed and there are no others available for the search."

"I accept. The search will begin immediately with no guarantees. If I am unable to locate them you will be notified through appropriate channels. I believe the terms are agreed upon?"

"Yes."

That said we are escorted back to our plane without further discussion and depart.

Once we are airborne the three of us sit in silence for almost an hour with Mr. Lark obviously deep in thought.

He breaks the silence with a question, "Your first impressions?"

I stay silent and Illych speaks first. "Whatever this Bright Child Genetic Initiative is it has nothing to do with those children being there voluntarily."

"That is obvious. What else."

"The building was scrubbed prior to our arrival. I suspect it was cleaned and equipment was removed."

"Agreed."

"They are genuine in their claim they do not know how these people disappeared."

Mr. Lark nodded, "Thomas, your impressions."

"The dormitories and class rooms made sense but what about the laboratories? What were the children working on?"

"Exactly! I recognized the technology. These children were working on advanced projects far from what is normal."

"Why would children ever work on such projects?" A valid question based on the complexity and size of the hardware involved.

"My apologies Thomas, my statement about not normal was not because they are being performed by children. The projects are not normal for any laboratory."

I continue, "I do not trust what Dr. Hess said. This disappearance may not be a normal kidnapping. It may have been an escape."

"Thank you Thomas, your insight makes me glad I brought you. As you probably suspect I was scanning with the Oculus during the inspection. The building has been cleaned. If they had not done so its appearance would have been radically different. The Oculus showed me that more than one-hundred people were ex-sanguinated in that building recently. Possibly as many as two hundred. The carnage left a significant amount of trace blood. I stopped counting after I found one-hundred separate contributors."

I had to ask, "Ex-sanguinated?"

"Murdered through blood loss, most likely with bladed weapons. I suspect the staff was slaughtered and the children taken or escaped."

Another long pause ensued.

"There are other things I observed which will take time for me to unravel. For now, we will return to the Citadel and prepare for your visit to Castle Houska. Upon your return I will have more to discuss about this investigation."

The flight back is quiet. I think we are all deep in thought about what we had just seen. It is a glimpse into something that left me feeling dirty just from having been close to it

Chapter 4

After landing in Miami, Illych and I quickly return to the Citadel to begin planning the Castle Houska mission. Mr. Lark says he needs time before starting the search for the Bright Child Genetic Initiative's lost personnel and I am fine not wandering the wilderness looking for what will either be children kidnapped by a gang of mass murderers, or a band of murderous children trying to escape their captors.

Neither version of the story will have a happy ending from where I am standing. The best outcome, in my humble opinion, is the children being found without my involvement.

For now, I am back in my lair in the library putting my notes on Castle Houska in order.

The good news is the visit to the castle will be a straightforward endeavor.

They have bus tours.

We buy tickets like normal people. No translating to a strange place in the dead of night while trying to not catch the attention of guards or monsters.

We are going in as tourists.

Illych informs me Held is my partner for the Castle reconnaissance. We will translate into the Czech Republic straight to the town nearest the castle and buy tickets for the castle tour. Held is an Oculus operator and will observe the castle. Afterwards we report everything to Mr. Lark.

We will be armed but only as a just-in-case. Being part of a tour group hopefully will make this an uneventful in-and-out mission. As I wrap up writing my notes, an idea comes to me. Leaving the library I go in search of Illych. There is a question that needs asking.

I find him in the first place I look, the cafeteria. Illych and Held are sitting together at a table discussing something over a cup of coffee. They both look up at me as I walk in.

I ask my question first, "Illych, what about Balthazar?"

Illych's blank expression tells me to add to my statement.

"Balthazar was around when Castle Houska was built and he owes us some favors. Why don't I visit him and ask about the castle? It cannot hurt our cause."

Illych nods his head and takes a quiet moment to consider what I had said, "I agree, we should gather every piece of intelligence available. I will check with Mr. Lark and see what he says."

That was the best I could ask for.

Illych asks me to join them at the table.
Coincidentally, he and Held are discussing the visit to
Castle Houska and they share with me everything is
ready. Based on my new request we will wait to leave for
the castle until Mr. Lark replies.

Illych leaves to send a message and I return to the
library to work on other things. There are no other
pressing issues calling for my attention so I settle into a
good book and relax. Mr. Lark has spent the last eight
years acquiring old books, text, codex's, and Lord knows
what else that was written hundreds or even thousands
of years ago. Now that I have joined the team and the
Citadel's library is setup I can spend the next several
years cataloguing and investigating the contents of the
shelves around me. If Mr. Lark never sends me into the
field again I will be ok with it.

That is where I am less than two hours later when
Held walks in. "Illych sent me to tell you Mr. Lark is
sending you to see Balthazar immediately. Collect what
you need to take with you and suit up."

As instructed I suit up in the all-black tactical gear
we wear when contact with the Created is possible. The
Created typically look for the radiated thoughts and
emotions when trying to find humans. Visual detection is
secondary for them. Mr. Lark has what he calls a 'crown'
installed in all of our heads to muffle most of our
thoughts and emotions to outside observers. The crown,
combined with all black clothing, reduces the chance we
draw attention of a nearby Created. Neither is a perfect
defense but it certainly moves the odds in our favor as to
who will see whom first.

I am ready in less than an hour. Illych tasks Held and Mike to escort me to the Compass. The three of us will translate to a location not more than an hour's drive from Balthazar's residence. We then wait at that location for another hour and a local vehicle and driver then delivers us to our destination.

Balthazar's home is located in what is almost wilderness near the Caspian Sea in Russian Federation territory. There are few towns or cities. What roads exist are rough and in many cases unpaved.

The vehicle is purely window dressing to maintain plausible deniability and we are not to talk to the driver. Balthazar does not know about the Ouiblet or translating and Mr. Lark will keep it that way.

Upon our arrival at the Kharkareth, Balthazar's residence, Held and Mike wait outside where our ride drops us off. They will wait for however long the meeting with Balthazar takes and will call for our transport to take us back when needed. I walk the rest of the way alone.

The good news is Balthazar had already been contacted by Mr. Lark and is expecting me.

The countryside around Balthazar's residence in the 'real' world is unremarkable. The nearest town is at least ten miles away. The terrain is open, with few trees and little in the way of signs of human presence.

The trip goes by the numbers and soon I am standing outside the location where the Kharkareth is located. The only landmark telling me I am in the correct location is a square pillar of aged and worn stone jutting from the ground.

Balthazar's residence exists in what Mr. Lark calls a non-Euclidean contraction. It remains part of the real world but was separated from it a long, long time ago. On a map it is just a point. When you cross over into it, though, you find it is a large circular space. It has weather, night and day and the sun shines down on it. You do, however, need a key to enter it when you reach the correct location.

I do not have a key.

So I stand and wait in what should be the right place. Not more than a minute later something shifts into view from the edge of my sight. The first time this happens it is disconcerting. I am expecting it though and do not react.

Standing in front of me is what mythology calls a Goblin. From my association with Mr. Lark I know it is really an ancient android of fantastic complexity. These androids make up a group of mythological entities Mr. Lark calls the Lesser Created.

The Lesser Created are very intelligent, physically stronger and much tougher than a human. They are also immortal. And dangerous, an uncontrolled encounter with a Lesser Created is usually fatal.

It was not because they are malicious. The Created, in spite of their intelligence, do not understand the concept of living creatures. They sort of play with humans, trying to figure them out, resulting in the subject's death.

This Goblin serves Balthazar. Standing at just over four feet tall, it has green skin and long thin arms and legs. Its gangly appearance is made all the more alien by its large mouth with crooked teeth poking out from between its thin lips. Add to this two very large solid black eyes and its appearance is very off-putting. The creature is dressed in what Balthazar probably considers a man-servants clothing.

It speaks to me in the voice of a young boy, "Mr. Davies, my master is prepared to meet with thee. Please enter. You are welcome in this place. Peace be upon you."

I bow to the creature and reply, "I am grateful for your master's consideration."

Without any further exchange of pleasantries, the Goblin turns away from me and takes a step.

And disappears.

I walk to the same location and in an instant I cross into the place where the residence of the House of Balthazar is to be found. In the distance, squats an enormous square ziggurat structure in the style of ancient Sumeria. This is no run-down ruin, however. The Kharkareth is in perfect condition and is made of polished stone with many windows and balconies. A stone road runs from under my feet to its front gates.

The residence has its own spirit and the building and the spirit are both called 'The Kharkareth'. If anyone in the real world knew of its existence, I guarantee it would be in the history books as a wonder of the world.

It has been over a month since my first and last visit. That had been our delivering Balthazar home after more than a 350 year absence. Back then the fields on one side of the road had been fallow for more than a century and the forest on the other side had grown tall and wild.

The fields are improved and show signs of care. The forest remains tall and dark.

Balthazar once had a full staff of mortal humans for the upkeep. His absence had been so long they had eventually been forced to leave.

I observe all of this as I walk towards the ziggurat.

The main gates are open and remain that way after our entry. Just past the great doors is an open space that extends all the way up to skylights overhead. During the day it is lit by the sun through the skylights. At night the stone pillars set into the walls luminesce and the white stone glows to provide light.

I expect to wait just inside the doors until I am called for. That is not to be. The Goblin waves me to follow it inside through another smaller, more human-sized, door, then another hall, and finally into a small sitting room with comfortable chairs. The lighting is dim but hardly dark and the Goblin indicates I should sit. The creature then leaves me alone without another sound.

The construction of the Kharkareth and everything contained within it are examples of what can be created when time and cost are not a limitation. I spend the next few minutes lost in the wonders on display in the room. Everything is a masterpiece, the furniture, tapestries and paintings mounted on the walls.

This is how Balthazar finds me when he enters, gawking at the decor. He is dressed in bone-colored robes. The Magi is short, maybe five and a half feet tall. His head is bare and he wears a golden skull-cap that seemed to be molded into his skull.

His eyes are dark and bright with intelligence and he walks with a confidence and fluidity usually seen in much younger men. Balthazar is a Magi, an ancient brotherhood whose members live well past a thousand years.

Balthazar had just returned from 350 years of exile on the phantom island of Hy-Brasil and looks none the worse for wear.

He bows and after straightening says, "Thomas, my savior, welcome to my home. I received Mr. Lark's message and replied immediately that I would receive you and fulfill part of my pledge to him."

"I must ask you to make your requests direct and specific. After so much time away I have no time for a social visit."

He then sits near me waiting for my questions.

So I begin, "We have been backtracking across Europe looking for the ones who tried to prevent returning here, to your home. There have been successes and we have rolled up most of the Abominations and Bound humans left behind. I also believe we have found a nexus where many of those who perished are connected. The place is Castle Houska in the Czech Republic. In the local tongue it is Hrad Houska. What can you tell me of it?"

The Magi does not reply immediately but is still while obviously considering what I have just said, "Yes, I know of it. To better understand what the castle is will require a brief history lesson. After the Roman Empire fell into ruin, Europe became a wild and dangerous place. Many of the things the Romans knew and kept in check were now free to cause mischief. Before the church stepped in to fill the void, a small fraternity of like-minded people banded together. They formed a militant and scholarly organization to contain the chaos. They were not political but rather more monastic and they founded a fortress to operate from."

"They called themselves the Scholomonari and their fortress the Scholomance and they were effective in preventing greater terrors from being unleashed. One of their last great works is Hrad Houska. Its purpose is to contain what is at the bottom of the pit beneath the castle. They could not close it and filling the hole in would not stop what is there from tunneling out. The castle is not just a physical barrier. It is also constructed using ancient knowledge to cap the gateway below. "

This explanation causes me to have more questions than answers.

"What is below the castle?"

"A description I have heard Mr. Lark use is appropriate if somewhat imprecise. He would call it a pocket dimension."

"The gateway to a pocket dimension is down in that pit? Why not just close it?"

"The Scholomanari lacked the ability to do so. They did the next best thing they could and capped the pit. The church turned on them shortly thereafter, believing the Scholomonari to be potential competitors. The Scholomance faded into history and the castle has stood as a barrier ever since."

"Do you know how to close it?"

"I do not share such knowledge. Not for reasons you may consider. That knowledge would reveal things better left unknown."

"Could the Adversary be using it as a place of power or to create its soldiers?"

"It is very possible. Mr. Lark must investigate the castle. If the Adversary controls what lies below the castle there will be more and worse trouble to come."

"What should we know about the things inside or what we might encounter?"

"Thomas, this will frustrate you but I have given you all the information you need."

"Please convey a message to Mr. Lark. He needs to enter the deeps below the castle. If the Adversary is there then it must be driven from it. There are ancient things below the castle that must be left in peace."

"You have nothing more we could use, like a map or a key or something?"

"It is time for you to leave now. I have enjoyed seeing you again. My servant will see you out."

Balthazar smiles, stands, and leaves without further interaction.

The Goblin servant shifts in from the edge of my field of vision again and indicates we are leaving. We retrace our steps and I am soon outside, back in the real world, trudging my way back to the others.

All Balthazar told me is the castle is there for a reason and it had been put there by an ancient brotherhood. It was bad if the Adversary is present and Mr. Lark must go there and clean up any mess we may find.

We are to storm the castle and fight the monsters beneath it. At least we did not have to rescue anyone.

And not die. Our other goal is to not die in the process.

Chapter 5

When the three of us return to the Citadel we find
Mr. Lark waiting in the library with Illych. He is sitting in a
chair paging through an old manuscript, his lips moving
while he reads. Illych is sitting a few seats away looking
bored.

Mr. Lark looks up upon our entry and nods to Illych
who picks up a ComDat from the table next to him and
says something I cannot hear into it.

Mr. Lark gets the first word in as he waves us to take
a seat. "Thomas, was your visit to Balthazar
educational? And more importantly, was it helpful to our
interests?"

I nod, "To a point. He gave me some of the history
behind the public story of the castle but his explanation
was short on specifics. At the end of our meeting he was
particular about sending a message to you though."

The expression on his face tells me this has peaked the old man's interest, "And the message?"

"You must visit the castle and determine what has happened there. His words, not mine."

Mr. Lark's face takes on a wistful expression and he is quiet for a minute while apparently thinking.

Tank takes this opportunity to walk into the library and choose a seat.

Tank is a Caucasian man just under six feet tall and a power lifter. He is proud of his Marine experience and is a combination of extraversion and belligerence that many people find irritating. The compulsion to lift weights has left him with a massive muscular frame. The ex-Marine's fearlessness is reassuring when fighting monsters or you need someone to carry your wounded body to safety. Personally, I think he is really obnoxious most of the time.

The big man looks at me as he enters, "Thomas, you are still in one piece. Good for you. What did I miss?"

Illych replies, "Thomas is just filling us in on what he learned on his visit to the Magi."

Tank is still looking at me, "And?"

Mr. Lark waves his hand, cutting everyone off, "Enough interruptions, Thomas, tell us everything."

I start at the beginning and relate everything Balthazar said. Everyone, even Tank, wait to comment until I am done.

Illych is first, "There is something to the place then."

Tank jumps in, "One thing is not clear: are we storming the castle or what is underneath it?"

Mr. Lark comments next, "The castle is a prophylactic for the real target. We need only concern ourselves with what is beneath, the 'deeps' as Balthazar calls them. With these Quixault traps just now coming to my attention, such as what Mike and Thomas experienced with the liger cutout in the mine, the normal method of translating directly in is not feasible. We will need to enter in a more traditional way. However the path to what is below is probably through the castle above."

"We will stay with the original plan of Held and Thomas performing a reconnaissance. Then we will break into the castle and storm whatever is beneath."

Everyone nods in agreement. If Mr. Lark says we are storming the castle then the castle is getting stormed.

He continues, "It is late and I need everyone rested. I have another task that requires the full team's attention for a single day. We leave in the morning."

This surprises me. We just established the Castle Houska mission is an immediate go and now we are doing something else. I had to ask, "The castle is going to wait?"

"Yes, Thomas, there is something more pressing to be resolved. The contract I accepted for those missing people in Argentina. While you were visiting Balthazar I did an extensive Oculus review of the facility we visited. The method involves translating an Oculus just underneath the target, taking a snap shot of a specific aspect and translating it back. A tedious process but undetectable by the subject."

I am sitting on the edge of my chair now, "You figured out how they were taken away?" This has intrigued me since our visit and I still have no clue. Plus, Mr. Lark's explanation of how the Oculus allowed him to spy on things is new and explanations from him are few and far between.

"Yes, I am uniquely knowledgeable on the method used. I have also conclusively determined they were not kidnapped. The children forcibly escaped."

"What about the teachers and staff? What happened to them?"

"The children murdered them all, violently. They then engineered an escape by a rather unusual use of physics. The murders of the staff, the technology in play, and the risk taking displayed by the children, demonstrate a remarkably high level of motivation. I suspect this research initiative has created something beyond their ability to control."

Illych interjects, "Are these children dangerous?"

"Yes, supremely so. They murdered almost two-hundred staff members in minutes and then affected their escape in a bizarre and almost impossible-to-duplicate way."

I had to ask, "So where are they?"

Mr. Lark continues, "I have located their exit point. Unfortunately, the method they used has left an after effect at the destination. I cannot get a scan with an Oculus. We will translate nearby and travel by foot to investigate."

That is not good. Any time the Oculus cannot see something means we are about to have, at the very least, a strange experience.

Mr. Lark has more to say, "So all of us will translate to a nearby location determined safe by the Oculus. Then we will hike a distance to this destination point and see what there is to see."

"This we do in the morning. I want the team rested and ready first thing in the morning after breakfast. That is all for now."

Everyone else, except Mr. Lark, stands up to leave. "Thomas, I wish to discuss your visit with Balthazar a bit more. Please remain."

I remain seated and watch the others leave.

Mr. Lark waits until the last man walks out before speaking.

"You have told me all the information you have gathered about the castle. Now tell me what you think and feel about the castle. I want insight."

He is being intense which makes me uncomfortable. "There has to be more to this than it just being a place where bad guys hide out. The way Balthazar talked about it, whatever is at the bottom of that pit cannot be disabled or killed, only contained. My takeaway from the Magi's explanation is that the Adversary did not always control whatever is beneath Castle Houska. This is a recent takeover. The bit about the Church turning on the Scholomance speaks to something more sinister happening."

Mr. Lark nods his head, "Thank you, Thomas, what you say aligns with my thoughts as well. "

I decide to ask a question. "What do you think is going on?" Asking Mr. Lark is always a hit or miss thing. He rarely shares his thoughts or plans but it can't hurt to ask.

"What you described are all excellent observations. Unfortunately, you can be naive in your world view. There are other, potentially diabolical, possibilities that I must include as contingencies in our planning. None of which is your concern."

"Off to bed, Thomas, we have work in the morning."

I do as instructed and consider his words as I walk to my room. As a child, I always wanted answers to every question. As an adult, I had become comfortable occasionally not knowing things. Since my service to Mr. Lark began I've prayed for ignorance. With that last thought I crawled into bed. Tomorrow is another day.

The next morning we all meet at the armory early and gear up, full tactical dress and weapons, all in black of course. Then breakfast followed by meeting in the open space just inside the gates at the specified time.

I expect the gates to open and Mr. Lark to come walking in from the Compass like he usually does. Instead he comes walking out from between some buildings inside the Citadel. This is surprising. It appears he spent the night at the Citadel and as far as I know Mr. Lark never does that. He is dressed and outfitted similarly to the team.

This unusual situation is not lost on my colleagues. There are sideways glances between everyone.

In my several months in his service I have spent little time with Mr. Lark. However, during the rush to return Balthazar to his home a little over a month ago, I spent several continuous days in close proximity to the old man. One thing I learned during that mission is that apparently Mr. Lark does not sleep. This leads to the question: why was he here at the Citadel all night while we were sleeping? I would ask him but decide it could be something I would regret knowing.

I shrug and mentally move on. Mr. Lark pauses for moment to look the team over. He then silently turns and walks out the doors that had just opened while he was still standing still.

The five of us follow in a box formation, four men in the four corners with me in the middle. We look like the number five on a six-sided dice.

It is a quiet walk to the Compass. This mission is blind and none of us has a clue what to expect. When we arrive at our destination, Mr. Lark hands out emergency return dongles to everyone. Then the six of us group together in the center of the stone circle.

The cold gloom of the Compass is instantly replaced with daylight with the team translating to open grassland. The skies are clear and blue and the sun is low in the east. The air is chilly with a slight breeze.

The nausea of the translation washes over me. Illych is right. I am getting used to it. The others still recover quicker though and Mr. Lark appears unaffected.

Our employer announces our destination. "We are in the Patagonian outback, so to speak. This place is approximately two-hundred miles from the Bright Child Genetic Initiative research center. The destination the children arrived at during their escape is ten kilometers from here. Due to the distortion and the remoteness of this place we will have to hike the distance."

Illych interrupts, "Will we be meeting anyone during our walk today?"

Mr. Lark starts walking and replies, "We are essentially in the middle of nowhere. We should be alone out here. The exception to that will be if the distortion masking the Oculus is hiding people at our destination."

Illych makes a hand gesture to Mike. Mike immediately jogs to the point position. Illych then looks at Tank who moves to take up the second position.

The rest of us spread out in a single file with Held bringing up the rear. Mr. Lark and I end up in the middle. Everyone is too far apart for there to be any talking and I know better than to engage in idle chit-chat in a tactical situation.

For the next four hours we hump, as my military trained colleagues call it, through the grassland. Mr. Lark uses the Oculus while walking thus no need to stop while our surroundings are scanned.

Our final destination turns out to be a low point in the ground like a crater. We walk up a grassy rise in the ground and find ourselves on a low hill overlooking a depression filled with water forming a shallow pond perhaps a hundred meters across.

From our vantage point we have a clear view of the entire pond.

I am confused for a bit. It looks like there are people in the pond and on its banks.

Then I realize they are not living people. They are the corpses of teenage children. From our elevated vantage point I can see bodies floating in the pond. Others are partially on the shore and precious few others are fully on the land.

They are bodies of children, teenagers, and there are far too many of them. I start counting as the team fans out, walking down to the edge of the pond. I stop the macabre exercise after counting thirty. It is too much to continue after realizing there are at least one hundred dead teenage boys and girls scattered about.

As we draw close to the pond I clearly see the children all wear a simple fitted body suit. Every child shows evidence of a violent death. Not from gunshots or other more obvious and traditional forms of violence. They have been twisted and torn. Some survived long enough to make it to the edge of the pond before passing. Regardless, they are all very dead.

It had been almost two weeks since their escape and the chilly air has slowed decomposition. It is still an awful sight and smell. Seeing so many perfectly healthy young people having their life extinguished at such a young age causes me to feel a visceral emotional reaction. I feel more anger and rage than sadness. This is a crime against humanity.

The others have more experience at things like this but everyone has a grave expression as they survey the scene.

Mr. Lark speaks first, "It is as I feared. The method used to escape has a high probability of fatal injury. If they were smart enough to conceive of it, then they knew the risks. Yet they did it anyway."

"Illych, I have the binder with the photos provided by Dr. Hess. I want each body brought onto the hillside to be identified."

The team stacks arms, placing their weapons in easy reach, and apply themselves to the grim task, including myself. Having never touched a dead body before, I gingerly imitate what the others were doing. Never have I been so thankful for having a pair of gloves on my person as I grab each corpse by its arms and drag it into position on the hill.

We make rows of corpses on the hillside and when all the children have been recovered from the shore and arranged, we wade into the pond to get the floaters.

I feel numb and mechanical dragging body after body into place. They are all in their middle teens and not terribly heavy but I cannot keep up with the others in the speed of the work. Our grisly task is complete in less than two hours.

It is not a competition and I want to remember what happened here and who it had happened to. These children had died desperately trying to escape from something and they should not be forgotten.

Mr. Lark stands on the hill and watches us work. He is referencing the binder and is checking off each photo as its owner is recovered. The final count is one-hundred and thirteen children with no adult staff members present.

That leaves forty-two children unaccounted for. There is no evidence of wild animals making off with any bodies. If I had to guess, this indicates there are survivors.

Shortly after the count is complete Mr. Lark announces what I have been thinking. There is a high probability of survivors. Now that we are here, witnessed the outcome of the escape, and counted the dead, our task is complete. Our employer announces a direct translation to the Compass will be error free from this location. We silently gather together and translate back to the Compass.

After the nausea passes I look around at the others and find them a grim lot. Walking back to the Citadel all are silent, including Mr. Lark. My colleagues all have similar expressions on their faces. They are sad and angry at whoever is responsible for what we have just seen. More mentally exhausted then physically tired and smelling like death we trudge through the Citadel gates. This is a day that started with blue skies and sunshine and ended in a very different place.

Mr. Lark's expression is its normal unreadable mask. Except for his eyes, there is something akin to a cold light coming from them. Not an actual light, more a projection of something inside the man.

Once we are through the gates and back in the light and warmth of the Citadel Mr. Lark finally speaks. "Thomas, Held, make arrangements to visit Castle Houska tomorrow. I will return for your report when you return."

That said he turns to leave. Something inside me made me talk. "That's it? We just move on?"

The four shooters all turn to look at me.

Karl Lark stops in his tracks and turns to look at me. The cold light in his eye transfixes me and I am frozen in place.

"Mr. Davies, it is not my place in the world to balance scales. Unless you wish to change your status within my organization I suggest you keep your thoughts on this matter to yourself."

I knew what that meant. I could feel it. Death is close and Mr. Lark is its hand.

When I say nothing else he turns and exits the Citadel.

After he is gone Illych breaks the silence. "Everyone to the cafeteria. Time to break out the spirits." He then looks at me, "Thomas, walk with me." And turns and walks away.

I join him and we walk in silence as we trace the inside perimeter of the Citadel.

After making it about half-way around Illych speaks, "I understand your emotions on this and I will share something I have learned from my eight-year association with Mr. Lark. That look in his eyes means he is dealing with the emotions the rest of us are more obvious about."

"He has feelings?" That is news to me. That man has been an impersonal robot since I met him. The closest thing to emotion Mr. Lark has ever showed is his contrived smile. I figure he is some form of a sociopath or psychopath, with his intelligence crowding out any room leftover for emotions.

"Not like us but yes, he has them. I think most of the time Mr. Lark is largely a person driven by his intellect. His emotions are small and quiet. When they come to his attention he has no experience with them and he does not handle them well."

"His intellectual side will not support efforts at vengeance as he views such activities as inefficient and misdirected. At the same time, his intellect will have a problem with events not in line with civilized behavior. If people treat children like this humanity cannot survive. None of which would be his concern except that by hiring Mr. Lark they succeeded in rubbing their stupid on him. And Mr. Lark does not appreciate someone sharing their stupid with him."

"I will not go into details but based on past experience I do not think this is over. He won't pursue it overtly but if the opportunity does present itself to 'balance the scales' so to speak, they will be balanced and with extreme prejudice."

"My advice to you: use a softer touch with Mr. Lark. At his core he is not an evil person. Now let's go to the cafeteria and join the others."

I appreciate the advice from Illych and ponder the consequences of genuinely making it onto Mr. Lark's shit list.

Back at the cafeteria the others are preparing dinner. The beer is already out, as well as scotch and bourbon. I already knew about the beer. We keep some really good stuff in stock. That is to be expected with a group of veterans residing in a pocket dimension. But the spirits must be from a secret stash.

There is a lot of emotional steam to blow off and the party lasts well into the night. This group is too mature for things to get out of hand but I will never forget Mike arm wrestling Tank with Held joining in to help. Tank still won.

The party breaks up in the wee hours of the night and I fall asleep the second my head hits the pillow. Tomorrow is a new day and it must be better than this one.

Chapter 6

My colleagues at the Citadel are skilled, experienced, and in excellent physical condition. They are however, not young men, except perhaps for Mike. Regardless, I arrive at breakfast to find that last night's excesses have come back to haunt everyone.

The scheduled morning calisthenics do not happen. Instead, the cafeteria contains five men who are not enjoying the after-effects of excessive alcohol consumption. I am the last up and upon shuffling in I can see everyone nursing a mug of coffee. Held and Mike have sunglasses on. Tank is sitting with his head in his hands, vocalizing the occasional moan and not looking happy. Illych has a baseball cap pulled low over his eyes. They are a sorry looking lot. The scene is the day after not young guys trying to party like its 1999.

I have a headache from a mild hangover but my condition is nowhere as bad as this sorry lot. Picking up a metal tray, I walk over to the table my colleagues are sitting at and loudly slap it down.

The sound elicits groans from several of the men mixed with a few curse words. Tank gets the humor of it though.

He glares at me, "How do you Brits say it? Piss off?"

"That is how we say it." I am smiling now. Something about irritating Tank first thing in the morning makes my day.

Sitting next to Held I sip my coffee. My practical joke put some life back into them and the level of conversation at the table picks up.

Held speaks next. His voice quieter than usual, "Thomas, perhaps this is a good time to discuss visiting that castle."

Nodding, I reply, "We can go anytime. The tours load up on a bus at a nearby town and it is a short drive to the castle. They stay for four hours, a long enough time window to check the place out."

"You mean we go there like the bus full of tourists who had their minds twisted and then sent on a suicidal rampage?"

Held has a point. The busses are being surveilled. That is something to watch for during our reconnaissance.

Held turns to Illych, "Can you get us dongles that return us to the Compass afterwards?"

"I will contact Mr. Lark. This is on the to-do list so we should have them quick."

Mike is listening in from down the table, "Do you need a third?" Illych's response shuts him down, "Three would be a crowd. The goal is a low-profile reconnaissance." Mike's expression shows he would have liked to join us. Probably just to get out of the Citadel and breathe the fresh air.

Held ads, "So we go in civilian clothes as tourists? It won't take long to get ready once we have the dongles."

Everyone nods in agreement. What just passed for breakfast breaks up and everyone leaves to clean up our gear from yesterday's nightmare. Afterwards, I head to the library to keep myself busy.

At dinner Illych informs us the dongles are waiting at the Compass and the castle mission is a go for tomorrow. He reinforces we are only to observe and report. If we run into trouble we are to return to the Compass. Held and I agree that due to the time difference we go in about six hours, middle of the night here at the Citadel but early morning in the Czech Republic. The Citadel exists in a pocket dimension and there is no sun to rise. For convenience this place runs on United States Eastern time.

Later that night, right on time, I arrive at the Citadel's main gate properly dressed in civilian clothes with good walking shoes and a light jacket. Held is dressed similarly and we both carry concealed M1911s nestled in shoulder rigs under our jackets. Better to be safe than sorry.

Feeling exposed without body armor and some Truestone in my pocket, I remind myself we are supposed to be tourists and do not want to draw attention. At least we each have a ComDat in a civilian backpack, just in case for emergencies. Held also carries his Oculus. Walking around with a four-inch diameter bronze sphere in your hand draws attention.

Illych and Mike join us for the walk to the Compass. They will remain there, waiting until our return. Our backup, just in case we get into trouble and need rescuing or we return injured.

Mr. Lark identified a geological feature on the edge of the Czech town we are translating to that makes an excellent entry point. From there we walk to the tourist shop and sign-up for the tour.

Today is Saturday and Held and I translate in and remain out of sight waiting for the nausea to end. Upon recovering, we walk out into the open. The sky is overcast, possibly threatening rain and the air crisp with cold. I expected this, it being early winter. Taking the light jacket is proving a wise choice.

Held and I maintain a brisk pace and we are in the heart of the town in less than a half-hour. There are people walking about, shoppers, those visiting a café, a few walking dogs, even children playing. They are all speaking a language I am unfamiliar with.

Held breaks our silence first. "I do like European women." He says this while watching the other pedestrians around us. Even in the chill the women dress to impress. I nod in agreement and keep walking and observing.

Both of us are trained to remain vigilant during these jaunts into the world. Between our training, weapons, the crown installed in our heads, and the escape dongles in our pockets, we are pretty safe from random street crime. It is still better to be safe than sorry.

We find the plaza where the shop selling tour tickets is located and our pace does not change as we walk across, maneuvering around civilians, to our destination.

An attractive English-speaking Czech woman exchanges our Euros for tickets. Only then do we discover the next bus will not leave for almost two hours. This does not match my internet research and we are told the number of busses was reduced due to the weather. An overcast day results in fewer tourists.

Held shrugs and points across the plaza to a café. We decide to sit outside at a small table in spite of the lack of sun and chilly temperature. The cold has driven everyone else inside, so it will just be the two of us.

First things first. I order coffee for warmth and while we wait Held puts his hand inside his backpack and closes his eyes to interface with the Oculus. Our coffee is served just as he finishes his scan. I give him an inquisitive look and he shakes his head indicating 'all clear'. Good. We can talk. No one else is listening.

The coffee raises my core body temperature, leaving me enjoying the feel of being warm inside and the sensation of the chill air outside.

Held speaks first, "You have been with Mr. Lark what, maybe five months now?"

"I have." My answer is short as I am distracted by some college-age women in high heels walking by. Most people spend their lives surrounded by an approximate fifty-fifty mix of men and women. Since I started spending so much time at the Citadel, decidedly an all-male experience, I find my interest in the fair sex heightened during missions to the real world. Based on observations of my colleagues, they feel the same way.

"Plan on trying to escape soon?"

That abruptly brought my attention back to the conversation.

"Uh, no. Why?"

"Well you know how in marriage they have the seven-year itch? For service to Mr. Lark it is the six-month itch. We have all had it. Except maybe Illych, he goes so far back and he was the first so who knows what his deal is."

"Well, yes, I have thought about it but Mr. Lark placed a great deal of emphasis on the murdering part if you should attempt to leave. Then there was that story you told me about the guy who wanted to leave and Mr. Lark disposed of him."

I pause for effect. "And quite honestly, a lot of the stuff we are doing is really interesting."

Held smiles at that, "Yes, that is what happened to the rest of us. You think about leaving and how difficult it would be, what with the high probability of death and all. Then balance that against the interesting things you would miss out on."

I nod, "I also figured the crown the Doctor installed in my head is probably a tracking device or something that self-destructs at Mr. Lark's command."

Held chuckles and we pause in our conversation while sipping our coffee.

I figure fortune favors the bold and all that so I just come out and ask, "So Held, what do you do on vacation?"

Human beings are not machines and Mr. Lark figured out his people need real rest. His solution is unique, three months service, followed by a one month vacation in the world. Expenses are covered, no matter how extreme the spend. The only rules are you do not talk about anything related to your day job and you return from vacation rested and healthy.

"Thomas, you are a decent guy and I enjoy your company but my vacation life is separate from my work life and I do not care to share it."

I nod. I guess sharing is out, "Understood."

After waiting for a few moments I ask my next question, "Would you be interested in discussing Balthazar?"

"Sure, why not. What should we discuss?" Held sighs, sounding resigned to discussing something to keep me entertained.

"Is he the real deal? A thousand-year-old secret protector of humanity?"

"You mean did he fake being trapped on Hy-Brasil for 350 years? And fake a horde of creatures trying to kill us while we returned him to his fantastic supernatural fortress on the foothills of Shahgah Mountain overlooking the Caspian Sea? Or that he made up popping in and out of that magic box he calls a Quixault?"

"Ok, when you say it like that."

"Thomas, you have been with Mr. Lark for less than six months. I have been with him for more than three very active years. If Balthazar is tripping your weird meter then you are in for a wild ride." Held is smiling now.

"You know, in the time I have been at the Citadel no one ever discusses Karl Lark. Why is that?"

"Why bother. Our lives are dedicated to his pursuit of knowledge interspersed with missions of a mostly criminal nature to generate revenue. Mr. Lark is an archeologist that found an alternate way to fund his research. Kudos to him. My experiences have guided me towards a more Zen approach and I just let life unfold. It would not surprise me if the others feel the same way. "

For the next half-hour we sit, sip coffee, and comment on our surroundings. Our bill is paid in cash and we catch our bus on time.

It is a big Mercedes coach, quiet, powerful, comfortable and only half-occupied. This makes it easier to eavesdrop on the conversations around us. From what I hear our fellow travelers are mostly Americans. Each person on the bus is reviewed as I have been trained to do. They are family units or groups of teenagers with a chaperone for the most part. No individuals or weird pairs of grown men sitting quietly. Basically, I am looking for people like Held and myself and come up empty. After completing my due diligence, I sit back, relax, and enjoy the remainder of the ride.

The drive is short and in no time the bus pulls up to the castle and we exit. The building itself is underwhelming, essentially appearing as a high square structure more resembling an apartment building or countryside manor. But this is the mystery of Castle Houska. It was never built as a traditional castle to defend against external threats. This castle was built to defend against or contain what is within.

The castle's external walls have windows, some of them fake and providing a view to a blank wall and nothing more. There are no towers or gates. No parapet or crenellations. As a castle it is unexplainable. And for it to survive in excellent condition for 750 years while providing no official useful function is difficult to make sense of.

Held and I exit the bus with the others and drift to the back of the group. The tour is informal. The handful of staff present field questions and lead small groups of visitors around. Nothing is cordoned off nor are there any mysterious locked doors. The floor plan is square-shaped and we walk the castle interior twice, visit the courtyard, and end up in the chapel.

Held pretends to be inspecting one of the many bizarre murals on the walls and then closes his eyes to interface with the Oculus.

While Held is busy I focus on the murals. The imagery depicted is incongruous. No story is being told. It strikes me as medieval graffiti. Random images painted on the walls.

Held's eyes open and he shakes his head. I move back to standing beside him.

"And?"

"Can't talk about it here but I took a snap-shot as a final observation for Mr. Lark to review." The Oculus is not a video recorder but it can store its last observation, a snap-shot, for later review.

With that part of our business out of the way, Held then wanders around the chapel leaving me standing alone. On the bus I had observed every single of our fellow riders and since our arrival I have done the same with all the staff members. However, entering the chapel is a man unfamiliar to me. He walks in through the entrance and stands there for several minutes.

Keeping him in the edge of my field of vision as I wander the chapel, I try to apply some critical thinking to the murals I see. Held does not appear to have noticed the man yet.

The interloper is average height and build, Caucasian and I guess him to be European from his pointy brown leather shoes. After standing motionless for a bit he turns and leaves without really looking around. The hairs on the back of my neck are standing up. I was going to get Held's attention but the man left too quickly.

The tour is overly long in duration as it does not take four hours to look at everything. After having seen everything, the visit devolves into random wandering around while waiting to leave. I am tempted to suggest to Held we find a quiet corner somewhere and use the return dongle and translate to the Compass. It is a mental indulgence with no chance of happening though.

Finally, all the tourists board the coach for the journey back. The bus ride and return to town are uneventful. During the short trip back I spend time looking around the bus for the strange man I saw back at the chapel. He is not on the bus and apparently no longer part of our tour group or more likely, never was.

After exiting the bus in town we swiftly walk to our departure point and soon find ourselves in the cold, dark embrace of the Compass. We recover from the translation nausea and meet up with Illych and Mike waiting for us in the vaults. Along the way back Held and I are informed we just missed Mr. Lark. He translated in not more than five minutes ago and headed for the Citadel. What a coincidence?

After being greeted by the Citadel's bright light as the gates open for us, I walk straight to the library. As I guessed, Mr. Lark is waiting in a comfortable chair, relaxing with his eyes closed.

Upon my entry his eyes open and he smiles a wide Cheshire cat grin. The man has many talents and strengths but people are his Kryptonite. He has developed what I believe is a form of compensation for being clueless in human interaction, he smiles. The smile is contrived and over done so I call it his Cheshire cat grin. It just means he is trying to be friendly is his own bizarre way.

Mr. Lark nods to me and waves a hand to the circle of chairs as an indication to join him. I nod in return and choose a seat directly across from him.

We sit silently knowing Mr. Lark will initiate conversation when he is ready. Shortly after taking a seat I learn the reason for the ongoing silence as Held and Illych walk in, witness our sitting and soundlessly join us.

Mr. Lark then speaks, "Was your investigation of the castle successful?"

Held replies, "I scanned the castle itself and everything in immediate proximity and within approximately a kilometer. The castle is an ordinary construct. No hidden passages, no multi-dimensional aspects detected, no Created."

Mr. Lark cuts him off, "Yes, but what of the pit below."

Held nods and continues, "The pit is real and easily seen by the Oculus. Incredibly deep, it ends hundreds of meters below the castle chapel. At the bottom of the pit is an open portal to a pocket dimension. The chapel was built atop an interlocking stone cap sealing the pit entrance. A snap-shot of the pit is still waiting in my Oculus. The rest of the castle is a normal construction but I could not figure out the cap."

Mr. Lark replies, "I reviewed the snap-shot prior to your entrance here at the library."

That statement caught my attention. We had only just arrived and he is saying what we are bringing with us has already been reviewed.

"The cap material is andesite stone built with interlocking pieces. There are spikes of material set deep into the bedrock around it. Combined with the thickness of the cap it would make it impossible to escape from the pit without digging through several hundred meters of bedrock or several meters of a capstone just a shade softer than diamonds."

Illych nods his head, "No one escapes."

Mr. Lark agrees, "Yes, no one escapes."

Held continues, "The pit has rough-hewn stone walls for maybe 100 meters down from the cap. Then the walls become a spiral stair case descending most of the way down the pit shaft. The stairs end at a platform some 100 meters above the portal carved into the shaft walls."

Held continues, "The pit, cap, stairs, and portal I all understand. The part that really did not understand is the granite tunnel at the top of the stairs."

This catches Mr. Lark's attention. He goes from casually paying attention to being instantaneously focused on what Held is saying.

"It looks like there used to be a tunnel from near the base of the rocky bluff the castle was built atop to the upper beginning of the spiral stairs. Then it was somehow filled with a laser straight cylinder of unbroken solid granite eight feet in diameter and running the full length of the tunnel. Where there was an open circular tunnel is now solid granite."

The three of us turn to look at Mr. Lark.

He thinks for most of a minute and then shares, "I have some theories I will not elaborate on for now."

Mr. Lark pauses again. "This is enough. I must consider our options going forward."

Our employer stands and looks directly at me, "Come, Thomas, I have something to show you."

A look of complete surprise, possibly tinged with terror, must be showing on my face.

"Your anxiety is unwarranted. This experience has been chosen to expand your knowledge, not end your existence."

I stand and follow Mr. Lark out of the library. My planned day of reading and library work just went away.

"Will this hurt?" With situations like this it pays to ask.

"It will not but should you sufficiently tax my patience with your dawdling I may change my mind."

Shortly I find myself walking side by side with my employer back to the Compass that I had just returned from.

"May I ask questions?"

"Good ones."

"Where are we going?"

"Ireland."

"What is my role in this outing?"

"To learn."

While walking the path between the Citadel and the Compass I do something I rarely do anymore. I look around. The spaces between and around the two locations in this pocket dimension the team uses are left wild and to some extent unexplored.

Outside the network of laser straight and flat stone roads the terrain is rough grey stone. There is no soil, nor any plant life to be found. It is a barren and almost impossible-to-travel wasteland. Randomly placed in that featureless expanse are buildings of alien architecture. There are Created out there and they make themselves visible if you look away from the path.

Today I do just that. In a break in the conversation with Mr. Lark I look out through the murk to observe one of the buildings closer to the road we are travelling. Standing near the building is a clown. It is not really a clown but some of the Created cannot interpret how we view each other. Instead they have some sort of internal scrambling filter and they make themselves appear as a clown thinking that is how we view each other.

The clown's appearance has a glamour effect to the uninitiated. Normal people, especially children, will see the clown and be compelled to go to it. Since Mr. Lark had the crown installed in my head, a circle of copper wire and who knows what else, it keeps me from being snared by such glamour. As we walk I can stare at the Created clown without concern.

"Thomas, if you keep staring it may decide you want it to come over and visit."

"I thought they are bound to their location and cannot move too far away."

"Some have an invitation escape clause. If you ask them to come and visit they can. Like a vampire needing an invitation to cross a threshold."

I look straight forward. If Mr. Lark had a sense of humor I might think he is making a joke. Considering the circumstances, discretion is the better part of valor.

Shortly thereafter we arrive at the Compass and walk straight into the circle and without delay, translate.

Arriving in a green grassy field, the air is cool but not cold and the day is late, approaching twilight. Looking around I see only green fields with waist high field stone walls separating them. Not far from where we stand is a densely wooded area.

Mr. Lark starts off at a slow pace towards the woods and I follow.

"What is this place?"

"I am taking you to a Faerie Circle."

"More Created?"

"Yes, but not in the way you have experienced up to now."

The woods are dense and overgrown. Even Mr. Lark struggles to push through. Soon both of us have scratches and tears in our clothes. My left hand has a particularly nasty bleeding cut by the time we make it to the grassy center.

"Why are these woods like this?"

"Because no one ever comes here. After centuries, if not millennia, of questionable regular events in this place, the locals allow it to grow completely wild and untrammeled."

Inside the wooded wildness hiding this place is a large open grassy space with a low mound in the center.

Halfway between the mound and the woods is a circle of small white flowers.

Mr. Lark acknowledges the flowers, "As long as we stay on this side of the flowers we are safe."

My employer looks around and finds a pair of stones between the woods and the circle of flowers. He sits upon one. My guess is I am to sit upon the other.

Twilight is here, with the night fast approaching, and my employer sits quietly watching the mound.

"I want you to see this. Your experience with the Created has been all monsters and immortal nightmares. But remember this, if you take one step within the circle of flowers there is nothing I can do for you."

As twilight changes to night, the mound changes into a miniature castle with an oversized gate right before my eyes. No sooner does this change occur and a short little man in brown overalls, slight of build and carrying a shovel, walks out. The little person is perhaps 18 inches tall with thin adult features. This is no child though, it is a man in miniature. The small man walks out to near the inside edge of the white flowers and plants his shovel in the ground, gives it a push with his foot and scoops out a tiny shovelful of dirt. Then he stops and pulls a red rag from a pocket and wipes his brow. This action of shoveling and pausing is repeated slowly, over and over again.

Now I hear music, high pitched, feminine and lilting. What instrument or orchestra is creating it I cannot tell but it is so beautiful it is almost painful to hear. I want to go to it, to touch and feel the music.

My reverie is broken by Mr. Lark's voice, "I call it the song of the sirens. It is not made by musical instruments or sung by anything living. It is how the Created reach out to anything nearby looking to connect. It is like the initializing tones of the old phone modems for internet connection, only so much more and so beautiful. How many humans have been inadvertently lured to their demise by that sweet sound? I can only imagine."

A parade of faerie figures, male and female, forming a troupe, march out from the gate. Some of their number walk, others are mounted on fanciful miniature mounts, even unicorns. Most of the female figures are in elaborate, colorful, flowing dresses. There are fewer men, dressed as if for a dance or ball. Part of the column marching out are small armored faeries mounted on armored steeds. Although mostly male a few female armored figures feature among the ranks.

The column breaks apart and three separate parts of the faerie circle are populated by colorful beings in their respective activities. One group is dancing in a circle, whirling and jumping, a riot of color and movement. The group of knights setup for jousting and begin taking turns knocking each other in turn from their mounts. The third smallest group takes up with the digging figure and seems to be planting something and encouraging it to grow.

At times the tiny figures move so fast they are a blur. When one of them performs exceptionally well there is cheering and clapping. The knights salute and wheel their mounts before they rear up and charge. The whole thing is a spectacle unlike anything I have ever witnessed.

Before I realize the passage of time the individual groups form themselves back into a column and return to the castle through its gate. I cannot help but feel loss as they leave. An idea comes to mind. I should follow and join them. It is a tiny voice but I can still feel or hear it. Telling the difference between it and my own thoughts is difficult.

I stay seated as the faerie with the shovel puts the small tool over his shoulder and is the last through the gate. Only now do I realize the night has ended and the first rays of the dawn sun are illuminating the tree tops of the woods around us. It is over in what seems like only an hour.

Looking at Mr. Lark the question must have been upon my face as he answered, "The night is over and only a single night. You felt the pull to follow them. The crown prevented its full power from affecting you. An unprotected human would have to follow."

"What happens if you follow?"

"They take you to a pocket dimension where you have a great time for what seems like forever. Then in seven years, or seventy years, perhaps even seven-hundred years you are returned to the world. Those who walk out only live for a day as the long-term exposure to the Faerie glamour and time distortion take effect."

"How often does this happen?"

"It is different for each Faerie circle but this one has a night like this every seven years. I was here for the last one."

The effects of the glamour are fading fast leaving a sad feeling behind.

"Let us go, Thomas."

Chapter 7

Due to the time difference that nights rest was cut short. Regardless, I walked into the Cafeteria the next morning feeling good, physically and mentally. Illych is here with the others, they are starting to plan today's activities. Some long-anticipated tactical gear arrived yesterday and we are to familiarize ourselves with it. The training will take up most of the day and I am not looking forward to it. My colleagues are all former military and love the toys. And Mr. Lark can afford the very best. I, however, am more interested in the books in the library. Since I am included in field missions, I need to be competent, thus the training.

Mr. Lark's entrance into the Cafeteria is the announcement that today's plans just changed.

The conversation at the breakfast table ends and we all look at Mr. Lark and silently wait.

He remains standing and without looking at any one of us in particular, begins speaking. "The Bright Child

Genetic Initiative contract is complete. The location of the dead children was submitted to the client and they paid in full. For three days of my time it was a more profitable opportunity than most."

I had to interrupt, "What about the children and staff unaccounted for?"

Mr. Lark nodded, "Yes, the client was informed that while I do not fully understand the means of the escape, I am fairly positive those means are what killed the children we found. The remains not accounted for were most likely obliterated during the escape attempt."

"And they believed that?"

"I care not one whit what they believe. I located that which they could not. They did not pay me to figure out the means of escape. The matter was complicated further by the client's lies regarding the disposition of the staff. They recovered two-thirds of what they sought and I have been paid."

Then Mr. Lark started smiling his big Cheshire cat grin.

"On another subject, I found the path of the remaining missing children. We will take a break from prosecuting the Castle Houska mission and spend a day or two searching for these children."

Another subject?

Illych got a perplexed look on his face and spoke up, "I thought the contract had been concluded?"

Mr. Lark continued smiling during his reply, "It is, but I am endlessly fascinated by what transpired at that lab in Patagonia. I want to meet one of the children and learn more."

Karl Lark wants to meet children? That is weird. And what, have ice cream with them?

"Are we kidnapping them?" I had to ask and regretted the question as soon I spoke it.

Mr. Lark's expression turns dark and he glares at me. "You will do as you're instructed Mr. Davies!"

He is still upset with me from my near rebellion a few days ago. Probably best to lie low and stop asking questions. I look over at Illych and he is nodding his head from side to side ever so slightly. Yes, it is time to shut up.

"Are there any other less-than-constructive comments?" Mr. Lark pauses for a moment. It turns out my colleagues at the Citadel are smarter than I am. If they have questions they keep them to themselves.

"I visited the Patagonia site and tracked the children's exodus to a small abandoned airport. It was cleaned up just enough to be functional. I then further consulted the radar logs at the nearest commercial airport. The children split up into three groups. We will be looking for the group that landed in the United States near Miami."

"Thomas and Illych will visit the airport in the guise of wealthy individuals looking for an airport to operate out of. The rest of us will be nearby in the event of unforeseen complications."

Illych spoke up, "How did they get planes to escape? I thought they were trapped in the lab with no outside contact?"

"That is one of the reasons we are following up. The children's desire and method of escape have a rational explanation. Their being able to meet up with planes at an abandoned airfield and just fly away cannot be explained."

Now I understand what is happening. Mr. Lark has found something he cannot explain, even with the Oculus. We will be hunting down the answers until we find them. If you look up 'relentless' in the dictionary you will find a picture of Mr. Lark included in the definition.

Since Mr. Lark integrated me into his organization, I am included in missions, like the one to Castle Houska or now this one to an airport, more often than I would have thought possible. There are five of us other than Mr. Lark. Considering how many combinations of pairs is possible from five individuals, including the fact the others all have military experience, why am I in almost every mission to the world?

Perhaps this is some passive aggressive attempt by Mr. Lark to dispose of me. Put me on enough missions and a bullet will get lucky eventually? I asked Illych about it once, hoping for some insight. Illych told me it was specifically because I was the only person on the team without military experience. That is why I am almost always part of the missions.

Later that day, all of us, including Mr. Lark, translate from the Compass to Miami and rent cars. Illych and I split off from the others and drive to the address provided by Mr. Lark. The private airport we are targeting covers a huge amount of ground area and is completely fenced in. The rent-a-cop at the main gate gives us a cursory looking over and lets us in while directing us to the company that organizes private flights in and out of this place.

The company goes by the humble name of Millionaire Flight Services. As we park the car out in front of the main doors I shake my head and think how this is only possible in America. Walking through the front doors, I take it all in. Everything is glass and chrome, shiny and clean and very modern. The stunning brunette sitting behind the receptionist desk could easily be a swim wear model.

She looks up at us standing in front of her desk, awaiting her attention. Her eyes flicker back and forth between Illych and me. I am familiar with this dance. She was determining if we should be here or if we were 'just looking'.

Our clothing showed quality and some money but it was the jewelry that gave it away. Both of us had high-end Rolex watches on our wrists. Not a Hublot or a Patek Philipe but also not your average Rolex either. Those who know, know, those who do not, do not.

The receptionist knew and her body language became warm, friendly, and inviting.

"Welcome to Millionaire Flight Services. My name is Mindy. How may I serve you?"

I decide to let Illych talk. We had not discussed it beforehand but I am not going to engage with Mindy. Nothing good could come from it. She is mind bending attractive and a man has to know his limits.

Illych accepted the challenge. "I am Jay Winslow and this is my friend Bart."

Bart? Why am I Bart?

"We are not from around here but are looking at flying here regularly in the near future. Could someone show us around and discuss the airport's features? If no-one is available we can make an appointment for a future visit."

"If your need is urgent," Mindy batts her eyelashes, "I am sure a member of our staff will be able to accommodate you. Please give me a moment. While you are waiting, refreshments are available." Mindy says this while waving to a drinks bar on one side of the reception area.

There are too many eyes and ears around for me to comment but I still glare at Illych, Bart indeed. Illych's lips curl in a knowing smile for a brief second and then he drops back into hyper vigilance mode. I do my best imitation of the same and the two of us sit at the bar sipping fruit juice and wait.

For an airport this size the foot traffic is light and during Mindy's brief phone conversation we see no other visitors or staff. Honestly, it is a little spooky. Mindy finishes her phone conversation in just a few minutes. Instead of calling to us from the receptionist desk she stands and walks over to us across the short distance on impossibly high heels. The glass receptionist desk had blurred the hemline of her skirt. Now that she is standing I can see how very short her skirt is.

She glides to us. "If you exit through the door you entered and turn right you will see a man with a clipboard. His name is Alan. He will discuss the airport and provide a tour.

As we thank Mindy and make for the exit she looks Illych's athletic form up and down and her parting words are, "I hope it is a good fit."

Wow.

After the doors close behind us I look at Illych, "What was that all about?"

"A distraction."

Alan with the clipboard is right where Mindy said he would be. He is a short, middle-aged, Caucasian guy with a pudgy look to him. He is red-faced and obviously hot in the Miami sun.

Illych takes the lead again by shaking the man's hand and Alan begins showing us around the airport.

Not long into our tour during the visit to the control tower I decide to ask a question. "What is security like?" At this point it is an appropriate enough question.

Alan nods, "Good question. We maintain armed security on site twenty-four hours a day. Our clients and their property are safe here." His reply had been armed security, with emphasis on the armed part.

They even have a small hotel on site. Alan walks us through and explains some clients are early for their flights and others want a room after a long flight.

Illych is not asking questions. I decide to ask another of my own. "How far do flights from this airport go?"

Alan's reply did not skip a beat, "The airport is rated for the largest jets. This gives our clients a global reach."

I had to admit, as tour guides go, Alan is a knowledgeable guy. We are seeing staff now but this is a curiously quiet place for the amount of airport around us.

Our guide's cell phone beeps and he glances at it briefly. We then continue to the next airport feature. As we are passing a hangar for smaller planes, Alan's phone beeps again.

"I beg your pardon but I need to use the phone inside this hangar for just a minute. Please follow me in as you cannot be left unescorted. This will take but a moment."

Illych and I look at each other and I shrug as we follow him.

The hangar main doors are closed and we enter through the man door off to one side. Alan makes a beeline straight for an office inside leaving Illych and I to stand around looking at the aircraft parked inside.

From dark corners and blind spots around the hangar six men appear as if choreographed. All are holding small compact submachine guns pointed at Illych and me. I fully understand that though we are armed, these guys would shred us before our weapons clear the holster.

The eight of us stand quietly staring at each other when a deep male voice challenges us from the door to the office.

"Why are you here?"

I turn to look and see a big, big man standing just outside the office. He is tall, Illych's height, but with much broader shoulders. Reddish curly hair and a red moustache add to the intimidation level.

Illych is unaffected by the big man's aggressive stance. "Who wants to know?"

The man takes several long strides, cutting the distance between us to less than ten feet. The men with the guns also close in, maneuvering to stay out of each other's line of fire.

The big man shakes his head, "I ask the questions here."

Illych's silence I take as a signal to do the same.

The big man walks right up to Illych and reaches inside my colleague's jacket, removing the weapon hidden there.

"You are going to tell us what we want to know, Illych Popovic."

The surprise must have been visible on my face and the big man chuckles.

"We run facial recognition on everyone who asks questions about this place. The little one here is nobody. But you Illych cause all kinds of red flags to pop up. First, you will tell us why you are here then I will turn you over to some people who have questions for you. They are offering a significant finder's fee for your live capture."

I do not appreciate being called a nobody. But the fact someone is willing to pay for Illych's capture is interesting.

Illych does not look all that concerned. "What is your name?"

"Call me Red."

"Red, you might think you are in control of the situation here but you are not."

"Really? It sure looks like I am. Now strip?"

This time I speak, "Beg your pardon?"

"Strip! It is the only way to be sure you don't have any transmitters or tracking devices. Quickly or I will cut your clothes off." While saying the last part Red produces a knife that looks both vicious and sharp.

Illych starts undressing and I follow suit. Soon we are standing naked in a dark hanger surrounded by seven men with guns and knives. This is now officially the most uncomfortable situation I have ever experienced and I do not like it at all.

One of the gunmen gathers up our clothes and disappears through a door at the back of the hangar. Just inside the hangar's main door is a windowless panel van and all of us climb in with Red driving. The men with the guns have seats to sit on. Illych and I are forced to crouch naked in between them on the van floor. During the brief drive Illych is silent and looking bored. I do not feel bored and I am pretty sure my anxiety is visible. The gunmen all have blank expressions and do not look at either of us.

The drive is short and I see through the front windshield we are arriving at a plane washing facility and Red is closing the hangar door behind us. This is not good. Water and drains probably means messy torture followed by a messy death. As we exit the van, I witness the inside of the plane wash hangar is brightly lit and empty of aircraft. It is just a wide open space. The two of us are led to the center of the floor grating. The torture already beginning, the steel floor grating under our bare feet is painful to stand on and getting more painful by the second. Our captors roll over a rack of some sort, our hands are bound, and then pulled above our heads, and attached to the rack.

Red pauses and then asks us again why we are here. Illych does not reply.

The big man grabs a hose from the wall and proceeds to spray us with ice cold water. As I am shivering my way to hypothermia, all I can think is where did they get ice cold water in Miami? The water pressure is painfully high and I make an unmanly noise when the stream of water passes over a certain tender area.

Two of the gunman hand off their weapons to the others and begin stretching, rotating their shoulders, and obviously getting ready for vigorous physical activity. I am pretty sure if it were not for the crown Mr. Lark had the Doctor installed in my head keeping me from talking, I would tell these guys anything they want to know.

The two men, after limbering up, walk to a metal cabinet and each pulls a length of hard rubber hose out. They give them a few test swings in full view of Illych and me. Based on the inertia in their arc, the hoses have some weight to them.

Red looks at us with a questioning look. Illych rolls his eyes, perhaps in contempt?

I am just starting to wonder who is going to get beaten first as the first blow arcs across my back. The pain is like being struck by lightning, the weight of the hose driving the pain deep into my body.

Perhaps I had some hope they would hit me once and ask a question. This was not to be. The blows came hard and fast across my back, chest, thighs and stomach. I cannot even cry out as I struggle to even breathe. After perhaps a score of blows I pass out. Only then does the beating stop. I am shocked back to consciousness by ice cold water to find myself hanging painfully by my arms.

Red dries off his hands and pulls a cell phone from a pants pocket. His finger swipes and pokes at it followed by his lifting it to his ear. "Yes, they have been prepared." One more poke of his finger and he holds the phone between us so we can hear.

The voice on the speaker phone is that of a young man.

"Illych, there is a significant bounty to provide you to certain interested parties alive. Do you see what was done to your colleague? That can be you in a few minutes. The bounty requires you alive. Nothing was said about undamaged." The voice on the phone pauses.

"Why are you here?"

My body feels like it is suspended in a tank of liquid pain. I still hang by my arms and I am also pretty sure I am drooling on myself. Through all this I vaguely make out Illych speaking to the person on the phone.

"We are looking for a plane load of children that landed here a few weeks ago. They arrived from Argentina. Patagonia to be specific."

I could have kissed Illych right now for saying that. Obstruction at this point is just going to get me beaten some more. .

"Why?"

"I was instructed to do so."

Loud booms in close succession shake the ground. This hangar has multiple man doors but I can only see one of them as I hang by my arms. Through blurry vision I witness one door blown off its hinges, fly ten feet and land flat on the floor.

Through the smoke of the breacher charge strides the unmistakable silhouette of Tank. Like an ancient God of War, Tank's muscled form, clad in black carapace armor, and his face hidden by a full face combat helmet, stalks into the hangar, the KRISS and its suppressor looking tiny in his hands. The weapons laser designator darts from target to target in short, precise movements. At each stop small tongues of flame emit from the suppressor as a burst is fired. I do not see the targets but I trust Tank is hitting them.

It is over in moments and my hearing returns a few seconds after.

The first thing I hear is Tank, "...there is a joke in here somewhere. Two guys are naked in a plane hangar. The first one says to the other one... It needs work I know but it will get there."

Mike is next to me now, "Thomas, I need you to stand and get weight off the bindings." I hear the sympathy in his voice and know the damage must look bad. The pain is impressive but bearable as I struggle to my feet. If I cry out Tank will never let me hear the end of it.

As Mike cuts my hands free I am able to look around. The gunmen and the guys with the hoses are all dead. Can't say I feel bad about that. Illych, Held, and Mr. Lark have Red in a corner with the cell phone in between them. Their conversation is brief before they drop the phone on the floor and Illych grabs the M1911 from Held's shoulder holster and shoots Red at point blank range multiple times.

Red slumps to the ground and Illych flips the safety back on while handing the weapon back to Held.

Mr. Lark is holding his characteristic cane with the over-sized brass sphere on top.

By now Mike has my right arm over his shoulder and is supporting my naked form.

Red and his team had not brought our clothes or equipment to this hangar and we are not going looking for them. The explosions and suppressed gunfire will be bringing visitors, preventing the search for lost items.

Mr. Lark announces, "We need to leave, now," while pulling a dongle from a pocket. The rest of us crowd in near him.

Tank glances at Illych's naked body as we fall in for the translation, "Don't point that thing at me." Illych then smiles. I am glad everyone still has their sense of humor.

The world goes black as the translation happens. The Compass is cold all the time, well below freezing. Arriving naked, wet and having just been beaten to a pulp is a bad way to be. Combined with the nausea of translation...

I go into shock.

Everything from there to waking up in the Doctor's waiting room is a blur. Apparently I almost died before making it to the Doctor's. That would have been bad because if you are dead before you get there you stay dead. The good news is I avoided dying.

When the Doctor is done you wake up perfectly healthy. I am a little peeved no one waited for me to be done. At least someone left me a jumpsuit and shower shoes so I did not have to walk naked to get clothes on. I dress and shuffle to where I know everyone will be: the cafeteria.

As I walk in the first thing I hear is Tank still working on his joke about Illych and me naked in the hangar. Tank is a solid guy to have around in a firefight and a braver man I have never met. Not that I would tell him. But his ongoing attempts at humor are demonstrating his true talents lie elsewhere.

Apparently Illych reached his limit. "Okay, Tank, keep working on it but let it go for now."

At this point my presence is acknowledged by head nods from everyone present.

After filling a tray with food and picking something to drink I sit next to the group.

Illych speaks first, "You look none the worse."

Mike adds, "I wish I had a picture. You were bruised to the point of not looking human. I am always amazed at the abuse the human body can suffer through and survive."

"I almost did not survive."

Mike shrugs.

I look at Illych, "Why were they beating me but asking you the questions?"

Illych did not return my gaze, "Three reasons: first was they wanted me to be able to give coherent answers. Next, they were showing me what I was in for if I did not cooperate. And finally, they beat you first in the hopes that I would be sympathetic and it would motivate me to talk."

"Were you sympathetic?"

Illych tilts his head back and sniffs, "Undecided."

Tank roars in laughter.

Bastard.

"So what they were doing made sense?"

"Completely, they wanted information from me quickly. The two men swinging the hoses coordinated their strikes on your body very nicely. They had definitely done this before."

"At least it worked. You told them what they asked for."

"I would have told them without the beating. By the time they asked I knew the others would be coming to our rescue and our interrogators would be dead in a few minutes.

"What was the deal about you being in a facial recognition database with a bounty?"

"Probably has to do with how I came to be working for Mr. Lark."

That is interesting. He had explained how he came to be with Mr. Lark during the flight to Patagonia.

"Translated out of Ft. Leavenworth with Mr. Lark in the dead of the night. They never knew how I escaped. Not a year later Mr. Lark and I had a run-in with the FBI. We kidnapped one of their senior people and he seemed to know my face. Since I am not on the most wanted list, my guess is there is a secret list that I am most definitely on."

My head is spinning. Illych is even more interesting than I had thought. Kidnapping FBI agents?

The group is silent for a minute while everything just said is fully realized.

One last detail, "What did you talk to that guy Red about before you shot him?"

"We talked to him and the person on the phone. Red did not have any answers. He was just doing as instructed. The person on the phone was a teenage boy named Heiko. He wanted to know what we want. Mr. Lark explained he is curious about what happened and wants to talk. Heiko requested to know how to get in touch and Mr. Lark shared a phone number to call. After that the line went dead."

If I have learned anything about the tenacious nature of Mr. Lark, I am pretty sure we have not seen the last of the escaped teenagers.

Chapter 8

The next two days at the Citadel are uneventful, mostly getting back into a calisthenics routine and catching up on chores. Things need to be cleaned, garbage removed, etcetera. I have never witnessed it myself but I have been warned that allowing organic matter to accumulate over time can result in unexpected consequences in a place like the Citadel. The Citadel's existence in a pocket dimension allows spirit forms to animate such refuse into something best avoided.

Three days after returning from Miami, just after breakfast, Illych is handing out work assignments when Mr. Lark walks into the cafeteria.

The main gates to the Citadel operate in complete silence. If you do not witness their opening or closing, you will never know when Mr. Lark is present until he reveals himself. At first his sudden appearances were startling. After some time your reaction changes to curiosity when he shows himself.

This leads me to wonder if Illych will let me attach bells to the main gate doors like those heard in a convenience store? At least we would know who is coming and going.

Mr. Lark is dressed in all-black tactical but still carries his cane, an odd combination. "Illych. You, Tank, and Thomas will accompany me to the Balthazar's residence. I have made arrangements for transportation and we will now withdraw my remaining gold."

Illych nods and points to me and then Tank. Tank levers his muscled form up from the table and the three of us head for the armory. There is no need to ask for details. Mr. Lark's state of dress tells us everything we need to know.

Twenty minutes later we catch up with our employer at the Citadel's main doors. Our state of dress now matches Mr. Lark's. We are armed but did not go all out with carapace body armor and heavy weapons.

Mr. Lark gives us an expressionless once over, turns, and walks to the opening main doors with the three of us falling in behind him.

I understand what we are doing. A few months ago, after rescuing the Magi Balthazar and assisting his return home, Mr. Lark was paid a ton of gold, literally a single ton, at least 2000 pounds, in gold bars. The SUV we brought the Magi home in could not be loaded that heavily. We took a significant portion when we left but the majority is still sitting in a vault underneath the Kharkareth. Apparently, now is the time to retrieve it.

From the Compass, Mr. Lark set it up for us to translate some distance from our destination. Keeping the fact that we could teleport anywhere a secret is once again inconvenient. Instead of just translating to the front door we will insert a two hour drive just to make it look like we traveled to our destination.

The vehicle Mr. Lark requisitioned for us is a box van with double row seating. The four of us pile in with Tank driving and Illych sitting shotgun.

Normally I would be apprehensive about driving around Russia with three American's armed to the teeth. But the area the Kharkareth is located in is mostly sparsely populated wilderness and we are traveling the back roads and across open country. Our chances of seeing another human being are slim, even less is the chance of a run in with the authorities.

It is a sunny winter day outside. Mr. Lark sits quietly with his eyes closed, obviously communing with his Oculus. The sunlight and warm truck cab, combined with the rumble of the big diesel engine, is very relaxing and I doze off at some point.

A closing truck door wakes me when we arrive. We have arrived at the weather beaten square pillar that marks our destination. Now we wait. If Balthazar wishes to let us in he will send a pet Goblin. It has not been long since my last visit asking for information about Castle Houska. It will be interesting to see how Balthazar handles so many interruptions in such a short period of time.

The wait is short and an approximately four-foot tall gangly green bipedal humanoid appears out of thin air next to the pillar. Dressed in poorly tailored clothing, that would have been more appropriate on a homeless child, the Goblin bows and waves for us to follow him.

Mr. Lark, Illych, and I have been here before. Tank however, has never been to the Kharkareth. Entry into the non-Euclidean distortion Balthazar's home resides in is easy enough. Just walk forward towards the point where the poorly dressed Goblin disappears.

One moment you are in wintry rural southern Russia; then one step later you are on the laser-straight, perfectly flat, stone road leading to the Kharkareth. Tank is not usually in awe of the things we experience in the service of Mr. Lark. This is different though. The giant trees the size of California Redwoods, just to the right of the road leading to Balthazar's home, are truly massive. Tank is looking intently at them and slowly falling behind our little group as we walk to the gates ahead.

At some point in our short walk, Tank realizes he is falling behind and stops his gawking to jog and catch up to us just as we arrive at the main gates. The portal soundlessly opens as we arrive, allowing our entry. Inside the main gates is several-story high foyer open to sky lights overhead. The skylights, statues, and stone work give Tank pause and have him staring in awe. I am sure the rest of us did the same the first time we were here. The similarity in operation between the Citadel main doors and the Kharkareth catches my attention again.

The gates remain open after our entry and our Goblin guide turns to us and in the high squeaky voice of a male child yet to reach puberty announces, "The master of the house will receive you soon." The Goblin then kind of sidesteps and just disappears.

Our small band breaks apart while we wait, wandering in different directions throughout the massive foyer. I studied this place in the past. Instead of gawking, I take a seat to relax and enjoy the mellow ambiance. Mr. Lark remains standing in one place, expressionless, while Illych and Tank slowly walk the perimeter of the room together talking quietly.

Just as our wait at the square pillar was short, so too is our wait for Balthazar. The perimeter of the entry-way contains several doors to other parts of the Kharkareth. One of those doorways, a tall double door, soundlessly opens and Balthazar strides forth. The short man is dressed in bone-colored robes with a hood covering his head. The Magi moves quickly and quietly towards Mr. Lark.

I stand as soon as the inside doors open and move to take my place next to Mr. Lark.

The Magi speaks first, "You are welcome in my house. Karl Lark, your gold is ready as you have requested. Is there more you wish of the House of Balthazar? "

"I have come for the gold and nothing else. I have no wish to disturb the peace of your house."

Balthazar regards Mr. Lark for a moment and then speaks again, "It is good you have come. There is work to be done beyond the limits of my domain. If it pleases you, I welcome you to sit so we can talk."

An extended sit down visit and taking on more work is not part of this mission. Based on Mr. Lark's attitude we are here to get the gold and get out.

Instead we sit-down on the stone benches and Illych and Tank join us. Balthazar is a powerful ally. If he wants to chat for a bit we will sit and chat.

"You have been successful in hunting down the servants of the Adversary, the monsters who tried to prevent my return home. Now I have another task righting some of the wrongs that occurred during my exile."

Balthazar pauses here, perhaps to gauge Mr. Lark's reaction. My employer says nothing, apparently waiting out the Magi's response. The result is a long awkward pause where no one speaks for almost a full minute.

Mr. Lark blinks first, "I did not come here looking for new tasks to perform but I will listen to what you propose. If my organization has the resources we will become involved." He is not smiling when he says this.

Balthazar nods his head slightly, "Since your last visit I have studied the exodus of my mortal servants by sending my ancient servants to explore the nearby town of Digora searching for clues of their whereabouts. After their exodus from the Kharkareth they resided locally for over one-hundred years. Perhaps a century ago there was a great political upheaval, a revolution you would call it. My servants and their descendants were labelled 'aristocrats' and forced to move away for their own safety. I know not where they have gone. This brings me to my request. Mr. Lark, I am asking you to look for them. Where ever they settled, whatever their fate, whomever remains."

The expression on the ancient Magi's face shows the emotion of loss. It really bothers the man his servants had been forced to leave.

I turn and look at Mr. Lark. He looks less than thrilled having something else added to the organization's current work list.

He says, "I do not consider this service part of past agreements."

This made me smile. He might be eccentric, obsessive, and controlling but like any good businessman he keeps his eye on the money and that short statement means he is interested.

Balthazar replies, "I will pay for expenses for an unsuccessful search and a small reward for finding where the last of them perished. My generosity will be incandescent should you find them numerous and in good health. Is that satisfactory Mr. Lark?"

Mr. Lark steps towards the Magi and extends his right hand. Balthazar follows suit and they silently shake on the deal.

"One question. You are positive your servants resided nearby?

"There are graves near a church that hold the remains of servants I left behind. They died of old age."

Mr. Lark nods.

"My ancient servants have moved your gold to your waiting conveyance and now stand guard awaiting your departure."

Mr. Lark nods to Balthazar, turns and walks towards the main entrance. I take one last look at the Magi and then turn to do the same. Too bad we could not stay for an extended visit. He is a fascinating character to talk to.

The four of us pass through the entryway and out onto the stone road leading to the edge of Balthazar's domain.

Mr. Lark is already planning the search for the missing servants, sharing his thoughts as we walk. "Illych, you and Thomas will handle this. We will return to the Citadel. You will prepare to visit the nearby town and I will assemble the needed dongles for your arrival and emergency escape if needed. Please be quick about this. I have other tasks for both of you."

One moment we are walking towards the mist at the edge of the non-Euclidean contraction and one step later we are standing next to the old square pillar looking at our vehicle.

There is no one around, supernatural or otherwise, and a peek in the back of the truck reveals a pile of gold bars neatly stacked. The weight should be eighteen-hundred pounds. Mr. Lark does not bother to count. If he wants to know he will just check with the Oculus while we are driving to the translation exit point.

The two hour drive gives Illych and me time to discuss what he is calling a dynamic search. I think it is a way of saying we do not have much information or planning to start with but we are going to pursue our goal anyway.

Illych shares an outline of a plan, "I am pretty sure when Balthazar says revolution and aristocrats he is talking about the Bolshevik revolution around 1918. Perhaps first we find out if any groups left the town in that time frame and hope something about where they went is known."

I am impressed, "You know your Russian history?"

"My grandfather was only two years old when he and his parents barely escaped the genocide that was the Russian Revolution. He taught my father and my father taught me, hence my name, Illych Popovic."

"What would be really helpful is if you spoke Russian."

"What would be really helpful, Thomas, is if you could read Russian."

Touché, he had me there. My use to the team is built around what I can read and we are going to a place where I will be handicapped.

In less than two hours we deliver the gold to the Compass, change into civilian attire, and pick up dongles and a pile of Russian rubles in cash. One more translation later and we are walking into the small Russian town of Digora, not ten miles from the Kharkareth. By small I mean less than twenty-thousand souls. The roads are in miserable condition and the buildings are a combination of old-world architecture which was well executed and attractive, if poorly maintained, and crumbling, ugly, multi-story Soviet era concrete apartment blocks.

While walking we discuss how to find evidence from a hundred years ago in a town where we do not speak the language.

Illych is optimistic. "Thomas, they lived here for at least a hundred years. That means records and Russians write everything down. It also means graves. Some of them died at some point. There will be an Orthodox church with records."

While we are talking and walking I notice there are few cars and fewer pedestrians around, even though it is mid-day. "Where is everyone?"

Illych replies, "This place is quieter than I would have expected. Let's find a quiet spot so I can look around with the Oculus."

The quiet spot ends up being a dead-end road with nothing around it. Illych stands there quietly with his eyes closed for ten minutes.

When his eyes open he tells me what he observed, "Found the church not a kilometer that way." He gestures off in the direction we had been walking.

It is an old Eastern Orthodox Church, quite beautiful and much larger than I expected. The outside is clean if not in pristine condition. The onion shaped spires are copper-clad and polished.

Walking up the steps to the front door, we find them unlocked. Passing through them to the inside we find ourselves in another world compared to what we have seen getting here. The inside is clean and dimly lit by candles. There are beautiful murals, statues and tapestries and the space around the altar is clad in gold scrollwork.

A priest is near the altar when we enter. I am caught up in the images of beauty around me and barely notice Illych walking away from me towards the priest.

The statues strategically placed about the open space inside the church are all Christian representations and very detailed. While studying one particular statue of Jesus I look at the floor. The floor is assembled from large flagstones precisely fitted in a display of fine stonework.

Curiously a square metal bar as thick as my thumb is recessed into the floor. Looking in both directions I witness the bar making a complete circle around the church floor.

I have seen such loops before. In the vaults at the Compass and in the floors of the stone circles Mr. Lark sets up for translating. No one had ever explained their purpose but I am thinking it is time I start asking. This thought breaks my reverie of studying and my eyes go to Illych who is now standing by the priest.

The priest is a tall man, close to Illych in height.

The two of them are in deep conversation and do not stop when I walk closer. As I draw near I make out the English words.

"…You know of what I speak?' Asks Illych?

"Da, when I first came here the most senior of the clergy required I study the history of this church and how it survived the purges and destruction brought by the Bolsheviks."

At this point they acknowledge my presence. Illych speaks next, "This is Sergei, one of the clergy watching over this church." Sergei has the typical Russian unemotional expression on his face.

"I am acolyte, not priest. I study now."

Illych nods and continues, "I have been discussing with him how our employer has us looking into a distant relative who can trace his roots to this town. They were forced to leave around 1918 and that unfortunately we do not have any names. This is what brought us to his church."

As lies go this one is not too bad. We are not asking for secret nuclear launch codes. We just want to know where some long dead people lived and where they went.

"Sergei, our employer provided us with money and is willing to fund church research if needed."

Sergei spoke, "The church records go back many hundreds of years. Few peoples coming here or leaving. Until recently, now they move away for better work. Long time ago, a man came to the priest of this church and asked if his family could live in town. They number less than hundred. They educated people, with money. The priest and town land owners say yes and they sell them land edge of town."

"They quiet people, only coming to town to buy things and attend church. Then the Bolshevik's came, questioning where their money come from, why they keep themselves separate, declaring their education showed them to be aristocrat."

"One day they are gone. The last one to leave, their headman, comes to this church with much money. He wants tapestry hanging in church. It is much money and priest says yes. Then they gone. They never return."

"Which tapestry?" I had to ask.

Sergei points to the space above the doors we entered through. A massive square of elaborately detailed cloth hangs there.

Illych points at it and looks at me. I get the hint and walk over to look at it.

The tapestry is perhaps four meters square and shows no signs of aging despite having hung there for a hundred years. Woven into the fabric is a scene from the Old Testament. While I was not raised Christian by my parents, my work requires detailed knowledge of the most printed book in history.

Woven into the tapestry is a column of people walking up out of water. On the side of the water they just came from are the pyramids of Egypt. The tapestry represents Moses leading the Israelites out of Egypt.

When I look closely at the pyramid I realize it is actually a stylized representation of a ziggurat. And what looks like a sea is actually farmland. In the sea is a sinking boat almost completely underwater. Only its masts could be seen. As I stare at the floundering ship in the sea I realize the masts are the onion steeples of the church I am standing in.

The column of people walking out from what I had at first thought was the sea, look to be dressed in robes. Except when I looked closely is now see they are dressed in normal 20th century clothing but are draped with possessions that made them look to be clothed in robes.

The man at the head of the column is pointing up to the sky. On the left side of the tapestry the sky is represented as day with a stylized sun visible. On the right side the sky is representing night with a stylized quarter moon on a firmament of stars. The man is pointing to the night side.

Except the quarter moon looked suspiciously like a Turkish crescent. I take out my notebook and sketch the crescent moon and the stars. The stars are all the same size except one. That one is half the size of the others.

I think I know where the servant exodus went and why they left the tapestry. It is a visual representation. The Ancient Created do not rely on visual sight the way humans do. A Goblin or Ciorii would never figure out the tapestry because they do not see it the way a human does. If the stars represent what I think they do, I know exactly where our next visit will be.

Illych remains talking to Sergei the whole time I am checking out the tapestry. I now rejoin him.

"Pay the man, Illych. It is time to go."

Illych looks at me, sees my expression, and addresses Sergei, "How may we donate to the church. Is there a donation box or would you prefer to hold the money for safety?"

"I will hold the money."

Illych reaches into his coat and pulls out a thick banded pack of Russian rubles. He fans the notes in front of Sergei to show they are all large denominations and slaps the pack down in the acolytes upturned hand. "We were never here." Sergei nods.

Illych and I turn and quickly leave. Upon exiting the church we see it is now twilight outside. Walking briskly to our exit point, we stop every now and then so Illych can use the Oculus. He is checking if we are being followed. No-one appears to be interested in us and we soon find ourselves once again in the cold and gloom of the Compass.

No sooner has the translation nausea passed and Illych asks, "What did you find?"

"If I am right, the next clue to their location will be in Turkey. I need to check a map about something first."

We are almost jogging from the sense of urgency to get to the Citadel. As we enter the light of the entry way I wave Illych to continue following me. The library door is frustrating me and I stop for a second and just breathe. Finally I slap the door open and stride across the interior of the library to pull a familiar book from the shelf it rests upon. A modern historical text studying the early Christian churches in Asia Minor is now held in my hands. After flipping to a dog eared page with a map of the churches locations, I place my sketch of the tapestry stars next to it.

It is a match

Pointing to a location determined by the small star in the sketch, I say. "There, that is what the tapestry is pointing towards. The stars in the tapestry are arrayed in the same pattern as the early Christian churches locations in what is today modern Turkey. I believe the single smaller star marks where we need to go looking next."

Illych nods, "Sure, why not, let me get this information to Mr. Lark. If he gives the green light then we are going to Turkey."

Chapter 9

Turns out there is an actual town called Ehgira at the location indicated by the symbols on the tapestry. Illych and I begin planning out the trip, setting ourselves up as tourists.

We fly in, arriving late in the afternoon, at the airport nearest our destination. Now a long car ride using a transportation service to drive us from the airport to our hotel in Ehgira. The town is so small the road leading in and out is also the main street. We travel past the fields surrounding the town on the way in. My knowledge of farming is close to zero but what I see resembles large orchards intermixed with planted fields and everything is green. My guess is the residents of Ehgira are a prosperous lot.

The town itself is a cluster of maybe forty buildings centered on the main road. The residences are two and three story affairs, flat-roofed, square buildings. I look for commercial venues on the way into town and only find a small grocery on the way in. On the other side of town is a single pump gas station. There are no cars in sight, parked or moving. The good news is the largest building in view is also a quaint old hotel and restaurant. At least we have a place to stay, giving some legitimacy to our visit.

While exiting our ride I find it warmer outside than I had expected, even though the sun is well on the way to its destination in the west. Illych tips the driver and we grab our bags. This is a day trip so we travel light, only one small travel case each.

Researching the town, both in print and on the internet, I found little to learn other than a bit about agriculture. This lack of information piques my interest. Sometimes it is not what you find when you look. Instead finding holes in the available information, where something should be, that holds my interest.

Standing outside the front of the hotel we take a few moments to observe what there is to see. When our transportation first delivered us there had been a few couples and children walking about. Now the street is completely deserted in just the few minutes it took to get out and secure our bags.

Illych and I look at each other. This cannot be good.

I speak first, "Maybe we will get lucky and find out they turn in early because they have a problem with vampires?"

"Why would that be lucky?" Illych does not sound impressed with my attempt at humor.

" Really? I can think of perhaps a half-a-dozen worse things than vampires that could happen in the next twenty-four hours. And there is a real probability one of them will actually happen. The townspeople could all be flesh eating zombies you know. So I figure a single vampire would be light work for us."

"Thomas, there is no such thing as vampires."

"How would you know?" Seriously, did Illych know something? Maybe Mr. Lark has looked into it.

"Let's discuss your irrational fear of the blood sucking undead another time."

I humbly disagree with his statement. Since joining Mr. Lark's organization, my fears could hardly be considered irrational.

Illych walks to the hotel door and waves for me to enter the hotel before him, "Ladies first."

Walking through the main double doors is a definite change in scenery. The décor has an east meets west thing going on. Or perhaps it is more like a country bed and breakfast with a Turkish theme. The entryway is wide open space to the small main desk. The rest of the front of the building is filled with evenly spaced tables for the restaurant. It is a lot of tables for such a small town. The only explanation I can think of is the space is used by the town residents for more than dining out.

In contrast to the ghost town outside, tables are being set and as many as five men and women of differing ages are moving about, engaged in tasks associated with getting ready for the dinner crowd. Past the dining area there are doors in the back, probably to the kitchen and rest rooms.

A tall woman, perhaps in her late thirties, finishes her table setting task and meets us at the main desk. She is pale, but not in an unhealthy way, not like she is a vampire. She wears her long dark hair back and her eye shine bright with intelligence. This is no small town hotel employee, I would bet real money on it.

We called ahead for reservations and Illych announces as much.

"English… and you are Americans?"

Illych continues to do all the talking, "I am American but my colleague is English."

"Your names?"

"I am Jim Winslow and this is Bart Smith." They are such bad fake names it makes it impossible to forget them.

"Your rooms are second floor overlooking the street. Please join us in the restaurant for dinner in an hour." No small talk, she is all business.

Illych nods and I smile at her.

There is no elevator, only stairs. I follow Illych climbing the stairs and down the hall.

I had to ask, "Illych, where are you going?"

"Second floor to my room."

"This is European numbering. This is the first floor. The second floor is what you Americans call the third floor."

He shakes his head while walking back past me. We walk up one more flight of stairs.

We are checked into separate rooms and split up. I cannot say the staff is friendly. Efficient and professional, yes, but not friendly. They look at us with a stare that says *why are you here?* Even the woman at the desk looked at us skeptically. I have never been to Turkey before, maybe it is a cultural thing?

Everything we had seen in this town so far is screaming that there are secrets kept here. Regardless, I clean up, washing the travel stink off. Then get ready for dinner. The food at the Citadel is excellent and certainly nothing to complain about but I and the others never pass on an opportunity for a meal in the outside world. Illych and I meet in the restaurant not thirty minutes later with the mouth-watering smell of cooking food calling to us.

The staff attempts to seat us in the center of the room. Neither Illych nor I are comfortable with this. Despite the protests of our host, we move to a corner table near the back door to the alley behind the building.

There are no menus. The waiter speaks broken English and explains how ordering works. Every evening the chef cooks and the guests are all served the same meal. Illych and I look at each other, shrug and then nod to the waiter this is acceptable. It does not matter what we want, only one choice is on the menu tonight. When in Rome…

Locals begin to filter in. Men and women, all adults, no children, sit at tables as couples or as groups. The wait staff, though few in number, is quite efficient and we all were quickly served. It struck me after about the fifth person walks in from the street. They are all dressed in all black clothing. Illych and I give each other a knowing look. That observation alone tells us we are probably in the right place to find Balthazar's lost servants.

There are enough people in the restaurant talking to provide background noise. Illych and I can whisper to each other with a reasonable expectation of privacy.

I start the conversation, "Is it just me or is everyone we have met since arriving staring at us?"

Illych is alert and watching everyone around us, "This place is setting off alarm bells in my head. They are talking but no one is laughing and they are spending too much time looking at us."

"Uh-huh and they wanted us seated in the middle of the room. I am sure of it."

Illych nods, "I agree. But what can we...." Illych's voice trails off as he turns his head back to look at me. He then shakes his head like he is dizzy. This strange behavior is followed by his turning his head all the way to the right and then slowly left while looking towards the open front door.

Illych repeats the head turning again, only this time he makes the return trip much slower.

Illych stands up and does the head thing again. The other restaurants patrons are staring at my companion behaving like a mentally ill person.

"Thomas, we have to go." Illych is now speaking in an urgent whisper.

"What do you see?"

"Get up, no time. Out the back door," Illych's fiercely whispers in reply.

That means trouble. I quickly stand up and bolt for the back door. Illych is right on my heels. When I glanced backwards he is also looking back and doing that head twitch thing. As we pass an empty table he grabs it, and a chair, pulling them down behind us, blocking the doorway after we run through it. He is acting like something is chasing us except there is nothing there.

Crap, it is invisible.

I have never encountered something invisible but I know there are ways to do it. Illych explained some stuff one time as has Mr. Lark. It was all very technical. Regardless, none of what they told me is helping right now.

I push open the door leading into an alley while drawing my pistol from under my sport coat. Illych slams the door shut behind us, his pistol ready in his hand. There are empty produce crates nearby and those are soon tossed in front of the door. Our pursuer may be invisible but the door and crates will have to move if they pursue us.

"What is going on?" I ask my companion.

"Weird invisible guy, at least I think it is human. I find that if I close my eyes and turn my head until it is out of my field of vision, then open my eyes and turn my head back, I can see it, as long as my head stays moving. If your head stops moving it disappears and then you have to start all over."

Illych said this while continuously spinning his head to one side with his eyes closed and then rotates his head back slowly with his eyes open.

Both of us keep our hand guns trained on the door. If that door opens, whatever is inside is going to have a bad experience.

After a minute Illych stops watching the door and started scanning the alley.

Illych spoke, "It is not coming through the door. We need to get out of the open and into an enclosed space. Why did I leave my Oculus back in our room?" He left it there because carrying around a four inch brass sphere in public draws unwanted attention and we were just getting dinner.

The alley runs in both directions for some distance. In the fading light of early evening the lack of outdoor lighting is obvious and more than a little sinister. It is just building after building, each with a single door into the alley. This is not a tactically advantageous place to be.

Two doors down, one of the nearby buildings back doors opens. Both of us drop into a shooting stance with our weapons pointing at the door. We must look like idiots, rotating our heads back and forth. If someone comes out that door they will be torn between fear from the weapons pointed at them and breaking into laughter from our bobble head imitation.

An elderly man walks out into the alley through the doorway. Bent with age and using a cane, not a prop like Mr. Lark does. His hair and beard are long, white, and full, and the clothes he wears are all black.

He raises the hand not on the cane and in a quiet and tired voice speaks, "I offer a peace bond to you both." English, accented yes, but since neither Illych nor I speak Turkish this is good.

Illych and I look at each other. Those are some of the first words spoken by the Magi Balthazar when we first met him on the island of Hy-Brasil.

Illych nods for me to reply.

"We accept your peace bond. Know this, should we not return our master will come looking for us. He would be most unreasonable if we are harmed." I am not lying. Mr. Lark reserves the murder of people working for him as his own exclusive right. No sharing.

A minute passes as the man hobbles towards us. He points to the door to the restaurant we just exited through. "Agreed, let us enter and sit. We will talk."

Illych shrugs and casually removes the crates he had just thrown down. He then holds the door open for the wizened old man whom we then follow back into the restaurant. The mess we made during our exit has been picked up. Most of the guests have left. A round table with six place settings is now in the middle of the floor.

Sitting in one chair is an elderly lady. At another chair is the woman who had checked us in. The third chair supports an adult man dressed in what appeared to be a pitch black full body leather suit with the hood pulled back exposing his face.

The elderly man moves to stand by the chair next to the elderly woman. Gesturing to her he says, "This is my companion Catherine, my name is Abraham. We are the oldest man and woman of our group. "The beautiful young woman sitting there," He says while gesturing to the younger woman. "She is here to remember what our old minds cannot. The man sitting there is Hector; he does what must be done to keep us safe."

Illych and I look at each other and take two adjacent chairs to sit down. Abraham slowly lowers himself into the remaining empty chair.

"You are the first to find us here. Few look and none solve the puzzle."

"How did you know we were coming?"

"The clergy at the church have been informing us when someone is seeking. Sergei is a good man. You," He said while pointing at me, "Said things that alarmed him and he sent word."

I nod. My outburst at the church almost got us killed. Sergei ratted us out even after we paid him very well. Of course, he probably expected we would never return.

Abraham pauses and then asks, "Who are you?"

Illych continues to defer to me in the conversation. "I am Thomas and this is Illych." Illych gives a little nod. He looks relaxed, sitting in the chair, but I know he is scanning, ready to become a blur of reaction if needed.

"How did you know?" Hector barks. Not quite yelling but still loud for being so close.

Illych is unruffled and calmly replies, "Perhaps we are not what we seem. Or maybe I saw you by chance. Either way, I will not share how you were revealed."

Abraham addresses Hector, "It does not matter. Servants of the Adversary would have killed everyone in the room. Not run out the back door."

"Wait, what was that guy going to do to us?" I already know the answer to my question when I ask it.

The old man answers, "Keeping our families safe is my only concern. Your deaths would have protected us."

Mr. Lark has a similar policy. No loose ends. Join or die.

"Why are you here?" Abraham asks.

It is a good question. We had not planned on making a scene. We had hoped to find more clues and report back. Not make full contact.

Thankfully Illych jumps in, "Why don't you explain who you are and we will then explain our goals in being here."

He is being careful and paranoid. We probably should make sure who they are. The fact they stopped trying to kill us is a good sign but without an Oculus we cannot know for sure who or what we are dealing with.

Abraham considers his words a few seconds and then speaks his next words carefully, "Yes, we must share for this meeting to work."

"I and the others in this room and in the town around us are the descendants of those who hung that tapestry in the church. Several hundred years ago those ancestors worked for a landowner near Digora. When the master unexpectedly disappeared one day, our ancestors carried on taking care of his lands. For over two hundred years they waited. When the Bolsheviks came it was not possible for them to separate those of us who served, from those they sought to destroy."

"Our ancestors left quickly and traveled to this place. They left behind that tapestry out of some misguided belief the master would return. We have lived here in peace ever since."

I interrupt, "Did this master have a name."

Abraham looks uncomfortable but answers regardless, "His name is Balthazar."

This should be interesting.

"The one your ancestor called their master has returned."

Hector jumps to his feet, "These are lies!"

Abraham's voice changed into something loud, like thunder, "You will sit and be silent."

He then addresses Illych and me, "Please forgive his outburst. He is young and does not remember the first ones like my parents did. Those who had stood in the presence of the master."

Hector sits and is silent.

"Why now? After all these years?" Abraham asks.

"That is along story," Illych replies. "Probably better told in person."

Illych pauses and then continues, "Abraham, we were not sent to contact you, only to find you and report back."

"You have found us. What will you do?"

It was my turn to speak, "I have a few more questions and then Illych and I will need to talk alone."

Chapter 10

"Abraham, what is that suit Hector wears?"

Abraham replies, "The first ones, our ancestors, when they left the lands of the master, brought artifacts with them. This suit prevents those who look upon it from seeing the suit and its wearer. Hector has trained long and through great difficulty to master its use. There is always one of us ready to put it on and deal with threats to our community. It has kept us safe through many trials."

Illych and I look at each other. No kidding, an invisible man protecting the community. That would shut down most threats pretty quick.

Abraham continues, "We have records of our ancestry to present to the master. Proof we descend from his loyal servants. I was a young man when we first arrived here."

That is difficult to believe and I feel clarification is called for, "You were a young man when you moved here, after leaving Russia? That was almost one-hundred years ago. You are a man of years but not that many years."

Abraham smiles and continues, "The first ones who served the master himself were changed in order to be more useful. We do not understand the craft of the change, but when the master accepts you, it will happen before you reach a score of years. Some do not survive but if you do, you will live a vital life past two-hundred years. The first ones left our masters land after he was absent some one-hundred fifty years. Only the youngest among those who had known the master remained."

"The change is passed onto your children but to a lesser degree. More so if both parents are of the chosen. If both parents are first-ones, then the child can expect to be vital past one-hundred and fifty. If only one parent, then one-hundred twenty years can be expected.

"My grand-mother had just celebrated her two-hundredth birthday shortly before my father was born. That was 1827 and my grandfather was an even older. My father lived for 164 years. The year of my birth was 1899; I was nineteen when we left Russia. This is my one-hundred and sixteenth year of life."

"I am the oldest man of our people who remains vital. Catherine is my companion as the oldest vital woman. Together we represent our people.

So far Catherine has not spoken. Regardless, I take Abraham's words as truth. At least I now understand why they live in this remote town. A group of people living a healthy life well past one-hundred years would draw unwelcome attention. I bet the people who conceived of the Bright Child Genetic Initiative would love to get their hands on some of the people in this town.

Now Catherine speaks. Her voice is quiet and soft. Abraham, Hector, and the yet unnamed younger woman listen intently.

She looks at me as she begins, "I cannot feel your emotions and your thoughts are hidden. Your words sound true but I cannot know. How is this done?"

The crown in my skull is shutting her probes out. When it was first installed I thought it a waste of time but since then it has proved useful.

I reply, "Our master has provided us protection against such craft. How are you able to do this?"

"That is a secret we will keep such as you keep yours. Only the ancient servants of old read as you do."

The Created, she is talking about the mythical creatures that are actually fantastically complex androids created long, long ago. They do not have emotions to radiate and I am sure whatever their thoughts are they would be completely alien to a human listening in.

Illych interjects at this point, "I believe the way in which our thoughts and emotions are shielded also interferes with the effect of your invisibility suit. Exactly how I have no idea.

Abraham is visibly tired and speaks next, "It is time for me to rest. Tomorrow we will discuss what happens next."

Illych nods, "We will confer with our master also."

Abraham and the others stand to leave. As he is walking out he says, "We will meet here in the morning for breakfast."

Illych and I retire upstairs to his room. After consulting his Oculus to make sure we are able to speak freely he switches on his ComDat.

"Held, are you listening?"

After a long pause Held's voice comes through loud and clear, "Yes and you are past due on your check-in."

"Things got complicated. We found Balthazar's people alive and well."

Mr. Lark's voice is next on the ComDat, "Excellent, we will bring this news to Balthazar."

Illych pauses to take a breath, "It is more complicated than that. We ended up making contact with them."

The silence is deafening before Mr. Lark's voice comes through, "That is not normal procedure. I trust there are extenuating circumstances?"

I took that as my queue, "An invisible man almost murdered us."

The ComDat was quiet for short while again and then Mr. Lark asks, "Is that so Mr. Davies? And based on your enthusiasm it appears you have survived. I will want the details of the invisibility incident."

Mr. Lark continues, "Since things have unexpectedly progressed we shall take them to their logical conclusion. Whomever you have made contact with, take them to Balthazar, assuming they will go willingly."

I reply to this, "We are not sure. They might be persuaded. Maybe." I look at Illych and shrug.

"Then be persuasive Mr. Davies. Contact me on the ComDat when you are a few hours from Balthazar's home."

Illych and Held briefly discuss potential travel plans and conclude the quickest way is by charter plane. We sign off and I walk straight to my room. Feeling positive there will be no trouble tonight, I only take reasonable precautions against unwanted visitors.

After a good night's rest, and further discussion of the circumstances, Illych and I go down for breakfast. The subsequent meeting is brief. Abraham and Catherine are informed of our intentions to take them to see Balthazar. I think both of them really want to see if all the things they had been told as children are true. Convincing them to travel to the Kharkareth ends almost as soon as it begins. They quickly agree and began making arrangements to leave immediately.

We live in a world where if you have enough money just about anything is achievable. And Mr. Lark makes sure we are well funded. Even by the standards of the truly wealthy we have access to significant liquidity. Both Illych and I carry 'black cards' with no credit limits. If necessary we can call certain banks that have lines of credit accessible around the globe. These are the kinds of lines of credit that guarantee payment no matter how silly the amounts we might ask for seem.

In this particular case, no feats of finance are needed. The airfield we arrived at on our way here has a normally priced charter available. This will deliver us to the nearest airport to the Kharkareth.

Illych and I pack up and are ready to exit in a short period of time. Abraham and Catherine are not far behind us. You do not usually see much in the way of giddiness in the elderly but these two are almost childlike with the prospect of meeting Balthazar.

The four of us are given one of the town's people's vehicles and in less than three hours we're airborne traveling towards Russian Federation airspace. None of us has passports or visas so you would think a Russian prison is in our future. Instead, Mr. Lark's contacts arrange for our safe passage, no questions asked. I am sure the fee is significant for this service but it is the cost of doing business in this part of the world. Most of the world runs on bribes and our employer knows where to pay.

The plane is a prop type and rather loud. The flight is several hours longer than our flight to Turkey had been, and we alternate between calm skies and uncomfortable turbulence. It is too noisy for conversation, so we fly through the afternoon without talking.

Before taking off, Abraham and Catherine both shared that this is their first experience flying. Illych and I wait to see how this will work out for our elderly passengers. When the first bout of turbulence hit I held my breath. They handled it like veteran fliers and continued looking relaxed and unconcerned. From where I am sitting it looks like being descended from the servants of an ancient Magi has its benefits.

Arrangements had been made for a vehicle to be waiting when we land. Within minutes of landing we are traveling what is beginning to become a familiar route while Illych contacts Mr. Lark to inform him of our arrival. The journey starts with rough roads and then out onto open country, finally ending at the familiar weather worn square pillar.

The four of us exit the vehicle. Illych and I lean back against the side of our transport while we wait. Catherine walks completely around us looking at the land within sight. Abraham shuffles to the square pillar and places a hand against it.

"It is true." The old man says. His face turns to us and there are tears running down his cheeks. I look at Catherine as she joins Abraham. She shudders and cries and the two hold each other.

Illych remains expressionless and I honestly do not know what to do. The display of emotion is making me uncomfortable. Abraham's statement does prompt me ask a question though.

"It is true? You doubted this existed?" They had an invisibility suit, what more proof is needed?

"We were taught so much as children, things too fantastic to be true. Yes, we had books and artifacts but we could not see or touch most of what we were taught. It was so much to take on faith."

"To be fair Abraham, you have not seen anything yet. This is just a square pillar standing in the middle of nowhere."

"No Thomas, a drawing of this pillar is one of the first lessons. Teaching how to know when you are at the front door."

As if Abraham's statement was their queue to enter, two Goblins shift into our vision from nowhere and begin circling us. Both have their usual appearance, green, gangly, clothed in a bad interpretation of children's clothing, but their mannerisms are different this time. When I first met them back on Hy-Brasil and every time since they are quiet, submissive, and very polite.

Now they would not stop moving. They are stalking around us and then even in between us. Abraham and Catherine are holding each other, visibly scared. Reading about the created in a textbook is wildly different than meeting the real thing.

One of the two stops moving and addresses us in the voice of a small boy, "You did not announce your visit." Its head and solid black eyes rotate to focus on Abraham and Catherine. "They are not with you. Did you bring strangers to the home of our master? It is not permitted."

I would have not thought Goblins could be agitated this way and anxiety grips me. Neither Illych nor I are prepared to deal with a single Goblin in close proximity much less two. Neither of us brought Truestone or a White Fang.

Just when how bad this situation really is starts to sink in, the spirit entity of the Kharkareth, seven feet tall, robes and all, shifts into view. It was highly unlikely we could have escaped from the Goblins. Now that this thing has arrived we are doomed.

I started running escape scenarios through my head same as I was sure Illych is doing, when the black clothed form of Balthazar appears. The Magi is not wearing his awesome robes or carrying his amazing staff. I am beginning to suspect we interrupted him in some way that might be considered rude.

The Magi closely looks at each of the four of us in turn.

"Thomas, have you brought me what I sought?"

"Yes. Balthazar please let me introduce the patriarch Abraham and matriarch Catherine. They are the descendants of the ones you seek. They traveled to meet with you and talk."

The elderly pair bow their heads towards Balthazar.

The Magi looks long and hard at all four of us, as does the spirit form of the Kharkareth. I suspect we are being scanned or somehow evaluated before being allowed to enter the non-Euclidean contraction that is Balthazar's domain.

Then without another word the Goblins shift away out of sight as does the spirit form. Even though we can no longer see them, my guess is they are close by.

Apparently nothing is found to cause alarm because Balthazar turns and waves for us to follow him. As a group we follow the Magi as he walks away from us, vanishing from my sight after taking two steps. The world vanishes and we are walking the stone road with the Kharkareth visible ahead. Abraham and Catherine are in awe, especially of the giant trees to our right, just as Tank had been a few days ago.

Balthazar's walking pace is quick, almost jogging, for the entire distance to the main gates. Catherine and Abraham are visibly struggling to keep up. The Goblins and the spirit of the Kharkareth occasionally shift in and out of the edge of vision as we walk. They are shadowing us.

Finally I had to ask, "Why the rush? Your visitors are having a difficult time."

Balthazar's reply is sharp, "Thomas, you were asked to find them, not bring them here. When I met you and Mr. Lark and the others I had time to observe you before you arrived. To make sure you were not tainted by the Adversary. Now you bring two people to my very doorstep without first receiving my leave to do such a thing. There may be consequences for this. You do not appreciate the subtlety of the Adversary."

The main gate doors opened soundlessly and we are led into the great main entryway.

Balthazar waives for the two elderly huffing and puffing members of our group to sit on a stone bench.

Balthazar continues the discussion, "They may have some mark or spoor upon them that does nothing until within my presence or within the presence of my residence. Now there is no time for subtlety or kindness. They are either untainted and will live, or marked and will die."

The Magi produces two glowing green stones in his right hand resembling oval emeralds. They possess a bright inner light that shines green on every nearby surface. Holding one in each hand he presents them to Abraham and Catherine.

"Take one and swallow it. Do it quickly!" Balthazar's impatience is obvious. This is shocking for me to watch. Every previous experience I have had with the old Magi he was mild and considerate. His current behavior is one step away from 'Mr. Intensity'.

Abraham and Catherine take their respective gems. Despite the jewels being rather large, they both try their best and succeed in quickly swallowing them.

Balthazar visibly relaxes. "We are safe now."

I look at the Magi and ask, "What was that all about?"

"The gems will seek any tampering and eliminate it and the host. It will be quick. We will know in a minute or two."

Abraham and Catherine are now holding hands and looking concerned. That was the problem with the Adversary. They could have been changed in some subtle way and not know it. Until they die…

The minutes tick slowly by and the look of concern slowly dissipates. They are not dead.

Balthazar signals the all clear by saying, "It is good."

Addressing Illych and myself he asks, "When will the rest of your organization arrive?"

Illych replies, "We expect Mr. Lark shortly. He knows of our estimated arrival time."

"How many descendants of my servants have survived?"

Abraham replies, "There are over three-hundred of us."

"And who is guarding the remaining descendants of my former servants?"

Illych's face became an instant mask of concern, "I beg your pardon?"

"You determined the precise location of their village while visiting Digora nearby. The Adversary will have a spy there. You were most certainly followed to Turkey. Mr. Lark should have anticipated this and provided protection after making contact and during the absence of these two."

I had a problem with this, "The adversary is able to maintain spies so close by?"

"The adversary is prevented from maintaining strength of any consequence within one-hundred leagues of where we stand. But a spy? Something small, this can get in."

Illych holds up his hands, "Ok, ok, I will return to our vehicle and contact Mr. Lark."

My colleague jogs away out through the gateway and out of sight. Balthazar is sitting with Abraham and Catherine quietly discussing who knows what. Leaving me to wonder what is taking Mr. Lark so long to get here? Illych contacted him on the way here and being the master of arriving right on time is one of his skills.

No sooner had those thoughts formed in my mind and Illych and Mr. Lark walk in through the gateway. Illych must have met him half-way to the vehicle.

Mr. Lark begins speaking as he walks in, his voice loud and clear, "Balthazar, I have posted security at Ehgira, the village in Turkey. Your people are safe for now."

Balthazar nods and shakes Mr. Lark's hand.

"Thank you for your diligence. A peace bond is offered to you and your servants. Please enter, I will offer hospitality and a more comfortable setting for our talk."

This should be interesting. During my previous visits I had only seen a library past the entryway and it did not qualify as a comfortable setting.

We leave the entryway and enter the Kharkareth proper. Catherine and Abraham gawk at the beauty of the place. History is recorded for the viewing in sculpture and murals as we walk long halls. The Goblins disappear but the spirit of the Kharkareth is never more than a handful of paces from Balthazar. The Magi is much more considerate now, moderating his pace for the benefit of his guests. The walk is short before we turn and walk through a doorway into what I would consider a much more comfortable room.

Perhaps you would call it Arabian style comfort. Large, heavy rugs cover the stone floors. A small fire pit is aflame in the center of the room. Large, firm, but comfortable pillows form places to sit half-reclined, having been arranged in a semi-circle around the fire.

Balthazar waves his hand across the open space. "Please sit and take rest."

Abraham and Catherine sit close to each other. Illych predictably takes the place closest to the door and I sit in between the elderly couple and Illych. Mr. Lark takes the other side of the door and Balthazar has his back to the wall opposite the doorway.

Once situated the talking begins. At least until the first Goblin servant shifts into sight and poor Catherine makes an undignified noise and Abraham's eyes go wide when it appears. They both watch it closely as the thing begins serving coffee and offering small breads and other food. Apparently their experience at the square pillar has not helped them with the peculiar way the creatures appear and disappear.

I now realize I am really, really hungry. During the plane ride and the long drive here there was no opportunity to eat. The small bites being gracefully served are excellent but there are not enough of them to be satisfying. I do not want to look like a glutton but I am hungry. The Goblins apparently determine my need without request and leave one of the trays by my chair.

After perhaps fifteen minutes of everyone becoming situated and relaxed, I notice Abraham apparently tell Catherine a joke and she giggles to the point of no longer being dignified.

The question on my face from this catches Balthazar's attention, "Yes Thomas, the green gem they swallowed has after effects. They will be very positive and light hearted is how I would guess you would say it, for some time."

"How long?"

"It disappears over a handful of days."

Mr. Lark speaks next, "Balthazar, Illych told me about an invisibility suit. If not for his ingenuity I would have been forced to find someone new for security and a new librarian."

Balthazar does not stop looking at me. "Have you ever been sitting, perhaps focused on another task and your head, almost without your control, turns and you see someone looking at you?"

I nod.

"The suit knows, just like you know, when it is being observed by human eyes. It removes itself from the sight of those who look upon it."

"Is that really being invisible?"

"Perhaps not, the light from the suit still reaches your eyes. The image is sent into your mind. The suit then manipulates your mind into not acknowledging its presence."

Reaching into my mind and turning things off. I do not like the sound of that.

"The crown Mr. Lark has placed into your head interferes with the suits effect."

No kidding, Hector was going to kill us.

A few quiet minutes pass. I believe the inaction is bothering Mr. Lark.

Balthazar finally speaks, "Mr. Lark, I spent much time in meditation on your behalf and wish to share more of what I have learned of Castle Houska.

Balthazar now has Mr. Lark's full attention.

"At the bottom of the pit is a gateway to another place. You call them pocket dimensions. The Magi have never entered this place. But I can tell you that Those Who Came Before gave life to living things there. When they were gone, the creation of living beings continued in an uncontrolled way. Things came from that pit."

"For you to fully understand I must instruct you on the order of life in our universe. There are the Angel's and Daemons, these are the Higher Ancient beings left here. A few have chosen to guide or destroy humanity. Then there is the pantheon of Goblins and Faeries, these are the Lesser Ancient ones. They are neutral and largely passive. All of the ancient's physical forms are not as ours. They are stronger, faster, and more resilient. They neither eat nor sleep. They follow the path set for them long ago and cannot change. In your understanding they lack free will so to speak. Their experience is not our experience."

"There are the spirits from the other side. When an Ancient one's physical form is destroyed their spirit endures in that place. They will form a new body for themselves here in our world over time. There are other spirits who cannot form a physical body. However they can involve themselves in the affairs of man by possessing a human either voluntarily or involuntarily. Those strong enough to fully control a human body are called the Possessed."

"Then there are the living, plants, animals, and humans. We live; we die, procreate and continue. This is as it should be."

"Abominations are the manipulation and warping of living things. Their creation is as the name states, an abomination. Such things should not be."

"What remains are the constructs. The Haemonculi and Golems created from what is available and motived by a spirit form coaxed into it from the other side. They can perform simple tasks or remember things and speak them back on command. They can be made by ancient or human hands using hidden knowledge."

"There are engines at the bottom of the pit beneath Castle Houska that allow for the creation of living things, abominations and constructs. Those same tools may provide for a rapid return to the physical world by ancients who have lost their physical form. The worst possibility is that humans can be taken there, their lives artificially ended, followed immediately by selective possession."

At this point I had to say something. "So why not just fill in the hole?"

"Yes, a straight forward solution. But no, the gateway will keep the shaft clear over time by eroding whatever is used to fill it."

"There is a cap on it now and it does not appear to be eroding." It seemed reasonable to point that out.

"There is truth in that, things have changed Thomas and I will explain now. Please be patient, such things cannot explained simply or quickly."

Balthazar composes himself and continues, "Upon the fall of the Roman empire much of the understanding of the ways things truly are and the protections the empire afforded was lost. A school of learning and protection was formed. In many ways it mirrored the efforts of the Magi even though they were not aware of us. The called themselves 'The Scholomance' and they did many great and good things until the church turned upon them and forced the breakup of the brotherhood."

"The last great work of the Scholomance was the construction of Castle Houska. They placed a Weaving of the Wyrd to fill the top of the pit. This allowed for a physical cap to be constructed without the pit being able erode it. The weaving also changes anything moving through it. This is why anyone lowered into the pit is horribly affected."

The Magi pauses and then finishes, "So it has been for seven hundred and fifty years."

Mr. Lark speaks next, "Then there is no way in?"

The Magi shakes his head, "The granite plug." The out-of-place long, perfect cylinder of granite below the castle connecting the pit to the outside world.

Even from where I am sitting I can see Mr. Lark's left eyebrow raise.

The Magi nods, "A solid unbroken piece of granite can be made permeable and physically traversed under the right conditions."

The way in is right there in plain sight for those who know how.

The tone of Balthazar's voice changes, "And now we come to the return of those whose ancestors served the House of Balthazar." He looks intently at the elderly couple sitting closely together.

"None of those currently living have served me. The expectation of service would be presumptuous on my part. Where you educated in the history of the House of Balthazar and the roles your ancestors played?"

Catherine spoke, "As children our lessons were based around the idea of the return to this place. Each generation has grown less attached to this history though. Those roles were demanding, including lifetime service. And then there is the matter of the change. We have children but they are involved in the modern world. It is possible a few would be interested in being inducted to your service."

Balthazar appears to be thinking deeply and then he replies, "It is as I suspected it would be. We cannot make all things happen in this one brief meeting. Please understand the joy in seeing the line of my servants endure even if they do not wish to return and I wish to present the opportunity even if it is rejected. I believe one must witness the Kharkareth and what could be, to fully understand the offer."

Catherine and Abraham, still smiling and energetic from consuming the detection gems, look at each other and back at Balthazar and nod in agreement.

Balthazar continues, "Then there is the consideration of security. If the Adversary is now aware of the village then everyone is in danger."

I feel compelled to ask a question, "Why did the Adversary not destroy them back in the 1800's? Surely if it could have followed us from Digora could it not have seen them leave the Kharkareth remaining nearby?"

"Thomas, there are many peculiarities from that time. Such as the Adversary knowing the perfect time to run me to ground during my journey to the new world? As for my former servants, they were not a threat to the Adversary when they left. Now, returning to me they become useful. That would be enough difference to compel their destruction now."

That makes sense. Why take the effort to destroy a group of people in a difficult to get to part of the world when they pose no threat?

"I wish you could stay and I could offer the comforts of my extended hospitality. However I feel compelled to ask you to return immediately and bring the people of Ehgira here. Not a moment must be wasted. Mr. Lark, you must make this happen quickly. We will discuss your fee after your success."

Wow, Balthazar sort of just gave Mr. Lark an order. I cannot wait to see how this will play out.

Mr. Lark stands and locks eyes with Balthazar. The sitting Magi does not blink or flinch. The two stare at each other and I swear if a piece of paper had somehow fallen between them it would have burst into flame.

I do not know what transpired between them during that minute but Mr. Lark broke eye contact first and says, "It will be done."

Balthazar does not accompany us to the main gate. One of the Goblins escorts us out and we follow Mr. Lark in a hasty exit.

As we are walking to our transportation Mr. Lark speaks again, "Illych, I will be unable to accompany you to Turkey. Arrangements must be made here at Digora and I will make the preparations for the return of however many chose to come. Tank, Held, and Mike are on-site in Turkey. Please update them of the situation and that trouble may be coming. After the arrangements here are complete I will join you."

Illych nods, "What will you really be doing in Digora?"

Mr. Lark smiles and says, "Making arrangements as I said. I will also be looking for that spy. Perhaps it will have something to tell us."

With that said we separate and begin the drive to the airport.

Chapter 11

Striking up a conversation with Abraham, who is sitting behind me in the vehicle, seems like the thing to do, so I turn my head and ask, "How many of your people are there in Ehgira?"

"Precisely 302 souls, including Catherine and myself. We track our numbers quite closely. There are some expectant mothers thus that number will change soon."

"Will any of them be interested in joining with Balthazar?"

"Who can know this? The first ones service to the House of Balthazar is a difficult enough subject. His disappearance impacted our ancestors with feelings of loss and abandonment. And now we meet Balthazar for this short time at the Kharkareth. It looking exactly as the legends say it should."

Sounds like this situation has been debated before and they did not reach a common agreement. "It was a lot to experience in such a short period of time but I am sure your people will have time to think and discuss amongst yourselves what to do. The important thing is Balthazar is back and the descendants of his first ones are alive and well."

That is the best positive spin I can think of.

Abraham asks a question, "Thomas, why was Balthazar gone all this time? There was never a chance to ask and the others will want to know. I want to know. Why did Balthazar abandon us for so long?"

So this is the hang up. They think Balthazar went on a 350 year walk-about and is just now coming home to check up on the old place. Talk about being as far from the truth as possible.

"Balthazar was trapped on a phantom island for 350 years, starting shortly after he left the Kharkareth. He could not return until we discovered and rescued him." I say this while pointing to Illych and myself. "The organization we are part of inadvertently discovered the Magi there. He then hired us to get him home."

Abraham is obviously thinking about what I just said. Shaking his head he shares his thoughts, "Thomas, the Magi are powerful, and possess wisdom derived from ancient knowledge. I do not believe Balthazar could be trapped in such a fashion."

"I almost agree with you but I believe there is a difference between riding out from the Kharkareth arrayed for battle versus being far from home and finding yourself thrust into an unanticipated conflict."

The conversation died away from there. We are tired and have another long, loud flight ahead of us.

We previously left Ehgira mid-morning. The flight to Russia, the visit with the Magi and our return flight brings us back to the village at first light, the day after we left.

As soon as we land Illych uses the ComDat to initiate contact with Tank, Mike, and Held. They are keeping to themselves in a vehicle outside of town. It is not comfortable but it allows them to keep watch without interacting with the townspeople. No need to have more unexplained newcomers waiving a red flag around in front of Hector.

So we, the four tired travelers, meet up with the three tired watchers no more than two miles outside of town. Abraham and Catherine are looking especially travel worn, being of an age that does not travel nor deal with sleep deprivation well.

The three watchers are standing by their off-road capable vehicle and drinking freshly brewed coffee. Both Mike and Held are trained to use the Oculus. For them it has a range of twenty kilometers or so. Thus no one is concerned about anyone or anything getting too close through covert means. It will show up on the Oculus long before it could be a threat.

When we stop to meet the others, Abraham and Catherine get out too stretch their legs. They immediately stop in their tracks when Tank walks around the vehicle and his broad shadow falls across the pair.

Both of them stare at his huge frame. Tank is a man of somewhat above-average height at six feet. He is also a maniacal powerlifter and he does not do it to make pretty muscles. The former Marine lifts weights like a guy who might have to go back to prison. If you are being held hostage and your naked body is being beaten into jelly with a big rubber hose like I was recently, the one profile you will be thankful seeing come through the door to rescue you will be Tank's.

Regardless, when the sun is low in the west and the shadows are long and you are meeting someone you have never met before and that someone turns out to be Tank, you might take a few steps backward.

Hands are shook, backs slapped, nods exchanged, coffee shared.

He likes to joke around, maybe sometimes a bit too much. Tank of course is not his real name but after almost six months with Mr. Lark I have yet to learn his real name. Note to self, keep trying.

Tank realizes the elderly couple is gawking at him. Not one to miss an opportunity, he stops to address their concern. Smiling he says, "What? You never seen a real man before? " He poses and flexes a bit followed by a brief laugh and then continuing on his way.

When our coffee clatch is finished we all mount up so Abraham and Catherine bring us into town. During the short drive in, Mike updates us over the ComDat about what was found during their viewing of the town through the Oculus. During the wait for our arrival they had hours to perform a detailed and thorough observation of the place.

"Most of the houses have something like a safe room underneath them. There are several secret rooms scattered about town and a tunnel from the hotel basement that ends a kilometer outside town. And gold coins, five locations, some are pretty deeply buried, significant quantities."

"Our secrets," Abraham says, "You know our secrets. How is this possible?"

Tank's voice came over the ComDat, "Cause we are that good, cause we are that good." I could hear his smile carrying over in his voice.

Mike cuts in, "The townspeople have posted about a dozen armed guards. They are either in lookout positions or patrolling as pairs. Otherwise all is quiet."

By this time we are rolling into Ehgira on what passes for main street. After parking in front of the hotel we witness greeters emerge from several buildings around us. They are not interested in interacting with anyone from the team, only Catherine and Abraham. The townspeople surround the older couple and guide them away. There is just enough time for Abraham to say we will meet for dinner in an hour and they are gone.

Illych implements rotating watches for the team, minimum two men, and one of the two needs to be skilled in Oculus operation. My shift starts just before dinner so I shuffle off to find a hotel room and hopefully get a half-an-hour of sleep.

My watch tells me not more than a handful of minutes of sleep have passed when I am awoken by yelling and a commotion downstairs. Somebody is making a lot of noise. I do not want to get up or get involved but figure it a good idea to go downstairs.

Besides, since falling into the service to Mr. Lark I have come to accept sleep deprivation as a way of life, why deny it now.

Grabbing my gear, I pull it on as I stumble down the stairs into the main dining room. By now the shouting had quieted down and I catch a glimpse of two of the townspeople running out the front door.

Illych and Mr. Lark are both standing and communing with their respective Oculus. When did the old man arrive?

Mike and Tank have brought in several large ballistic cases. Tables and chairs are thrown out of the way so the cases could be set down in the clear and opened. Once their contents are made visible I can see what is inside looks like a toy chest for the God of War. Grenades, breaching charges, directional fragmentary charges, a 40mm grenade launcher, and a German MG4 with backpack ammo feed.

"Good, sleeping beauty is up," Tank snarks at me.

"Why is it the world always goes to hell whenever I fall asleep?"

Held walks in through the backdoor, "No time for chit chat. Gear up, the fight is coming to us."

Illych begins shaking his head as he disconnects from the Oculus. "This town sits on a single road that passes straight through it. There are two busses coming, one each from both directions. At least eighty hostiles each. There is no way to escape. We stand and fight."

"Hostiles will be within range in less than ten minutes. The good news is they have no heavy weapons, only AK's and a lot of ammo"

I slip into my body armor and start strapping on my gear. "Who is coming?"

Illych walks over to a ballistic shield leaning against the wall. "Bad guys Thomas, men will evil intent coming to kill everyone in this town including you. Get with the program or this is going to turn into the Alamo."

Mr. Lark starts speaking, addressing no one particular, "The men on those busses are bound with a terrible rage against everyone in this town. They will kill every man, woman, and child if they can."

Illych speaks, his voice loud and clear, "Tank, Held, the west, Mike and I will take the East. Thomas you will remain inside the town and hunt down stragglers." No sooner did he stop speaking and the four men pull helmets into place and file out the door.

I am alone with Mr. Lark. He is not wearing the ancient armor he wore when Balthazar took me hostage. Nor is he wearing the ballistic carapace the team is wearing. All he has on is black tactical dress with a single M1911 holstered under his left arm. I know better than to ask. He will do whatever he is going to do. I witnessed him shutdown an attacking Djinn in the caves below the Ellora temple complex. Human gunman will not be much of a challenge to him.

As for me, I am not going to let a bunch of butchers kill innocent people just because a supernatural force from another dimension permanently twisted them into sadistic killers. I grab my KRISS and walk out the front door.

The street is empty, all the doors are shut and many windows have aluminum shutters over them. The town is small enough, and with hotel centered in the town, means I can see the town limits in both directions from where I am standing.

I flip on my ComDat, "Comm check, this is Thomas."

Mike replies, "Roger that, you are loud and clear." I am surprised, he does not sound stressed at all. This always surprises me about my colleagues. When something like this happens they always seemed to have lifted spirits like they are doing something they have been looking forward to.

Based on the position of the sun above the horizon we have, at most, an hour of sunlight left. This is an impromptu attack because the eastern group will have the sun in their eyes as they advance. No military commander would do that on purpose. While looking west I see the bus come over the last hill before reaching town. Quickly looking east I see another bus come into view. They are big Mercedes Euro tour busses. Nice transportation for bloodthirsty berserkers.

Startled a bit, I realize Mr. Lark is standing next to me in the middle of the street. His expression flat neutral.

"Any advice Mr. Lark?"

"Kill them before they kill you?"

We stand there watching. The team's lack of long range firepower leaves us helplessly watching our approaching doom. The busses stop about half a kilometer outside of town and the men in them begin debarking. From where we stand we witness both situations unfold. The Bound quickly form a long line abreast, faced to the village. The flat terrain allows us to see them but they are out of range for anything other than a sniper rifle.

Broad daylight, open terrain, our foe had expected the benefit of total surprise and no ready resistance. Yah, score one for the Oculus. These guys are about to meet resistance. Even so, there are at least one-hundred and sixty of them. Once they make it to town, if they still have numbers, we will get swarmed and cut down.

As soon as the busses are empty, as if on cue, both enemy lines begin to advance with a quick gait. It is quiet, no birds chirping, there is not even a breeze. Just still quiet air. Hundreds of people in motion and not a sound to be heard.

Shotguns and a KRISS are probably limited to an effective range between one-hundred and two-hundred meters. But the MG4 with a bipod Tank carried out to the west side on his shoulder is perfectly comfortable with targets at five-hundred meters. The silence ends in a demonstration of the effective range of an MG4.

Tank fires a short burst to find the range and sight in his weapon. I cannot see where he is firing from or the effect it has on the target. Following are long bursts. Through spaces between buildings I watch the advancing men to the west. They do not pause in their advance, marching right into Tank's kill zone.

Mr. Lark's voice is crystal clear over the ComDat, "These men are cruelly bound. Wounds will not stop them. Only kill shots."

Illych's voice is next on the ComDat, "Thanks for the confirmation."

Both lines of attackers break into a sprint. They are fast, really fast. From my limited viewpoint I was able to see a burst from Tank's weapon knock down a section of the attacker's line. Most of the fallen just get back up and start limping, walking, or running towards the town again. Kill shots indeed, now I understand.

I look back to Mr. Lark to ask a question and find him completely gone from my sight. This leads me to wonder if Hector is out there in that suit. I turn my head back and forth a few times to see if he is nearby. No Hector, no Mr. Lark.

The running lines make it to less than one-hundred meters from the edge of town and they are moving like Olympic sprinters, the binding driving them to super human feats. As they reach the first buildings the road narrows my field of vision to nothing and I lose sight of most of the attackers. Looking back and forth down both roads I can see a group of attackers from both directions making a sort of a wedge formation on the road with the apparent intent of sprinting straight into town.

Each wedge is a handful of men, a fire team of five or six. Once inside the edge of town they split up left and right and run to the front doors of the first residences they come to. Finding the doors locked they used their weapons to shoot the locks open and charge into the homes. It is happening so fast and I am still standing in the middle of the road in front of the hotel.

Tank growls over the ComDat, "Held's wounded and we are pinned down in a house. I am keeping them out for now but we are trapped and out of the fight. They seem content with holding us in here and attacking the civilians."

Illych spoke next , "Roger that. We are still maneuvering but we are taking a lot of fire. Same here with the civilians."

I move to one side of the street and begin jogging east. A group of attackers came out of a house reloading their weapons. I shoulder my weapon, took aim, and began firing short bursts. Two of the three men went down and then promptly got back up. All three lifted their just reloaded weapons to their shoulders and began firing. A round grazes a ballistic plate on my right thigh, knocking my leg out from under me.

My body does a weird spiral spin and I land on my back with the wind knocked out of me. The men who had just shot me must have thought me dead and begin walking away. I use the short pause in gunfire to get back on my feet and reload my KRISS. The men are slow leaving, apparently considering what to do next or perhaps their wounds are catching up with them?

For one man, the latter is true, he walks a few steps and then collapses to the ground going completely still. The other two keep shuffling away with their backs to me. I shrug, aim at the healthier of the two and pull the trigger on my KRISS. After five rounds I shift the weapon to the last man and let the brass jacketed .45ACP rounds do the work. Both men crumple to the ground.

Shooting them in the back is not the honorable thing for me to do. However, being shot really hurts, pushing me more towards an effective solution.

Continuing east along the row of buildings I come across something I did not expect. A spaced out line of dead attackers running some distance between the buildings, made up of perhaps as many as eight corpses. I suspect this is Hector's handiwork, starts at the back end of a line and silently work his way forward.

Tank's voice comes over the ComDat, "Hector is over here with that invisibility suit thing you talked about. It is a little weird to see guys getting knifed but you can't see who is doing it. The guy is quick too. Shows up, eviscerates a half-a-dozen guys and is gone. Held is in a bad way, we need to evac soon if he is going to be saved."

Illych is next, "Roger that. As soon as we are clear, transport will come your way."

Curiosity got the best of me, "Anyone seen Mr. Lark?"

A chorus of, "No's" reply over the ComDat.

While listening I am weaving between buildings looking for bad guys. The sound of gunfire is coming from all directions, combined with echoing from the buildings makes it impossible to pinpoint the nearest attackers.

Turning a corner I am just in time to witness four men enter the front door into a residence. From the condition of the door they must have gunned the lock open to gain entry. Sprinting to catch them I cover the space to the doorway in seconds. The door is up a few steps which I take in one leap and barrel through the doorway full steam. There is no guard at the door for me to deal with. I hear screaming coming from a nearby room subsequently cut short by ragged automatic weapons fire. Maneuvering through the rooms at the front of the house as fast as possible, I turn a corner and stop not five feet from the four gunman.

They just finished their goal of murdering a family hiding in a back room. I cannot see everything through the doorway but I see enough to know not to look closer.

My KRISS has a fresh magazine and the gunmen are empty. The first two go down to single headshots.

Sane men might have begged for mercy or tried jumping out a window while their compatriots are being shot. These gunman are not sane however, their minds bent and twisted to hate and kill. As the first two men are crumpling to the floor, the two furthest from me charge.

It is then that I realize I am too close to them. They swing their empty rifles like caveman clubs. The impacts do not hurt much, the body armor and helmet preventing any real injury. They do knock my KRISS from my hands though. Without my weapon I have a problem. In their maddened state there was no way I can hurt my attackers enough with my hands to win a straight up fist fight. Eventually they will figure out how to beat me to death.

So I decide on the crazy way out. Maybe if I had more time I would have been cleverer, instead my right hand pops a fragmentation grenade loose from a harness pouch, pulling the pin. I open my hand letting it fall to the floor. Out of the corner of my eye I see it lazily rolling on the floor to rest against a wall perhaps three feet away.

The gunmen take no notice of the grenade and keep clubbing me with their rifles. Even with the body armor absorbing most of it, the impacts are getting painful. I do not look forward to the soreness I will feel tomorrow, if I live that long.

Grenades are not like in the movies. There is no wall of flame and walls are not leveled. There is just a really loud crack and a puff of black smoke. I am betting my armor will stop the detonation from killing me.

It works, sort of. The gunmen take a lot of shrapnel. One just perishes, falling down and remaining still, the other is now a bloody mess on the floor screaming this unholy high pitched squeal.

My gamble pays off, I am still alive. However something got through one of the seams where my chest carapace meets the plates at my waist. It hurts and burns at the same time. I touch the area with my hand and it comes back bloody. There is nothing I can do for now but keep going.

Picking up my KRISS, I confirm it is still operable. One shot later and the mess on the floor is no longer screaming.

Illych's voice is clear through the ComDat, "Status everyone, sound off!"

Tank is first, "This is Tank. I am uninjured. Held is injured and alive but can't speak."

Mike was next, "This is Mike. I will live."

There is a pause and Illych says, "Thomas?"

Illych asks again, "Thomas?"

"Oh yeah, I am bleeding a little but still here."

"Tank hold your position, Mike is bringing transportation to you."

"Thomas where are you?"

I looked around the wreck of the house I am in. "I am in a house. Heading back out to the main street."

Now it is quiet outside. Since the grenade went off there has been no gunfire. Maybe it is over?

My side hurts with each step but I see no more hostiles or to be honest anyone at all as I shuffle back to the main street. I pop the facemask on my helmet to get a breath of fresh air and immediately regret it. The smell that greets me is of cordite from weapons fire mixed with a whiff of death. The helmet filters had been keeping it from me.

Once back on main street I head for the hotel. Mike waves as he drives past continuing on to the west edge of town. Tank strides out from between buildings with Held over his shoulder. Mike and Tank carefully put Held in the vehicle. Both men then jump in the front seats and the vehicle leaves town going west. I know what they are doing. Once they make it about ten miles away they will translate back to the Compass. There, Held will be loaded into the electric cart and raced back to the Citadel and the Doctor. My guess is he will be OK.

Turning back, I continue to walk to the hotel which now seems so very far away. One foot in front of the other, it is the only way I will get there. Half-way I realize Mr. Lark is now walking next to me. A quick glance tells me he is uninjured. Apparently none the worse for the experience. Typical.

"Thomas, I am pleased you survived." The tone of his voice does have a pleased tone to it.

"The day is not over yet Mr. Lark."

The old man nods, "Not yet but the sun is setting as we speak." What he says is true. The battle for Ehgira lasted less than thirty minutes. It is now dusk and lights across the town are becoming visible.

I continue, "I came across some of Hector's work. A whole line of gunmen with their throats cut. Looks like he took them down, one at a time, in quick succession."

"Yes, invisibility gives a number of advantages. Your enemy is not expecting you because they cannot see you coming. This helps with the coup de gras, the killing blow. They do not see it so they do not try to defend against it. There is an old Roman proverb, *how many throats can a running man cut in one day.*"

Mr. Lark then smiled his overly broad smile, "I wager Hector could provide an answer to that proverb."

Pleased and then creepy. Yes, the day is not over.

We arrive at the hotel and find Illych inside. Hector, Catherine, and that dark haired lady from our first visit are all sitting in chairs. Illych's armor is mostly stripped away and he sports bandages on his neck, both arms, and he is holding a sterile pad to his left side. He looks tired, in pain, and happy, all at the same time.

"All the gunmen are dead Mr. Lark."

Our employer nods.

Catherine's mild voice spoke next, "This would not have happened if you had not come. They followed you."

Mr. Lark's voice is harsh and cutting in his reply, "Such reasoning is for fools. If your people had remained in Russia they would have been close enough for Balthazar to protect them. If this town had been properly fortified, casualties would have been minimalized. Or for that matter private security could have been hired considering your communities vast wealth. Shall we go on?"

Gotta leave it to the old guy, when he snaps he snaps. The room is deathly silent for awhile until Illych speaks, "Estimated one-Hundred Sixty gunmen. Between the team, a handful of townspeople, and Hector, we did pretty well. My estimate had them overrunning the team and killing everyone. Especially after they demonstrated they could run so fast and only kill shots were putting them down."

Crap, Illych thought we were all going to die.

In a reasonable tone Mr. Lark asked, "What are the civilian casualties?"

Catherine replies, "We are still counting. We estimate slightly greater than one-hundred dead so far. There are very few wounded. The gunmen put significant effort into making sure each of their victims perished."

Hector decides to contribute his opinion to the discussion, his tone accusatory, "What about you Mr. Lark? Where were you during the battle? You look as if you were hiding!"

Easy there mister, this is one bull you do not wave a red flag in front of.

Mr. Lark's head turns slowly and his cold eyes transfix Hector. Everyone present witness the invisible man blanching under that gaze. "Making sure we did not lose."

There is a pause in the conversation and then Mr. Lark starts giving commands, "Catherine, prepare your people to move. All the survivors are going to the airport and on to Russia. Take only what they can carry. Movers will be hired to come in and pack up the whole town and transport your belongings to Digora. This location is not safe."

Hector, Catherine, and the dark haired lady began speaking to each other in a language I did not recognize. It is a fast paced, staccato like language unlike anything I have heard before. Their conversation is short and Hector and the dark haired lady both stand and quickly leave.

Catherine finally responds, "We will do as you wish."

It finally registers with me, someone is missing.

"Where is Abraham?"

Catherine's voice becomes a whisper, "He is dead. He was with his family in one of the first home's the gunmen broke into. There were no survivors."

I nod and breathe deeply, turn and walk outside. It is twilight becoming night and I can feel the air cooling off from the heat of the day. Just a few minutes ago it had been dead quiet. Now there is activity everywhere. My side is starting to bother me more. It needs to be looked at soon. The old man's death is affecting me. Knowing I can never talk to him again.

I watch as vehicles appear from garages and families began loading them with children and belongings. Illych is already making the arrangements for chartered flights and a no-questions asked entry to Russia. So much effort and sacrifice to get a group of people to move. I hope Balthazar values what has been paid for in blood today.

Tank's voice comes over the ComDat to tell us Held had seen a doctor and is recovering. His statement is code for Held having been completely healed by the Lesser Created Doctor. Lucky bastards are probably sitting in the cafeteria drinking beer while they clean their gear.

The evacuation proceeds quickly. A motley caravan of cars and vans form a long line as we drive to the airport. Each bump makes me wince but I am needed for now and cannot leave. Healing will come later. Right now we need to get these people on a plane.

It turns out three planes will fly through the night. We arrive in Russia and load into busses at dawn. A village of people who had just survived a firefight, followed by being ripped from the only homes they had ever known to fly through the night to a foreign land. And after landing, more travel for hours over rough roads to their final destination.

One-hundred Ninety-two survivors arrive in Digora. Since over the last ten years the village population had been dwindling, it is easy to find accommodations for everyone.

The current town residents are curious about the sudden arrival of new residents. After Illych had a conversation with the local clergy and money changed hands a wave of positive enthusiasm for the newcomers washed across the village.

It had been decided the official story would be that the new arrivals are descended from former residents who had moved away in the distant past and were now returning and bringing their prosperity with them. Strangely enough this is not far from the truth.

Finally, hours after night has fallen, Illych, Mr. Lark and I leave and go in search of a quiet place to translate away. Within the hour I am limping into the Citadel. Thirty minutes later my healed body is enjoying dinner with the rest of the team. It is a short party, everyone's exhausted and I am asleep seconds after my head hits the pillow.

Tomorrow will be another day.

Chapter 12

The last few weeks have been over the top. Multiple visits to see Balthazar and the search for his missing servants ending in a gruesome firefight. For being a librarian by trade, I am spending a lot of time traveling and meeting people. Sometimes killing them, mostly in self-defense, mostly.

Waking up the day after the big firefight, I find I am not inclined towards leaving my bed, much less getting up to go to work. In spite of my visit to the Doctor yesterday healing my wounds, the effects of over-exertion and sleep deprivation are afflicting me to the point of being a handicap. With no small effort I lift my left arm and consult my watch.

Illych gave me this watch on my first day at the Citadel. One of Mr. Lark's creations, its internal operation is based exclusively on light. Another example of our employer's aversion to electronics, the result is an oversized, heavy, and strange looking wrist watch. The reading of minutes and hours is non-standard but still relatively straight forward enough to easily understand. After a moment focusing my eyes, I determine I just slept for fourteen hours.

Fourteen hours is enough. Any longer is like inviting Tank to enter my room with a bucket of ice water. Time to struggle from bed and begin my morning ablutions.

Twenty minutes later my tired feet shuffle into the cafeteria. My colleagues, other than Illych, are all clustered together at one table engaged in an intense conversation. They are in disagreement over something and it is getting heated. Staying out of it seems a wise course and I head for the coffee.

Mike is now shouting at Tank, "The long range ones do not count. We only count the ones that made it to town. Not all of us had a long barreled machine gun. "

Tank bellows back, "I was pinned down with Held after that. Just because you are too weak and tiny to handle a man sized weapon is not my fault."

Really? They are arguing over who had the higher kill count yesterday. That is kind of tacky. Americans…

Illych walks in at a brisk pace and I feel my exhaustion weighing even heavier. He has something for us to do, I just know it. I can tell from his walk. At least the others stop their arguing when he enters.

All four of us watch and wait. Illych ignores us and our sudden silence, serving himself a cup of coffee and sits by the others. I take this as a cue and join them.

Illych speaks with a clear direct voice, "Stop looking at me like you are about to be punished. We are all tired but that does not stop us moving forward. The good news is we have a whole day to cleanup and rest."

Everyone visibly decompresses at those words, Tank and Mike even high-five each other.

"Except for Thomas and myself." Crap, what fresh Hell am I about to be forced into?

"We leave for the Kharkareth in an hour. Those remaining are responsible for cleaning his gear from yesterday."

The Kharkareth again? Mr. Lark may want to consider getting me a room there.

Illych looks at his own abomination of a time piece and announces I now have fifty-eight minutes left to prepare and meet him at the gates ready to go. He stands and leaves, taking his coffee with him.

Breakfast is quick and I end up arriving early at the front gate. No dress code was specified so I went with all black tactical.

Illych shows up dressed similarly. We turn to leave and the gates open without command in anticipation of our exit. My companion does not seem to be in a hurry and the hike to the Compass is at a reasonable pace. I take the opportunity to find out why we are travelling to Balthazar's, again.

His reply, "No kidding, we are there at least once a week lately."

"What is the reason this time?"

"Mr. Lark is being rewarded, just as Balthazar promised. Since we were able to get most of the servant's descendant's home safe, something the old

Magi promised he would be extra generous for. This should be interesting to witness."

I snort a reply, "What, more piles of gold? I would like to see some of those books in the Magi's library during our first visit. Or the books he let me read on Hy-Brasil while I was held hostage. I never finished and their contents are unique."

We walk in silence for a few minutes.

Breaking the silence again I mention, "That was intense yesterday."

Illych looks over at me, "Small talk Thomas? Perhaps we can discuss the weather. Here at the Compass it is cold, dark, and gloomy."

"Ok, ok, I just feel like you are not telling me everything about this visit."

"I do not tell you everything about everything, get used to it."

That said I keep silent during the next hours traveling to the square pillar marking the entrance to Balthazar's home.

We are expected and the Goblin sent to bring us in is non-threatening. Even the non-Euclidean contraction the Kharkareth resides in is beginning to experience the cold bite of winter. There is a light dusting of snow on the road as we walk.

Half-way to our destination I stop and look back.

Illych walks a few paces and stops, "Thomas, what are you doing?"

"Look at the snow. You can see our footprints."

Illych gives me a look he reserves for fools and idiots.

"Where are the Goblins prints?"

That look disappears when he realizes we made footprints in the snow.

But the Goblin left no prints.

We look at each other and resume our walk. I file my observation away for future consideration. It might mean something or it might mean nothing.

Leaving the chill air behind us as we enter the Kharkareth, stomping snow from our boots we continue following our guide. Our course brings us to the same room Abraham and Catherine sat in just a few days ago. The lighting is more subdued now and most of the room's red colored illumination is from the small fire pit in the center of the room. The effect is not much different than being in a red-lit cave.

The Goblins do not enter with us, instead remaining outside in the hall, shifting in and out of sight. Seated inside is Balthazar, and standing close behind its master, the spirit of the Kharkareth. Mr. Lark beat us here. He is seated next to Balthazar on large pillows, rather close to Balthazar, discussing something in low tones.

Our entry interrupts their discussion and in a strong clear voice Balthazar speaks, "Please enter and sit. Your master has accepted my offer of a peace bond and hospitality. Tonight we feast and celebrate my return to the Kharkareth, the return of my servants, and the success of your many labors since my return. Payment and reward is now due from the House of Balthazar."

Illych takes a seat near to the door. The room is too small to be truly far from anyone present. I take a place on the other side of Balthazar opposite from Mr. Lark. My choice of seating pleases the old Magi. Even Mr.

Lark is acting almost happy, in his own expressionless way.

Fine crystal goblets filled with wine appear without warning, the work of the Goblins. While remaining seated Balthazar raises his glass, "A salute to your success. The Adversary's efforts have recently been blunted more than once. This is a rare thing to witness and it was done with great cleverness." The Magi empties his glass which is quickly refilled.

I follow his example in draining my glass. The wine is too good and I suspect this party is going to be interesting as my glass is also quickly refilled.

For the next three hours we feast and drink. The food is amazing and varied beyond my ability to remember it all. When Balthazar goes all out it is amazing.

By the end of the feast I sit back in a relaxed pose, my mind more than a little foggy. The wine really is that good. Illych fully participated and is now half-sitting, half-lying in relaxed bliss. Even Mr. Lark enjoyed himself, as much as that is possible, taking on the look of a satisfied and relaxed predator. If that had been the point of the feast, it succeeded.

Without warning Balthazar stands straight up and claps his hands together. Addressing us in a clear voice, "Now is the time for you to receive what is justly due."

"The first gift is for the soldier and warrior, the tip of the spear, the chief of the guard, Illych Popovich."

This catches Illych and me completely by surprise. We figured Balthazar would roll out a pile of gold and some knickknacks for Mr. Lark to deposit in a vault somewhere. Instead Illych is being personally rewarded.

The somewhat inebriated former Green Beret carefully raises himself to his feet.

A Goblin enters through the doorway keeping a slow and deliberate pace. His poorly fitting, low quality, imitation children's clothing replaced by manservant finery of a bygone era. The diminutive Goblin is effortlessly carrying a wooden chest almost as large as himself. The chest is carefully set at Illych's feet.

"As you are aware, the effects of time, as you understand it, can be slowed after a fashion. It is not the true slowing of time but resembles it as most everything happening around us is affected. A very longtime ago, in a different age, an ancient master delved deep into the knowledge of what was known about the long sleep and the apparent slowing of time. He chose to take this knowledge in another direction."

"He wrought a set of vambraces, forged to increase the speed of the wearer. This increase is small when compared to the greater universe. But for the man wearing them, the effect is impressive. You will be faster and stronger. Your movement will challenge even some ancient servants. A warning I give with this gift: though you wear the vambraces, you remain human. Your body will strain as normal. Your bones will break should you push them hard enough. Use this gift only in dire necessity. This was chosen for you as I perceive you have need of it in your future labors."

Illych bends down and opens the box. From where I am standing I am unable see the contents until they are lifted free. The vambraces are shiny silver half-shells that fit to the owner's forearms. Displaying good judgement, he does not try to put them on right now.

Instead he nods to Balthazar in thanks, returns them to the chest and sits back down.

As gifts go that was pretty awesome. I feel like a child nearing Christmas. Hopefully I get something like Hector's invisibility suit. Translating into a trouble spot fully invisible, I would be unstoppable. And the pranks I would pull on Tank would be legendary.

The overdressed Goblin returns with another box to be placed at my feet. I look at Balthazar and he, without the history preamble, nods for me to proceed. I open the wooden chest carefully. Inside it is lined with felt and upon the felt is a pair of dull grey balls, each perhaps four inches in diameter, connected by a flexible braided copper cable. The cable must have been at least seven feet long.

I reach into the chest to bring out my gift and show the others when the Magi interrupts me. "Please wait Thomas while I explain your gift of humble appearance."

"Not all material in the universe is as substantial as other material. The earth beneath our feet, affected by gravity and magnetism is quite substantial. Other things less conductive are not as in the present as they would seem. Stone of certain types are an excellent example."

"What is in that chest will change a human, normally quite substantial, into something less than the earth beneath his feet. The effect lasts for precisely twenty-three seconds during which you can physically pass through homogenous objects, mostly stone materials of flawless quality."

"It is activated by holding one ball in each hand and outstretching your arms at shoulder height to achieve the desired effect. You will see and feel the change. If you are partially within something when the time runs out you will be ejected into free air. Even if it means you are to be crushed should the space you are delivered to is too small. If you are completely within something solid when the duration ends, then there you shall remain, mixed with the stone."

I nod to Balthazar in thanks. Now I can walk through walls.

Now it is Mr. Lark's turn. Based on how amazing Illych and my gifts are, what comes next could be truly epic.

"Karl Lark, the services you have provided to the House of Balthazar have required great effort and risk on your part. You have been generously compensated with gold in the past. The recent return of my servant's descendants requires you be rewarded and this time not with common gold."

"I worried the treasure halls and vaults beneath the Kharkareth for days, reviewing the inventory collected there over the eons. The choice for your gift is driven by the need to combine something sufficiently exceptional to match your accomplishments, and useful in the future endeavors I may ask of you. Perhaps somewhat self-serving on my part, but necessary."

"You already have efficient methods for dealing with ancient servants, but your tools against the Possessed are limited to destroying the human body they inhabit. For this I gift you an ancient and diabolical weapon feared by the Possessed."

The goblin enters the room again, this time with a much smaller chest. As he slowly walks towards Mr. Lark my mind races with the possibilities of what could be within that chest. The Goblin holds the container in front of Mr. Lark and Balthazar nods for him to open it.

Mr. Lark opens the chest and lifts his gift free for all to see. It is a small baton of crystal, perhaps a foot long. From where I am standing its liquid contents are visible.

"What you hold will bring a Possessed to its knees. When the contents are sprinkled upon them they feel true pain. In all their millions of years of existence they have rarely felt true pain. The effect ruins the host body forever and their phenomenal physical abilities are destroyed. The contents are self-renewing over time."

"I warn you now. Using such a thing on a Possessed will bring upon you the eternal hatred of something that it would best never know you. If you can achieve your goals by other means, I suggest you do so."

I look around the room and consider the gifts Balthazar has given us. Illych will be stronger and faster than probably any living person. I can now walk through walls and Mr. Lark has received a magical holy water sprinkler. Not a bad haul.

"Our feast is over and the gifts are given. Mr. Lark you have the matter of what is beneath Castle Houska to resolve. I will take my leave now. My servant will show you out."

Balthazar walks to the doorway with the spirit of the Kharkareth close behind. A goblin, clothed like a homeless child again, shifts into view waiting for us. Without a word we collect our gifts and began the journey home.

Chapter 13

The next day back at the Citadel, the whole team, including Mr. Lark, gathers in the open space near the main gates to experiment with the gifts from Balthazar. All witness as Illych, dressed in exercise clothes, straps the vambraces to his forearms.

The former Green Beret comments, ""They are warm. I can feel them connecting through my arms and chest." Illych's speech and movements become choppy, the sounds starting to not make sense.

Then he moves, running away from us while taking the inside loop of the Citadel. He is a blur of speed, at least twice as fast as normal man could run. Arriving back where he began, he stops and tears at the vambraces to get them off, throwing them to the ground.

"Ow, that hurts," He shares while rubbing his legs.

Mike asks, "What was it like?"

"Try them for yourself. I was fast and I knew it. But after I started to run it began to hurt. The pain grows the faster and farther I went. You might want to stretch first."

Mike nods, walks over, picks them up from the ground and snaps them in place. After a few moments to acclimate, the former Ranger takes off running at a terrifying pace. He also runs the inside perimeter arriving back in even less time than Illych had. Mike skids to a stop, tears the vambraces off and throws them to the ground, mirroring Illych's actions.

"Oww is right."

Illych looks around at the rest of us, "Any other takers?"

Held, Tank, and myself wave our hands and decline, "No thank you, I will pass."

Mr. Lark had been passive, silently standing while watching the spectacle. Now he speaks, "So that is how that works. We may need to bring more painkillers. Mr. Davies, your turn. Walk through that buildings wall." He points to a nearby small stone structure.

I look at the coiled up ball and cable contraption in my hands.

"Why is it so weird?" It is bugging me how strangely constructed it is. Why not some box with a switch? Two balls you hold with your hands outstretched? What a goofy way to activate it.

Mr. Lark is unimpressed by my statement. "It was made by those who never watched science fiction on television and are intimately aware of a large multi-dimensional universe. The reason for the cable being seven feet long I thought is fairly obvious."

He pauses and appears to not be planning to elaborate.

He is forcing me to state my ignorance, "What is obvious? That it cannot be used by anyone taller than seven feet?" This is the only reason I can think of and I felt just as dumb saying it as I had been in thinking it. The distance between your outstretched hands is typically the same as your height. Since your hands must be fully outstretched for the device to be activated and the cable is seven feet long, no one taller than seven feet will be able to activate it.

"Excellent Thomas. Yes, to prevent giants from using it should it fall into their hands. You must consider that over the course of Earth's history many creatures have walked this land and many of them did not follow the Homo Sapiens norm. Now try out your gift."

Holding one each of the heavy stone balls in separate hands, I outstretch my hands, lifting them to shoulder height. A warmth spreads from the balls to the palms of my hands, and then across my horizontal arms, finally meeting between my shoulder blades. It only takes a second. I know the process is complete when my colleagues gasp and take a step back.

"What? Am I invisible?"

"No, you are still visible but only as a blur," Illych's replies.

"Remember, you only have 23 seconds." This comment came from Mr. Lark.

The nearest stone wall of the targeted garden shed sized building is not five paces away. I run at it, positioning myself to bounce off with my shoulder if this does not work. Instead I pass through the wall. It is like sliding through something thick and heavy. As I pass through I feel the pressure of the walls material pushing in on me. Then I am through to the other side standing inside a dark room. The effect having worn off, it is then I realize I dropped the device outside just after it took effect.

Feeling my way to the door I find it locked, from the inside or outside is hard to tell in the pitch black. I start banging on the door while calling out to my colleagues. In return I faintly hear some laughing outside and then the sound of something moving, like a lock being turned. The door opens outward and I walk out into the brightly lit interior of the Citadel just in time to witness Michael outstretch his arms and change into a blur. The blur is poorly defined, making your eyes hurt as you concentrate to see it.

The blur quickly shifts through the wall I had just had traversed, followed by a visible Mike walking out the other side and back into view through the door. He nods and comments on it being a positive experience. One by one everyone gives it a try, even Mr. Lark.

Mr. Lark concludes, "This is how we gain entry to Castle Houska. Each of us will hold this device in turn and then immediately traverse the granite plug. Plan on leaving for Castle Houska tomorrow morning after breakfast." He then turns; exiting through the Citadel's silently operating main gates.

Illych takes this as his cue, "Full gear check after lunch at two. Weapons check at 5. Dinner and then bed. Everyone needs to be rested for this event."

As the others walk away I move towards Illych. "Did you notice he did not try out his holy water sprinkler?"

"Neither of us is Possessed and I suspect the stuff that comes out of that thing has no effect on normal people."

"You are probably right. What do you think of the mission?"

"Very positively Thomas, it is like the story of two men walking together in the woods and they come across a bear. One of the men says to the other, we cannot hope to out run a bear. To which the other man replies, I do not need to outrun the bear, I only need to outrun you. After all, if anything goes wrong I can just put on my shiny new bracelets and run away." Illych is smiling now.

"Ha ha, funny." I am sure is joking.

The rest of the afternoon is spent checking gear, live weapons check, and more checks. It went on and on. I do not know if American military people are the same as other nations but they are thorough to the point of the ridiculous. We are five guys, how many times can we check the same equipment?

After the final check we virtually marched, under Illych's watchful eye, with all our gear still on, to the main gate. There, all lined up in a row we strip our gear down into our own individual piles. Since we are the only humans at the Citadel, our equipment will be waiting right where we left it tomorrow morning. There is a collective sign when this chore is complete.

Dinner is lively. After so much controlled time it feels good to goof off a bit. As much as a group of experienced veterans goof off. Regardless, dinner is short and I take my leave early. Fall asleep reading a book that has been on my to-read list for a long time.

A gentle knock on my door in the morning is my wakeup. It is Illych of course, I know without looking. It is time to get going. Breakfast first, ablutions, and then game time.

I am the last to the main gate. The others are obviously excited and there is an anticipatory energy to them and I feel invigorated by it. Now is time to put our preparations to use. By 0900 East Coast time we are ready. At 0901 the gates open and Mr. Lark walks in. He wears that strange all black banded armor I am told he found somewhere in Mexico. Illych would not say much more, only that it was in an abandoned non-Euclidean contraction similar to the one where the phantom island of Hy-Brasil or the Kharkareth reside in. The material it is made from looks like black glass. Every joint is articulated and the plate behind Mr. Larks head is part of the back piece coming up over his white hair and forward to his forehead. The closest thing to it I can think of to describe it is medieval armor blended with a cosmonauts suit. His face remains exposed but otherwise every inch is encased by suit.

I witnessed him wearing it once before, when he came to get me back from Balthazar. At first contact with Balthazar, the Magi took me hostage to force a meeting with Mr. Lark. Upon seeing the armor Balthazar recognized it and told Mr. Lark not everything walking the face of the planet will be pleased to see such armor survived. Mr. Lark is a man who cares little for the opinions of others, thus he continues to wear the armor.

Mr. Lark makes a cursory examination of the team ending with a nod to Illych who returns the nod back. It is time. As we exit the gates the demeanor of each person changes. The hypervigilance shows on their faces and their gait changes to something more direct and purposeful. They are now a wolf pack on the hunt. Weapons that had been left in holsters or dangled casually from a harness are now properly gripped in the ready position and game faces are on full display. The team is ready to ruin the day of anyone or anything that gets between them and whatever goal Mr. Lark assigns.

When we go to battle there are no air strikes, no main battle tanks, and certainly no large movement of troops. We come in the back door, quick and quiet. Accomplish our goals by any means necessary. You can forget about fair play or being nice, these men play to win.

The walk to the Compass is silent and quick. Once there Mr. Lark hands out the one piece of gear we did not already have, our escape dongles. The small bronze batons are secured differently by each man. Some use a pistol magazine pouch; others casually stuff it in a pocket. That is my preferred method, right pants pocket.

There is no pause in our movement upon arriving at the Compass. We walk straight through the standing stones and circle. No sooner than we stop and Mr. Lark's hands do the dongle flip.

Castle Houska's time zone put it at mid-afternoon when we translate close to the edge of the bluff the castle sits upon. Trees and bushes provide ample cover for our arrival. There are no trails near the granite plug. While the team and myself recover from translation sickness Mr. Lark is already scanning with his Oculus.

He speaks less than a minute after our arrival, "As long as we stay close to the face of the bluff there is no one even remotely able to witness our position."

As soon as each man is fully recovered, we shift not twenty feet to the smooth face of the granite plug. I had not realized it is recessed into the bluff a few feet and the native stone frames the plug in a natural looking way. The exposed face of the plug is not much larger than an irregularly shaped doorway.

Translating to the other side of the plug would have been quicker. Unfortunately the experience in the Black Forest with the Quixault trap makes that a hazardous choice. The Adversary would most likely not have a lethal trap or guard out here in the world where a random hiker could end up fatally disturbing it. But inside, there could be something.

Hence the need to walk through walls.

Mr. Lark has some last minute information to share as he begins speaking, "Once past this granite barrier the Oculus will become less useful. The 'Wyrd' as Balthazar puts it, at the top of the shaft, just below the plug under the chapel, interferes with its normal operation. Some aspects of the device remain useful to me but I suspect most of you will not find your Oculus functional once we enter. It is possible they will regain functionality at the bottom of the pit as it is such a long drop to the portal."

Everyone nods in acknowledgment.

"Thomas, the device if you please."

That is my cue. I drop the rucksack from my back and pull the coiled artifact clear.

"Illych will determine the order of entry. Upon clearing the other side we will expect a verbal confirmation of success over the ComDat."

Illych points at Mike, "Private Snuffy, you go first." Mike nods, and grabs the artifact. Placing a ball in each hand he begins to outstretch his arms.

Mr. Lark shares one last piece of information, "The plug is less than ten feet long. No more than four or five paces."

No sooner did Mike nod in the affirmative and his arms reached their full spread. He disappears, replaced with a vague blur. The artifact reappears as Mike drops it and the blur moves the few feet to the granite face, merges into it, and disappears.

I involuntarily begin counting seconds and make it to five when Mike's voice comes over the ComDat, "I am through." He still has time until the effect wears off.

Illych queries, "What do you see?"

"No contacts, and no lights, it is a hall hacked from native stone. The floor is clean and smooth, like a lot of feet have walked through here in the past."

Held is next, followed by Mr. Lark. Then Tank and finally me, Illych is the last and he is to bring the artifact with him. The practice on the stone walls in the Citadel makes sure this part of the plan is a success. The granite plug is a lot thicker than the building walls back at the Citadel and there is a point when traversing, having left the entry way behind but not yet made to the other side when you are completely encased in granite. At this point your only protection is the effect of the device Balthazar gifted me. His warning of the consequences of being completely encased forever, should I not make it to the other side in time, whispers to me as I push through.

Relief washes over me as I cross back into open air and stand there waiting for the effects to wear off. The others moved down the hallway a good twenty or more feet and I join them. Tank slaps my back as a show of success in making it. Not even a minute later Illych arrives with the artifact still in his hands.

In addition to the full body armor we are all wearing we also have full face ballistic helmets that incorporate the ComDat, microphone hearing, night vision, and filtration protection against air borne threats. The gear we wear costs a fortune.

Night vision gear in the real world is designed to operate in low light conditions. Some light is necessary. Here in this tunnel it is pitch black with zero light of any kind. In order for our night vision to function properly all of us have a low output LED light clipped to our right forearms. This fully illuminates everything for the night vision while remaining barely visible to the naked eye.

Mr. Lark's voice comes over the ComDat, "The granite plug, platform, and spiral stairs were added after the castle above us was built. Someone or something wanted access to what is below."

Illych makes some hand motions and Mike and Held take point. They had already begun moving forward to the platform indented into the shaft. This is where the long spiral staircase downward is carved into the walls of the pit begins. The other end is more than a hundred building floors distance down. It would take so long to fall to the bottom that you would need to pause and inhale a few times to keep screaming all the way down.

The spacing between each member of the team is wide. If anything like the Liger from the Black Forest adventure pops out it could only get one us before the others react.

Mr. Lark is taking his time getting to the platform. He is operating the Oculus continuously at this point and is only able to walk slowly while being so engaged. Every so many paces he pauses as some detail consumes his full attention. The rest of us continue moving forward, weapons at the ready, providing security. This is probably the most dangerous part of the mission. We are essentially trapped in a solid stone cul de sac. It took time to get through the granite plug. If we were attacked by a dedicated foe right now it would get really ugly real quick.

Mr. Lark stops his shuffling and disengages from the Oculus as he makes it to the middle of the platform. Mike and Held are now covering the stairs going down. The others watch the edge of the pit. There is no railing, just smooth stone floors and a better than a thousand foot drop.

Even the stairs are just a recessed spiral in the wall of the shaft going down. No railing on the stairs either, just regularly spaced pillars at the edge. Apparently safety was not part of the design considerations back in the day.

Mr. Lark's voice breaks the silence, "No guards at the door. I find that odd. And no evidence of detection or observation of our entry. There is no evidence of regular use either. This indicates there is at least one other entry point."

I thought about it and then comment, "Maybe getting through the granite is a rare knowledge."

Tank spoke next, "Or maybe everyone smart enough to get past the front door is not dumb enough to challenge what is down those stairs."

Mr. Lark nods at Illych. This starts the journey down into the dark below. Illych directs Mike and Held to space themselves out in front and stay close to the wall. After that we form a line with Illych, Mr. Lark, I and Tank bringing up the rear.

The trip down is nothing like in the movies. We are quiet the whole time. The full face helmets and the ComDat help with that by allowing us to communicate normally with each other while remaining completely silent to an outsider. The night vision we are using is very effective in preventing missteps or poor footing.

And nobody accidentally or otherwise tosses anything out into the pit. No stones, buckets, or light sticks are casually released and then watched as they fell. Because that. Would. Be. Stupid.

It takes hours to walk down the enormous number of stairs to the bottom. The stairs themselves are not uniform in height or width. This made moving along them difficult. You would not think uneven stairs could be a problem until experienced first-hand. Combined with the hazard of no railing, everyone is extra cautious.

The entire trip down is uneventful. No scary shadows or booming drums. As creepy as this place is I would have accepted hearing an evil cackling soundtrack. There are no bones, trash, or disturbing splashes of blood anywhere. From what I can tell this place is long abandoned.

With the spacing so far apart, the team is completely wrapped around the pit and I can look across and down to see Mike and Held ahead and below me, allowing me to witness their arrival at the lower platform. Since we are not throwing things in and we are not shining lights around there is no way to check how close we are to the bottom. The psychological effect of this is to make the journey feel like it is taking forever.

Our arrival at the lower platform ends that.

Mike's voice comes over the Comdat,"Arrived at the lower platform. Another recessed space open to the shaft. There is also an archway leading somewhere on the inside wall of the landing. How should we proceed?"

Illych replies, "Everyone advance and quick secure the landing and whatever is through that arch. We have been taking it slow long enough. Let's move quick and maybe we can surprise someone."

All of us surge forward. What had been a slow and careful advance changes instantly into a rapid movement. In seconds we are all on the platform. The pit edge is similar to that of the landing above. Except the pillars here all had these perches sculpted onto them sufficiently below the ceiling to accommodate gargoyle statues, three to each pillar. The pillars ring the entire landing resulting in dozens of gargoyles staring at us.

The pit is still there but I know from earlier discussions we are close to the bottom now. From here there is a shorter fully encased spiral stairs to the bottom.

Tank and Illych are keeping an eye on the landing and the pit, so I join Mr. Lark in observing what is past the arch on the inside of the landing.

Mike and Held had already entered the small room beyond the arch. Looking in I see it is a small chapel. Or at least it had been. The smooth stone floor does not cover much more space than a large room in an average home. But the ceiling soars far above. There is defaced stone work everywhere and the pillars along the walls have those same perches as the pillars out on the landing. Except these pillars have no statues on them…

"Mr. Lark?" I started pointing at a pillar and the empty space above the perch. He does not respond immediately and I realize his eyes are closed and he is engaging with the Oculus.

The others are looking at the empty perch and realization begins to move through the team. Why are these empty?

Mike comments, "I have a bad feeling about this."

Held yells to the others still out on the landing, "Tank, Illych, get in here!" Yelling, of course, is completely unnecessary due the ComDat and the sound deadening provided by our helmet speakers. The emphasis on the need to move quickly however, is not removed by the tech.

Mr. Lark lets out an uncharacteristic sound and speaks, "Someone knows we are here. A burst of energy came up from below and split up with a single tendril ending in each gargoyle statue outside. I think they are some kind of golem or haemonculi. Regardless they are probably going to start moving."

"Everything out there registered at almost zero anything and then this burst lights up the Oculus. It was not painful but it did startle me."

Illych and Tank jog in through the archway, "The statues out there are about to come to life." Both men shrug. It is about to get weird. What else is new?

Illych speaks next, "Go heavy people." That was the cue to hook the KRISS currently in your hands to your harness, swapping it out for a heavier weapon in or on your pack. Mike and Held had M79 40mm grenade launchers. They are single shot, break open weapons. Both men produce a bandolier of 40mm shells from inside their packs, slinging it across their chest. This was followed by one large shell being seated in the weapon and the action snapped shut.

I half expected Illych to pull out the vambraces and a big hammer. Instead he retrieves two sections of a double rifle from his pack. They easily connected together leaving the former Green Beret holding what looked like a heavy double-barreled shotgun. In fact, it is a double rifle in .600 calibre. Rifles like this are for hunting really big game, the kind where if the first shot did not work you might end up eaten. The brass shells Illych is feeding into the weapon are the size of cigars, each one incorporating a tungsten penetrator into its tip.

Mr. Lark moves to the center of the room and appears to be keeping his hands free. I know better than to ask what he plans to do.

Gripping my KRISS tightly, I look around for Tank. Upon finding him I almost started laughing. The big man has a Prohibition era, gangster style, Thompson submachine gun in his hands. Drum magazine and all. In the hands of the burly ex-marine it would shred just about anything it is aimed at.

The thud out on the landing, as the first stone golem walked off its plinth and lands on the stone floor, can be heard as well as felt as vibration in the floor. That first thud is followed by others, so many others. There is no counting them all. Had to be at least fifty, maybe more, based on counting the pillars from memory.

The first one walks into the archway less than a minute later. At only four feet tall with rounded features they look like something from a children's book. Except for the claws, they are longer than before and the thing has its hands up in a slashing position as it advances.

Mr. Lark calls out, "Illych."

I am still looking at the stone creature when the first shot from the double-rifle detonates. I can hear it and feel the rapport. Being in close quarters, my night vision clearly shows a jet of flame emitted from the weapons barrel extending almost to its target.

The round punches straight through, leaving a baseball sized hole in the gargoyle's chest.

The second shot closely follows the second. The creature's loss of so much structural integrity is too much and the thing folds in on itself, crumpling to the floor.

Two more gargoyles walk in behind it, pushing the ruins of the first out of their way.

Illych calls out to Tank.

Thank God for the hearing protection. The weapons being used would destroy a person's unprotected hearing in such a close space. Tank plants his feet, cradles the Tommy gun and proceeds to carve the first and then the second gargoyle each into pieces. Chunks of stone gargoyle are flying everywhere.

Pieces of three stone creatures litter the space around the entryway. Stone dust and weapons exhaust fill the chapel with dust and smoke.

Illych gives the command to fire at will.

The next few minutes are a blistering cacophony of weapons fire. Our night vision equipment is barely coping with the constant strobing of bright light produced by weapons discharge. The pile of gargoyle bits is really starting to take up space inside the chapel. If we are not careful our foe will bury us alive under their corpses.

Illych announces we will try to push out onto the landing and get the grenade launchers into play. Throughout all of this I have been an observer. Between Illych and Tank there is not much left for the rest of us to shoot at. Kicking aside gargoyle chunks we move forward. Looking through the doorway I see dozens of the creatures advancing.

Mike and Held aim and fire. At this range and considering the enemies numbers missing would have been a difficult feat. They are firing shaped charges that made a loud crack sound when detonated on one of the stone creatures. These rounds had been designed to put the hurt on a lesser created. The gargoyles stone construction meant nothing compared to that level of durability.

Each shell shatters a single gargoyle. This allows us to push fully out onto the landing. Not a bad place to be if we decide to evacuate up the stairs. Tank snaps his last drum magazine in place and hoses four more monsters to the floor. He sets the smoking weapon down and grabs his KRISS.

Illych's updates the team, "They are getting ready to rush us. Either we go up the stairs or back into the chapel. Based on the numbers we may run out of ammo before we run out of targets."

Mr. Lark spoke one word, "Stairs."

The path to the stairs is relatively lightly defended. Only a handful of the slow moving things block our escape route. Those obstacles are violently removed in short order. Soon Mr. Lark and I are up the stairs. The other four are alternating pairs, shooting and falling back. I am not a slacker in all of this either. Throughout the engagement so far I have put down three of the monsters.

It is a bit irking how Mr. Lark does not actively participate. He just watches. Occasionally, he shifts his position for a better view or to accommodate someone who is actually fighting. From prior experience I know the man can fight. Apparently that is not part of the plan this trip. No one's life in any danger yet so it was not worth getting too excited about.

The stairs are wide enough to accommodate five gargoyles abreast as demonstrated by how they are advancing up the stairs. As each one is destroyed, another pushes its fallen stone body aside and takes its place.

The grenade launchers and the double rifle are discarded, their ammunition spent. Everyone is using their KRISS now. A full automatic burst consuming an entire magazine delivered center mass had fifty-fifty odds of putting one of the creatures down. The flashes from the gunfire continue, illuminating everything around us. From my higher vantage point on the stairs, I see the end of the creatures. There are only a few rows left, so at most there are thirty of these things left to kill. If kill is the right way to say it, maybe deconstruct would be a better way to say it. I announce what I am seeing over the ComDat. The others give positive affirmatives back.

While looking down the shaft to the other side at the lower landing we just left I see something in the dark. It is long in body and moving with supernatural speed and agility, scrabbling up the pit's stone walls. The body of the thing shows no signs of clothing or weapons. It reaches the landing, crawls up onto it and disappears.

Looking back at the battle I notice the others, including Mr. Lark now, are working to maintain a certain volume of fire to keep the things back. Realizing my participation will help, I shoulder my KRISS and open fire.

This went on for another minutes while we back slowly up the stairs. The gargoyle ranks have thinned to almost nothing. Only two partials rows left. This is good because I have used up half my KRISS ammo loadout.

These are just the guards at the front door. Who knows what else we will have to deal with down there.

Instead of continuing to fall back, Illych calls out for us to hold position and finish the stone monsters. This engagement has gone well, no one is injured, and we have proven ourselves more than the equal of a pack of stone gargoyles.

For some reason I am not feeling particularly victorious, like I missed something. There is unfinished business here somewhere. Then I remember the thing crawling across the walls down by the landing. We were a considerable distance higher now but the others need to know something might be hiding down there waiting for us.

The helmets we wear are designed to filter out noises and protect our hearing. During a gun battle like the one that was just now winding down, all I hear is muted gunfire. Now that the weapons are going silent other noises become apparent.

There are scratching noises, like claws on stone. I focus and look around below us for the source of the noise. It becomes evident the sound is actually above me, above and behind me. I turn in time to see a Ciorii hanging by one claw from the edge of the pit above the stairway.

It releases its hold on the stone and lands on its two feet not three strides from where I am standing, while drawing itself to its full height.

Ciorii have solid rectangular bodies with long spindly arms and legs. At full height the monster is at least seven feet tall. They do not have a neck per se; their heads are just set atop its body. Set high in its head are two very large solid black eyes. These things have no mouth or nose. Just a long string of short tentacles from where its nose should be, down to where its navel would be, if it had one.

It is looking right at me, freezing me with fear. My first and only experience with a Ciorii was back in my flat in London, in my last few minutes as my own man. If anything my fear of these things has increased since then.

It moves towards me in a blur, slamming it chest flat against mine while wrapping its ridiculously long arms tight around me. With a small lift my feet no longer touch the floor.

Without pausing it runs right off out into the open pit with my struggling body still in its arms.

Chapter 14

The next few moments are me screaming uncontrollably as I fall to my death clutched to the bosom of a monster. My colleagues get an earful on their ComDats as I fall.

My reaction is based on my belief the Ciorii has grabbed me and jumped out into the shaft to drop me to my death. Instead, I remain firmly clamped to its chest, face to face with the thing, able to barely make out its inhuman features before the blackness of our descent takes away my sight.

How far we fell I am unsure, maybe fifty feet. Then we contact the walls of the shaft and the foot claws of the Ciorii make a loud scratching noise as our descent slows. The thing pushes off out into the darkness, our descent again increasing in velocity. This process of jumping from side to side continues, falling a considerable distance between each contact with the wall.

My initial screaming terror is replaced with silent, cold, dread. I faintly hear my colleagues over the ComDat trying to contact me as I fall through the darkness.

The dry, cold air has a dusty metallic smell as it rushes past us in the dark. The Ciorii clutches me so closely to its unnatural form I feel the short stubby tentacles on the things chest probing and twisting against my body armor. They grip ammo pouches and rip them free from my tactical harness. The ComDat goes silent as its solid metallic form is found and ripped away, the voices of my colleagues suddenly cut off.

It is so revolting, combined with the never ending drops into nothing, broken up by sudden, scraping deceleration that I felt my gorge begin to rise.

The nausea's point of no return has almost arrived and I was considering the impact it would have on our relationship were I to somehow open my helmet faceplate and vomit in the face of the Ciorii. I am saved from those consequences by landing on a hard flat surface with a bone jarring thump. The monster then just opens its arms so I can flop from its chest onto hard ground.

There is light here. Not much, just enough to look up and see the Ciorri's alien form standing over me. The thing bent at its waist and appears to be regarding me with its oversized solid black eyes.

Ciorii are watchers, kidnappers or assassins and I am not sure which role this one is performing yet.

The thing then crouches down, bending its knees and leaps straight up into the shaft opening above us. I can hear it scrabbling and scratching its way up for maybe half-a-minute and then it is gone.

The faint light in this place comes from fluorescent amber patches the size of hand prints randomly placed on the walls and ceiling around the chamber. From this feeble light I can tell the place I am in is roughly circular and the ceiling is at least thirty feet above me. The Ciorri made a vertical jump around five times its height, a scary thing to know. The fluorescent patches, combined with the illuminator connected to my armor, provide enough light for my night vision to operate. I will not be able to read signs but it is enough to keep me from tripping over stones or falling into holes.

The chamber I am standing in the middle of is really big, like the one with the stasis machine back in the Ellora cave complex, at least a hundred feet across with three equal sized openings indicating tunnels for exits. The surfaces of the interior of the chamber look to have been clawed from bedrock. The floor beneath my feet is rough, but flat enough for walking without tripping or twisting an ankle. I will still need to be careful though. As I look around I see stones the size of my fist randomly scattered about.

The gear stripped from my harness during our descent continued falling with us, Looking down I see their smashed remains scattered about where I am standing. My KRISS has shattered into several pieces, that is not good. My only firearm is now the M1911 under my left arm. The ComDat's metal form appears none the worse for wear from the drop. But when I try to reconnect it I discover the microphone cable torn out. There will be no calling for help.

Standing still and holding my breath I concentrate on listening until all I could hear is my own heartbeat. There are no other sounds. It is dark and quiet and the whole place gives me a creepy vibe like I am being watched. It is even worse than when walking between the Compass and the Citadel. The air is cold and dry with no condensation visible on any of the rock surfaces.

Walking to the first tunnel exit, I peer down its visible length. After about fifty feet the tunnel makes a gentle turn. With a shrug of my shoulders, I inspect in turn the possibilities to be found in the other two openings with similar results. All the exit tunnels run for a short distance and turn.

Figuring the Ciorii either left me here because it intends to come back later or someone told it to drop me here and disliking either prospect I consider my options. I have Truestone and a White Fang. With a little warning I might be able to put down the Ciorii. The one Mr. Lark, Held, and Mike destroyed in my flat, back when I still belonged to myself, took a tremendous amount of abuse before the White Fang could be used. And even then they barely pulled it off before the effects of the Truestone wore off.

Staying put and waiting for the Ciorii to return for its snack seems like a bad idea.

The Americans have a peculiar saying, 'The best defense is a good offense." Right now that is the closest thing to a plan I can think of. After descending hundreds feet in a virtual free-fall and almost vomiting in the face of a monster perhaps it is time to go on the offensive. Drawing my M1911 from its place under my left arm I retrieve a smaller version of the torch on my wrist and attach it to the pistol. Now I will be able to easily illuminate what I am shooting.

During all these calibrations and arrangements I have been shuffling closer to a wall and now my back is flat against it. My mind is starting to consider things other than the Ciorii. What about that Liger back in the Black Forest? What if there is one of those down here? Or something like those ghastly things in that pool of water in the Ellora caves?

At this point I actually slap the side of my helmet, a symbolic gesture to be sure. I need to focus and thinking about the laundry list of horrible ways I may meet my end deep underground, alone, with no one to hear me scream... Possibly in the next few minutes, is not helping.

I consciously slow my breathing and try to clear my mind and focus.

A scrape of something on stone echoes across from one of the exits to the chamber.

Now I am focused for real.

My left hand snatches a flare from my left leg and with remarkable dexterity ignites it and despite my being right-handed makes a fair left-handed throw into the center of the chamber. The red light of the flare illuminates everything in sight. Against the walls, the light takes on a blood red quality and the sputtering of the flare ads an unpleasant visual dynamic.

The flare's sudden appearance must have startled something because the scraping noises are now happening in quick succession. They are getting closer and I catch myself muttering under my breath, "Please don't be a spider, please don't be a spider, please don't be a spider."

The source of the scrapping noise leaves the shelter of an exit opening and walks into the flares light. The good news: it is not a spider, nor a liger. It is however ten feet tall and walking on two legs. I thought it was a really tall human male at first, until my eyes focused on its form. It is no man, even in the dim light of the flare I could see the lack of symmetry in its malformation.

Its two legs are of noticeably different lengths, as are its arms. Its head is off-center from its torso. The creatures overall form gives the impression of having been assembled from parts that did not match. It also resembles what had been described as crawling from the pit, minus wings, back in the 13th century when the castle was constructed.

Although difficult to be sure of in the red light, I have the impression its skin tone is ink black. The things oval head is rotating back and forth, looking for me. In its right hand is what appears to be a six-foot long iron bar. Based on the things hand and arm movements, the bar is heavy, and heavy for a ten-feet tall monstrosity probably equals bone-crushingly heavy when it is used to beat me to death.

Time to go.

At various points on my tactical loadout are six fragmentary grenades, all with three second fuses. It only takes me a second to get one out, pull the pin and throw it at whatever that thing is. It lands short, as I intended, bounces, rolls and then detonates.

The monster lets out a loud rumbling roar. By this time I had stopped looking, having turned to the nearest exit and begun running. The thing behind me could easily follow the light from my pistol. Nothing can be done about that, it is the only way I can see while I am running. Desperately waving my weapon back and forth checking for targets, I am looking for a tunnel, doorway, even a crack in the rock wall I can enter to bottleneck my much larger foe with.

The tunnel runs uninterrupted for at least one-hundred feet, then a ninety degree bend and a short straight run ending in a tee. I stop, stand still and in-spite of having just sprinted for over a hundred feet in full gear, stop my heavy breathing and listen. Based on the volume of its roaring, the thing is getting closer but does not seem to be pursuing. The two tunnels, left and right, are not different as far as I can tell.

So I turn right and started jogging into it. The rough walls are not precise in their layout and the tunnel dimensions change, getting wider and then narrower without rhyme or reason. I chalk it up to poor quality control when this place was dug out. It is disorienting whenever the walls narrow causing me to subconsciously slow down and then speed up when the tunnel widens. There are some gentle changes in direction and then one sharp ninety degree turn.

My grenade must have really made that thing really angry as it keeps roaring. Despite my running away from the source I am unable tell if it is getting closer or not. The sound from the roaring echoes back through the tunnels making direction and proximity impossible to determine.

Running through the next ninety-degree turn, I try to maintain my pace. The goal is to put as much distance between myself and the ten-foot tall thing back in that chamber.

I fail in that goal.

In the rush to get away I had not been paying attention to distance and turning angles. The path I had taken delivered me right back to the chamber I had started at. No sooner did I turn the corner and I realize this. Of course by the time it registers to me I am standing in the opening at the edge of the chamber, looking at the monster standing over the flare in the middle of the open space.

It stops roaring and makes snuffling noises, its torso and head shaking a bit. I think it is laughing at me. And then it charges. Even with uneven legs the thing has longshanks that would make a professional basketball player proud. Each stride eats up the distance between us.

My M1911 takes on a life of its own. I drop into a shooting stance, aim center mass and deliver seven rounds in short order. Some of the rounds impact and the thing stumbles in its charge. The opportunity to drop another grenade presents itself and I take it, tossing the small bomb, minus its pin. Turning, I run back the way I had just come from, barely making the turn before the crack of the grenade detonating can be heard. It is so close I feel it as much as hear it. The tunnel acts like a shrapnel funnel with ball bearings from the grenade bouncing their way towards me, sending sparks out with every impact. No small few strike my body armor without which I would have been at the very least seriously injured.

After two grenade blasts and several .45ACP hits and I can still hear it behind me roaring. The micro-phones in my helmet pick up the footfalls of pursuit. The thing is following me. I sprint as fast as I can while retracing my steps until I reach the tee where last time I chose to go right. Without slowing down I barrel straight into the other tunnel.

The footfalls behind me are getting closer. Another grenade drop seems a good idea as I navigate my way forward. Three seconds later the crack of the grenade is followed by another roar of discomfort. This grenade thing is working for me but I doubt a fatal blow can be dealt without taping a grenade to its head or something similar. Perhaps I can wound it though and slow it down.

The tunnel ends in another chamber, perhaps a quarter the size of the one I fell into. Off to one side a heavy steel door is recessed deep into the wall with no knob or handle in sight. Above the door also set into the solid stone is a single, brightly lit, caged lightbulb. My guess is that is the way out. Unfortunately I am unable to stop and investigate. The footsteps are getting closer again.

Already reloaded while I had been running, my M1911 and I decide to give bullets another chance. On the opposite side of the chamber is a similar opening in the rock. After settling into a shooting position using the wall for support I wait. The wait is short, as my foe approaches the lighted chamber its pace slows. It purposefully strides into the well-lit chamber, bar in hand. The light is bright enough for me to get my first clear view of the monster.

Its skin is truly ink black. Prominent scars are visible across its chest, arms, and shoulders. Wings appear to have once sprouted from its back but they had been torn or chewed away leaving little more than large stumps to show they once existed. Its legs and body sport as many as a dozen recent puncture wounds all leaking dark blood. My shooting is finding its mark but none of the wounds appear to be causing much damage.

I wait until it had taken two solid steps into the light before opening fire. Seven rounds in quick succession. My eyes remain open during the shooting and I see as many as five or more shots hit their target. The shooting visibly affects the monster. Without a second thought grenade four is tossed into the chamber and I take off down the tunnel I hope ends somewhere I can escape from my pursuer.

The midnight black giant resumes its pursuit, as I again hear the footfalls behind me. This tunnel has a lower ceiling, hopefully slowing my pursuer. The tunnel splits into three relatively equal tunnels. Without slowing down I run straight into the center one. After perhaps a hundred feet the three tunnels rejoin, run straight for a bit and then take a solid ninety-degree turn. I continue sprinting but I am getting close to hyperventilating and cannot keep this up much longer. If only this tunnel leads to another door or a crevasse I can hide in. Digging deep I push myself to keep the sprint up, taking another turn without breaking rhythm and keep going…

Right back into the chamber I had originally been brought to by the Ciorri.

All three exits are interconnected and other than the room with the light and the steel door or back up the pit shaft to the castle above there is no other way out. I am truly trapped in this small labyrinth with that thing. Wandering out into the chamber, chest heaving, I stand near the still sputtering flare casually reloading my weapon.

What to do? Perhaps I have seriously wounded the creature because its pursuit is less pressing. Or perhaps it is because this place is relatively small and there is no way I can escape. It is just taking its time.

It likes to play with its prey, like a cat?

My adversary walks around the turn and into the same corridor I had just entered the chamber from. It is limping a bit but otherwise its vigor appears unchanged by four grenades and fourteen rounds from my handgun. I drop into a shooting stance Illych would have been proud of, take aim and drill more rounds into the creature. Its body jerks under their impact but keeps coming.

The creature pauses in its advance, regarding me malevolently, and I take the opportunity to reload my M1911 and prepare my secret weapon. Now, instead of running away I confidently advance towards the dark giant. My aggressiveness is noticed and the creature takes a step back, an odd reaction for one of the Created. Regardless, my advance continues until I am, at most, twenty feet from the monster.

The things head cocks to the side as if thinking, its decision is made in less than a second. The hulking demogorgon steps forward while raising that great iron bar above its head. This is the moment to make my move and I do, my right hand punches outwards, releasing a piece of Truestone right at the giant in front of me. The thing is monstrously huge and it will be impossible to miss.

But I still mess up the throw, somehow the Truestone ends up flying high and left over my adversaries shoulder. It does not matter; Truestone is like a magnet to the Created. Even when the initial throw would miss, the white stone will correct its path and shift to its target like a heat seeking missile.

Except this not what happens. The Truestone just flies over the giant's left shoulder. My foe had paused when I threw the stone and stands still while watching it fly past him. He then turns to face me and continues his upward swing with the bar which I am guessing will soon be followed by a fatal downward swing. I doubt my helmet will prevent much injury when at least a hundred pounds of iron comes crashing down.

In that split second before my almost certain death, I realize that if the Truestone did not work, then the misshapen creature before me is not a Created, it is a living thing. And living things can be killed.

Dropping into my shooting stance, just as the bar reaches its apex above the monsters head, I open fire. The shots are point blank and I can clearly see each one impact the creature's chest. At the edge of my vision I also see the bar beginning its downward stroke. We are so close to each other I see my adversary's muscles contract as it brings down the bar.

The slide on my weapon locks open.

The muscles that had been furiously contracting to bring about my end suddenly go slack. As if in slow motion, the creature begins to fall down, almost folding up on itself. My determined shooting had hit something critical. I am not going to die with an iron bar beating my brains out.

Looking at my now dead adversary, knowing this was a living creature changes everything. When I had arrived in the arms of a Ciorri and immediately saw the dark giant I just assumed it was another lesser created to contend with. Although when it laughed I should have realized something was different. Supernatural androids from eons past can do many things but they do not understand humor or laugh.

Another living thing like the Liger back in the Black Forest twisted to serve another's will. I cannot say I am proud to have killed the giant but at least it is at peace.

My torch finds the white of the Truestone on the floor and I retrieve it. The stuff is bloody rare and not to be wasted.

The firefight up on the platform, the descent with the Ciorii, and now the dead giant in front of me. My clothes are soaked with sweat and I am shaking from exhaustion. Backing up to a wall; I slide down to a seated position on the floor.

A bottle of water and a reloaded weapon later and I begin to think about what I should do next.

A booming noise reverberates through the cavern like a big door slamming shut. The only door I saw was that one in the smaller side chamber with the light above it. Something must have entered the labyrinth. Now what? I am too tired to run around again.

The tunnel from the chamber closest to the exit door shows an approaching light source. Standing up I palm grenade number 5. Figure I will start with that and then switch to the pistol. Losing the KRISS is a real problem; the seven rounds in the M1911 would be gone in less than a second whereas the twenty-five in the carbine would be really useful in my current situation.

The light creeps closer and I hear the scuffling of shoes or boots on stone. Finally a man walks around the corner. He is average height, perhaps mid-thirties, dressed in casual civilian attire and carries a bright lamp.

Curiously he does not appear to be carrying any weapons and looks to be a proper modern human.

He keeps his distance as he walks into the chamber, and speaks to me in a neutral tone, his accent English, "If you would come with me there is someone who wants to meet you." He then turns to leave, not checking to see if I follow.

Guessing the man's job is to deliver the message and guide me to a certain destination, I decide to jog and catch up with him. If I choose not to follow he would just leave me here, perhaps as a snack for the Ciorii should it return. Opening my helmet faceplate to remove my helmet completely, I attach it to my harness.

Falling in on the man's right side I start with my questions.

"Perhaps you could tell me whom I am to meet?"

Silence.

"Your name at least?"

"I am Gregory and you should be silent until spoken to." Despite his apparent defenselessness and the obvious armament I carried, my guide is completely fearless in his tone and mannerisms.

So silence it is. After everything that has happened in the last hour, I can do that.

Chapter 15

As we walk I keep myself a few steps behind
Gregory. Travelling along the rough-hewn stone
corridors he occasionally waves his hand one way or the
other as the direction in which to proceed. During our
short walk we see no other living thing. Or perhaps I
should say there was nothing else moving. After maybe
ten minutes of walking dimly lit corridors the hallway
ends in a circular hole in the wall the size of a bank vault
with a massive stone rolled into place closing it. Seeing
me standing far back from the stone door, Gregory
roughly grabs my arm, pulls me closer to door, then
turns, and walks away leaving me there.

After watching him walk away down the hall I turn
back to face the vault door. The circular stone face rolls
sideways into a slot in the wall. Beyond the circular
opening is a short hallway ending in a brightly lit room.

Not seeing any other options I shrug my shoulders
and start walking towards the light. I consider my

situation: I am not dead yet and if whomever or whatever is down here decides to do away with me I doubt my objection or meagre resistance will slow down my ending. Nothing left to do but roll with the punches and see what happens.

Stepping into the light, so to speak, I observe an open space that is neat, clean, carpeted, and furnished with comfortable chairs around a beautiful wooden table. The walls are tastefully covered in colorful tapestries and paintings, that my brief analysis determines are of a historical nature. The lights overhead are similar to the large crystal units suspended from the ceiling back at the Citadel. They produce a clear white light will little shadowing, allowing for every detail to be seen.

"Welcome Thomas Davies!"

Sitting in the center of all this beauty is a tall, handsome, muscular African man who just demonstrated he knows my name. He stands up from a large wood and leather chair magnificently constructed for comfort and style.

It is too much, leaving me speechless. My host is close to seven feet tall and blessed with the deep black skin tone of someone from central Africa. The man gestures for me to enter further into the room. He is dressed in an open chested vest and voluminous pants giving the impression of an Arabian genie. His voice and visible physique are exceptional by any standard.

It is a lot to take in but I am catching up. It also registers there are normal looking humans in servant roles about the room.

"Thomas, please sit. After your victory you will need refreshment." The man's immense hands slap together twice with a sound so loud it hurts my ears. Two mortal servants, both African and impeccably dressed in a manner similar to my host, move with a speed and precision normally seen in world class sport competitions. Gentle hands guide me to a seat and I turn to find one of the servants carefully guiding me. A small table appears at my right. A crystal goblet upon it is soon filled with what looks like water. Next, a plate with a variety of small fruits beautifully arranged is brought to me.

"Please Thomas, consider yourself my guest. Refresh yourself while I answer your questions before you ask them."

Old world hospitality, If I do not eat and drink my host will become offended. On the other hand if I accept his hospitality I will be under his protection. Plus, I am intrigued by how he will answer my questions before I ask them.

"I accept your kind offer of hospitality." The words sound nice but I barely croak them out.

The big man sits down and continues talking. "In this world I am called Leveque. You would not understand, much less be able to speak, my true name."

"This language, English, is crude and difficult to communicate with but it will still allow you to understand most things. To answer your next question: I am only Leveque, no more, no less. As addressing me in the familiar may be uncomfortable for you, perhaps addressing me as Mr. Leveque would be more comfortable. Unfortunately, I find Mr. Leveque tedious and require you address my form as Leveque."

That probably was going to be my next question and addressing this man or thing, in the familiar did not feel right. Regardless, when in Rome...

"Thomas, I have chosen you to serve me."

To the point, ok, and based on the situation this was going to be a short and fatal first date. Serving these monsters was not even remotely in my desired future.

"Thank you for the kind offer Leveque but I am currently retained by another."

I cringe inside a bit as I decline. This is usually when the pain begins.

Leveque laughs, a big, warm and friendly, barrel chested laugh. The sound of it leaves me feeling more positive in spite of the dire situation.

"I knew you would not accept. My kind walked this Earth when it was a lifeless ball of rock. We remember Those Who Came Before. I was there when the first of your kind, your predecessors the Mannu, came into being. You are not the first to sit in that chair and decline my offer. You would have been killed if you had accepted in some misguided attempt to save your precious skin. There is no place here for the weak."

"Now we will sit and talk. Then you will be my guest for a single day. Then we will talk again. After that, if you still refuse me I will release you unharmed to the nearest group of dwellings."

That last part, 'nearest group of dwellings' I think he means a town, regardless, I do not believe any of what he is saying.

"Twenty-four hours and I leave unchanged and unharmed?"

The toothy smile leaves his face as he replies, "Do not question me Thomas. It is an insult that I should give my word to one of your kind. I have time, forever from your viewpoint, so yes, unchanged and unharmed."

Holding my hands up in front of me, I look at them. They are filthy from the battle in the labyrinth. One of the nearby servants, silently anticipating my needs, places a warm, damp cloth across my hands. I scrub them vigorously, cleaning them. The servant deftly removes the soiled cloth. Picking up the crystal goblet from the table I take a sip. It is cool clean water. Selecting an especially plump grape from the tray I put it in my mouth, finding it delicious.

Welcome to the dark side, we have cookies.

A thought occurs to me and even though I felt it would be better left unasked I ask anyway. "Mr. Leveque, why not possess my body and send me back?"

"This is a fool's question. None of my kind is able to conduct ourselves in your world. I have claimed many a vessel over the long march and am among the most skilled of my kind in keeping up proper appearances. Even I cannot perform such subterfuge for long. Once among your people they will quickly realize you are not you. And why ask such a thing? You would be killed for the possession to occur. Do you not know this?"

I recall Mr. Lark trying to give me the technical explanation how possession worked. When he was done my understanding was less than complete.

"I am only vaguely familiar with the process."

Leveque smiles a dazzling white toothy grin, "You would be dead from your point of view with the part of you given by the divine gone. One of my kind then enters your lifeless corpse and takes control."

I mumble, "Dead."

"Yes, what you call death. Your kind has known your dead can be possessed since the beginning. With proper ritual and prepared participants it is quick. The chance for success with just any corpse is less likely. The circumstances of the deceased body come into play. Why do you think your kind has such odd rituals for your dead? Some cultures require the body be buried within 24 hours and the fondness for coffins, tombs and deep burial? If the body cannot be buried quickly the process of embalming is employed making it impossible for my kind to possess a body. Others burn the dead or firmly bind them. Do you not find these rituals strange and unnecessary for something that is supposedly inert and awaiting decomposition?"

Well, yes, when you say it like that it is all creepy and weird.

"My control of this body does not end with the death of the flesh. We have much work to do and my kind is limited on how soon after the last possession we can possess another form. Thus we keep the bodies as long as possible."

"Can you possess the living against their will?"

"Only the young and the sick, we cannot forcibly possess a healthy adult. That would violate how you are created. We can be invited in however, a mutually beneficial relationship as it were."

The big man continues, "I brought you here for a reason. You are not like the others. You are intelligent, better educated, more reasoned. Mr. Lark has imprisoned you, taken your freedom. With me you can be free again. The strength you demonstrated in the labyrinth will take you far."

Not only does he know my name but he knows Mr. Lark's as well.

"And you will help me out of the goodness of your heart?" Choke on that Leveque.

"Don't be stupid, charity is for the weak. If you truly wish to be free Thomas, I will reveal a path to you, for one who is strong, so you can take your freedom."

It is a nice speech and has a certain appeal. I miss my old flat in London and would like to return to living there. What about the catch? There is always some fine print making the dream impossible. "This is not just about me and my dreams though. What are your dreams Leveque, what do you wish freedom from?"

Since I had arrived Leveque had been the poster child of happiness, health, and positive energy. For the briefest instance his face showed something that was perhaps sadness. I cannot be sure because it was so fleeting and these creatures can fake everything so easily.

"Your question is well asked and I will answer. To know this you must receive a history lesson. Prepare yourself little human. Such truths have driven your kind into madness."

At this point I am hoping Leveque gets started with the 'truths leading to madness' portion of this discussion because his monologue is right out of a bad movie.

"I was there in the beginning, when the foundations of this world were laid, and everything was truth and light. Eons I spent in the presence of the creator, witnessing miracles you are unable to comprehend. Even if I wished to share what I witnessed it is not possible. This crude language you communicate with will not allow for such an exchange."

"I am neither the greatest, nor the least of my kind, neither the first nor the last. I will tell you this: the greatest of us was the last created. We are the sum of our creation, nothing more. Our actions preordained for all eternity."

"Those Who Came Before became interested in outcomes not determined at creation, what you call free will. The last and greatest of us was touched with the beginnings of this. Then our creators turned from us and hacked your kind from the mud. This work was different than the perfect works that came before. It was as if imperfection was intended as part of the design."

"In the creation of your world every plant and creature was planned. Each had a place they were made for. But your kind did not fit anywhere. The first were called the Mannu. They were all the same, what you call clones. Each was made in turn and their lives would span almost 1000 years. The sameness caused discontent among the Mannu. This combined with the need to create each individual almost fully grown inspired an even more revolting development."

"The Mannu, the first, were neither male nor female. They were changed then, male sex organs were added, a simple change. Then, using the Mannu template, the first females were created. These first humans began to reproduce."

My guess is the reproduction part required little encouragement.

"Humanity is created with a higher order of intelligence than most everything on Earth but you are still mentally retarded compared to such as myself. What gave offence was when the creators revealed the Mannu and subsequently, humanity, had been blessed with the divine. The outrage that creations as complex as monkeys and cursed with a painfully short existence, not more than a blink of an eye to my kind, changed the natural order of things."

"We, their chosen servants, created by them, in our perfection forever connected to the divine. But you..." Leveque is now displaying anger. Taking note I keep quiet. Apparently even after millions, if not billions of years, he is still carrying a grudge."

"Then the error is acknowledged by the creators, and those among us who had seen the incongruity felt reason return to the universe. If your kind lives too long they can learn enough to reach for, and touch, the divine. This cannot be allowed."

"Except the removal of the divine from humanity was not the solution chosen, Instead humanities life span was decreased from a single millennia to at most, a century of years. The last and greatest among us was then sent to observe your pathetic race multiply across the face of the Earth. He witnesses your puniness, your petty irrational existence and decided to take up the challenge of making humanity better."

Say what? I have never heard this version of the fallen Angel story.

"For millions of years we have pushed humanity to grow and improve. Now I want you to join with us and contribute to humanities success."

That is a mind bending story and the twist at the end is over the top. What if it is true? I cannot think of anything that will disprove it. Leveque is into a form of tough love, culling the weak and rewarding the strong.

I am speechless and Leveque sits quietly observing my reactions. During this pause I look around the room trying to think of something to say.

Finally a reply comes to mind, "And Balthazar, the Magi?"

"A line established to keep humanity in place, frozen, and under control. They are like an old man in his dotage, set in his ways and unable to change. If not for their efforts our goal would have been achieved long ago."

"Please clarify that goal if you could. It was not clear from the history lesson."

"Guiding humanity to become worthy of the divine within them."

"That sounds like a worthy goal, as you say. But I wonder about the tough love intentions?"

"Thomas, I can see you need rest and time to consider my offer"

"Is there a piece of paper where I sign away my soul?" I had to ask.

Leveque laughs that booming, warm laugh of his. "No Thomas, I have no interest in your soul. My interest in you is almost philanthropic. I will teach you things and you will pay for such knowledge with knowledge of your own. It is important you make your own way in the world, would you not agree?"

"And if I refuse?"

"You are then free to leave. You are more interesting than most of your kind and I think a meeting to talk in the future is something that I will enjoy. After all, I have forever." His forever comment came out as more of a taunt. I do not know if immortal androids can become mentally-ill but from his stated puny humans viewpoint Leveque is demonstrating a megalomaniacal superiority complex.

"You have met many of the other-than-human. I can smell it on you."

He speaks the truth. A greater created, a Djinn, in the recent past had said the same thing, *I can smell it on you*. I do not believe it is the proper use of the word but I understand. My guess is the English word for 'smell' is the closest thing to what they are experiencing.

The man Gregory, who escorted me here from the labyrinth, reappears. Not actually appearing in the Goblin sense. He walked in without being announced and I just notice him now.

Leveque smiles his dazzling smile again and booms, "You see Thomas, Gregory is one of your kind and he joined our cause freely. There is neither lien nor geas upon him." He says this while nodding to Gregory.

That is the signal for Gregory to escort me away.

Leveque gets in the last word, "We will talk again soon Mister Thomas Davies."

Chapter 16

As we walk out from Leveque's quarters I decide to get some answers from Gregory.

"How long have you served Leveque?"

My escort takes his time in answering as we keep walking. Eventually he replies, "I am not bound to Leveque. I serve the goals of the group."

"You volunteered for this?"

"I was approached when I was younger, in university, to participate in something important."

Gregory speaks English with both English and American accents but his speech uses more European terminology.

"Where are you from? Your passport country?"

Gregory shakes his head, "That is enough questions for now. I have been directed to temporarily house you in the Quarters. This tunnel complex is very large and very old. Only a small part of the many places within it are used. You will be safe in the Quarters. Do not wander off. There are few safe paths and if you enter areas best left alone you will most likely die."

Sounds like the path from the Compass to the Citadel. Do not wander from the yellow brick road Dorothy.

"You are being given a great opportunity to work with like-minded people. Despite what you have been told we are working to make the world a better place."

My guess is Gregory is a true believer.

The path from Leveque's throne room to the Quarter's is a convoluted journey of finished stone halls, winding rough stone passages, and finally a vault-like steel door.

"Before we enter, I will warn you. None of us entertain the weak. You have been left in possession of your weapons because you may need them. Show respect and you will receive respect. Leveque has declared a feast in your honor. You are encouraged to ask any question you wish of the participants and they must answer. Leveque considers you a great prize for us to win. But should you show weakness they will fall upon you with his blessing."

"The feast will begin within the hour. Until then you will remain in the place I have brought you to. The others know you are coming and will expect to meet you. Let them come to you. Do not get up and move around. During the feast I will assist in your introduction. Until then, try to not give anyone a reason for your death."

Honestly, whatever positive boost Leveque had instilled in me is now gone.

Gregory faces the vault door and produces from his sleeve what looks like a classic magician's wand. He waves it in a pattern and the vault door soundlessly swings open.

With my escort leading the way, we walk inside. The room on the other side of the vault door is mammoth, easily the size of a smaller sports stadium. There is elevated bleacher seats recessed around the perimeter of the room, at an elevation just above the doorways. The open space is warmly lit, not as brightly as the throne room, but more than enough to be able to clearly see.

Sections of the open space are defined by the furniture within them. Apparently there are factions and each has an area selected for them to conduct court. The furniture styles are varieties of wood and leather, nothing extreme nor anything soft looking. A quick count comes up with nine factions.

Gregory guides me only a short distance in. A small, flat, backless seat had been brought for me to sit on. Not much more than a stool really.

"You will remain here until I return. " I nod my understanding and watch the bearded man walk away. He crosses the room, skillfully navigating the borders between the factions and finally exits through a door on the far side of the space.

Those few present do not make much of my arrival. A few heads turn and briefly take note me before turning back to whatever business they are involved in. The vault entrance is elevated with respect to the rest of the room and when sitting there on my stool I enjoy a good view of all nine factions.

Five of the spaces are devoid of occupants. One of the territories has only two or three people seated and surrounded by ten of what I would call servants, to handle their every need.

One territory appeared to be the 'general' grouping. The five individuals in this section do not appear to follow a uniform dress code like those in the others groups. One territory has a single, severe, priestly looking fellow dressed all in black. The last occupied territory is the most disturbing, with a low altar at its center. Surrounding it are seven individuals alternating between prostrating themselves to the altar, to sitting and engaging in an active discussion.

My conclusion: I am surrounded by a significant amount of weirdness right now.

Two doors on the opposite side of the room open and a stream of men in identical uniforms walk out through them. They take to rearranging the territories, allowing for a long dining table to be brought in, pointing at the vault door and centered in the room. Apparently feast preparations have begun.

The single individual all dressed in black, is forced to move and he decides this is the time to meet the new guy. The figure is covered from head to toe, including gloves and balaklava that leaves just his face exposed. He is not particularly tall, at most six feet and from what I could see of his face his age is short of forty years. His Caucasian features do not give away a more specific heritage. His smooth gait navigates the territories, bringing him to me quickly.

I have spent my most recent six months with dangerous men. How they hold themselves, the walk, and the look in their eyes.

The man looks at me as he walks closer.

This is a very dangerous man.

He stops a respectable distance from me and nods his head once while stomping his feet.

"So you are the one who made it possible for the Magi to return?" His voice is strong and direct.

My reply, "Not just me, I mean it was a team effort."

Now that he is standing closer I see several bladed weapons sheathed in various places in his attire. This man is heavily armed.

He continues to look at me while standing there silently. It is unnerving. Unable to withstand the quiet any longer I ask his name, "My name is Thomas Davies. And yours?"

"Your name, this is known, and that of your employer, Karl Lark. My name is Hugo Soldat."

Behind him the preparations for the feast continue at high speed. Not much longer and I will be meeting the entire menagerie.

"Mr. Soldat, what is your role in this place?"

"I am an ambassador. This is high conclave and those who remain true must send someone."

"What about those empty spaces? Is there a loyalty shortage?"

Hugo nods and continues, "Yes, a few did not heed the call. This is expected when more than a hundred years have passed since the last gathering."

"One-hundred years? That seems a long time to go between meeting each other?"

"It is all that is necessary. The last high conclave met after the final Magi was done away with. Now that one of them has returned we must meet. This conclave is also a test of loyalty. We work towards a common purpose with immortal creations. If we cannot keep focus for a few hundred years what are we worth?"

Hugo pauses and then continues, "You recognize me as a man of violence. This means you know such men. Looking at you I know you are not such a man. What are you Mr. Davies?"

"A librarian."

Hugo makes a choking noise that could pass for a suppressed laugh.

"Let me ask you a question Hugo. That outfit you are wearing, you cannot possibly walk around in the world wearing that."

"No, certainly not. This is the traditional costume of what you might call a cult or a secret society. I wear it here as it is known by the others present. In the world, as you say, I wear a suit."

"There are others like you?"

"There are many of us. Chosen at the age of seven we are taken from our families and spend the next ten years enduring training similar to the Spartan Agoge. The survivors are then tested for loyalty. The loyal remain and begin their contribution to the work."

"And the less than loyal?"

"A childish question Thomas, I am sure you already know the cost of being less than loyal. How else can you be assured? Your Mr. Lark must do something similar."

Don't I know it, "Yes, he does."

That said I can see the preparations for dinner being completed and others entering the room to join in. They take seats as small groups at different locations along the long table. Hugo also takes notice. "We will speak more at the feast." He nods to take his leave, spins on his heels and starts towards the table.

This leaves me still sitting alone when Gregory appears. The man changed into a tailored suit. As a matter of fact, everyone participating in the feast dressed for a gala event. This contrasts with my black tactical uniform, armored chest carapace, and full face helmet clipped to my belt. For armament I still have my M1911, a couple of grenades, and a combat knife.

For my being from the 'other team' they are leaving me awfully well armed. I would also be willing to bet Hugo or any number of the others present could solve the problem of a librarian acting out pretty quick.

Gregory walks up to me and requests I follow him to the long table. Bringing me to head of the table, "You are the guest of honor, you will sit here."

Cool. "Should I wait for the others before I take a seat?" It is hard to tell as most of the guests are still standing while a small minority had already seated themselves. With a group like this etiquette is probably all over the place.

"Do as you please." Gregory says while taking the chair to my right. Surprisingly Hugo returns and sits on my left. Now that preparations are complete the groups present claim their sections of the table. A group of people in 'normal' formal event clothing take seats further down the table on my left side. A number of individuals, and a few two's or three's show up. The last large group is half-naked, wear turbans, and sport bold tattoos and occult jewelry. They sit at the far side of the table to my right.

When all are seated, Gregory stands and bows to everyone at the table, "Leveque will not be joining us." If this means anything to the other guests, no one shows it. "At this time of conclave Leveque is presenting a unique opportunity in the form of Thomas Davies. It is believed that with correct persuasion Mr. Davies will choose to join us in the improvement of this world. As a show of good faith Leveque has extended a guarantee of safe passage to our guest." That statement brings a reaction. Several people quickly hold short, quiet discussions.

"A representative from each group is to make introductions."

Hugo makes no move to stand as we have already been introduced. The normal looking people seated to my left have a female representative stand. She is an attractive blond, tall and athletic in a striking light grey fitted blouse and pencil skirt. "Mr. Davies, greetings. I speak for the families who continue to work for our greater good in making the world a better place. We are members of houses and bloodlines ancient and storied, our ambitions uninterrupted for centuries or even millennia for some."

Greater good? Make the world a better place? Who are these weirdos?

After the attractive woman, who noticeably did not share her name, sat down one of the turbaned men from the end of the table began speaking.

"We are the seekers of truth. Humanity cannot understand its place in the universe until we first understand the universe. A man such as you, who seeks knowledge, would find our association an easy one."

I think that might be a job offer. None of the introductions is long or particularly informative. The remaining individuals who speak are even less forthcoming. Apparently just because Leveque gives an order does not mean those present will do much about it.

Gregory and Hugo are expressionless throughout the introductions. No sooner did the last person speak and servants rush in through the doors to begin serving. Dinner is a practiced affair with food served from a common dish. Wine and spirits are available, of which I have none.

Out of concern that I might be rude, combined with my impressive hunger, motivates me to partake and I do. Gregory nods in approval when I start to eat.

The guests do not speak amongst themselves or to the group nearest them. All the groups and individuals have left empty chairs between themselves and the others sitting close to them. I sense distrust in the room.

Sitting in silence, eating what is turning out to be a truly magnificent dinner is not my forte. "Excuse me Gregory; I do not detect affinity between the different groups present."

"We believe in competition. Also, the different groups present have talents wildly divergent from each other."

Hugo contributes next in his forceful staccato, a voice accustomed to giving orders. "I and my brothers provide security that can be trusted."

Gregory continues, "Yes, Hugo's brothers have a philosophy that perhaps could be considered similar to Sikhism, only more militant. Their word is their bond."

I jump in at this point to give my observation, "My guess is the well-dressed people to my left are the wealthy aristocracy."

"It is rather obvious but yes. They represent the bankers and those most wealthy."

"What about you Gregory? What do you do?"

"Thomas, my story is not much different than yours. I was studying anthropology with a focus in archaeology. Then I met a man who had a task for me, a very special task."

I understood before he said it. "This is your place. You came here to study it."

"That is part of my responsibilities. I am more of a facilities manager who gets time to do some research on the side. This place is rarely this busy or fully occupied. When the official operations have been handled I have time to explore and document this place."

He is correct. His story is not much different than mine.

Through the main doors, which are currently closed, I hear a loud noise. The sound is difficult to categorize but something is happening.

Those same doors open quickly and a small host of armed men in uniform walk in. The gates close just as quickly behind them. Select individuals separate from the uniformed host and approach each group of seated guests. Short discussions are quickly held. The instant the message, whatever it is, is delivered, the group change from seated and enjoying a civilized dinner to a flurry of activity focused on quickly leaving.

Some of the uniformed host had begun taking up firing positions near the main doors according to some preplanned positioning. Their movements are practiced and efficient. Honestly, it reminds me of watching my Citadel colleagues work together. Except that here, there are significantly more of them.

A uniformed messenger speaks to Hugo briefly. Standing free of the table the fighting man confidently strides to a place by the wall, perhaps twenty feet from the main doors. He is standing still with his back flat to the wall when his image goes fuzzy. I can sort of see him if I do not take my eyes away. If I look away and then look back it takes a couple of seconds to find him.

Gregory finally comments on the situation. "Your colleagues have entered the complex and are apparently searching for you."

I bet and the Oculus will show them right where I am too.

"Leveque wants you to have the full twenty-four hours. Please come with me as we evacuate."

"What about Hugo?"

"He is tasked as our vanguard. After all the dignitaries have been evacuated he will follow."

I stand and follow Gregory. The evacuation is quiet and well organized. The important people and their entourages exit first. My place is at the tail end of the movement. Then the uniformed men and Hugo begin a controlled fallback behind us.

The distant sounds had changed from the occasional loud boom to now and then I can hear the staccato of gunfire. Someone is raising Hell out there.

My strategy is to slow walk myself to the very back of the group and then break free and make a run for it. All that is needed is an opportunity. This frustrates Gregory to no end and after several attempts to motivate me to move faster he unexpectedly leaves me behind.

Soon I am mixing in with the vanguard and Hugo. The uniformed men are following proper military protocol. Half falling back to take cover with weapons pointed in the direction the enemy is expected to come from. Then the other half follows and does the same. In the middle of this is a nearly invisible Hugo.

My tardiness eventually pushes me right to edge of the vanguard. A couple of steps and I will be free.

Keenly looking for my opportunity, I miss Hugo materializing right next to me. He deactivated whatever it was making him hard to see. Covering the remaining distance in an instant he grabs my arm.

"You wish to leave?" His grip is vicelike and the man's fierce eyes reinforce the question.

I do but not permanently from life. It escapes me how to answer.

"Librarian, as I see it our pursuers are after you. If we keep you who knows the carnage that may be unleashed. If you were to escape to your friends they will most likely stop pursuing."

Looking at Hugo's expression, completely devoid of any hint as to what he was thinking, I have no idea what is going to happen next.

"Go to your colleague's librarian." He nods to me, turns, and quickly walks away.

As I turn to leave I hear the fighting man say, "We will meet again."

The few remaining uniformed men look at me with confused expressions. I shrug and say, "Follow him." They look back and forth at each other and then break and follow Hugo.

After the last of them disappears around a corner I realize I am alone with no idea where I am. My concentration up to now was focused on escaping. Now I am in some random hallway, not knowing which way to go.

In the distance is another boom followed by the sound of a machine gun firing. Most people run away from such noises. In this unique situation I feel my best course of action is to run towards the battle. Putting my helmet back on I draw my M1911. Hugging the wall, I begin stalking towards the battle.

It occurs to me the reason the sounds of battle have been getting closer and closer is because my comrades are following my changing position on the Oculus. All I need to do is stand still and wait and they will find me.

Pressing myself into a corner for cover, I wait.

Chapter 17

I do not wait long. In less than five minutes a familiar figure in full body armor and a helmet walks around a corner into the hall I am sort of hiding in.

Seeing me he lowers his weapon and when he is close enough, offers me his hand. I take it. My mood is significantly improved when Mike flips up his face plate and I can see his smile.

"Captured and held for hours, a banquet in his honor, and not a scratch on him. You are one lucky bastard."

The others soon make a tactical movement into the area, taking up positions at each exit. Illych and Mr. Lark arrive last. Their gear is dustier and more battered than when I had seen them last. You know, as I was being dragged out into the abyss by a Ciorii.

Otherwise they look none the less for wear. No one is seriously injured from what I can tell. That is a blessing I guess.

Mr. Lark pauses for a moment to consult his Oculus. Then he speaks with his usual matter of fact deadpan, "We must retreat to an exit. Now that they have moved the dignitaries safely away, the security forces are moving towards us en mass."

Illych makes several quick hand gestures and Mike breaks from his position and jogs back out the way he just entered from.

"Illych gives more instructions, "Held, trap this corridor. We are not coming back this way." The rest of us follow Mike in single file with Held bringing up the rear. He pulls a device from his rucksack as he walks something square and olive green. Mr. Lark is starting to have custom explosives and fragmentary devices made for the team, under Illych and Helds direction. This particular device has twice the explosive mass of the standard claymore mine. And instead of setting it on the floor, it has this super adhesive you peel the film from and it will stick instantly to just about any surface.

As he starts around the ninety degree turn at the end of the hall, the device is pressed against the stone wall at about chest height. After fiddling with the controls on the side for a second, Held jogs to catch up with us. My last visual of the mine is a green light turning red. Anything following us will now go boom.

With the adversaries security forces closing in there is no time for staged movement. Instead Mike acts as Private Snuffy. He runs ahead of the rest of us. If he draws fire we will respond while he finds cover. So far though, there have been no contacts.

In a few short minutes we are back in the banquet hall. The remains of the feast in my honor are still on the table. So much has changed in the last half-an-hour.

While passing through the relatively open space of the hall my colleagues start grabbing things from my gear. Now I know what a plant feels like when locusts descend on it. Having lost my KRISS back in the labyrinth, the teams takes turns grabbing my spare magazines. There are other useful things in my rucksack that they also grab. By the time we reach the gate I feel my carried weight significantly reduced.

We pass through the gates and begin navigating our way to the entry portal. The path we are taking is not in the direction of the portal to the spiral staircase.

The need to point this out forces me to comment. "Is this a different path to the portal?"

"We are not leaving by that portal," Is Mr. Lark's terse reply. That portal? There are others?

My silence prompts Mr. Lark to fill in the blanks.

"Our original point of entry is too complicated and time consuming to support all the people encountered in here. This understanding is reinforced by the Oculus having shown the path through the granite plug as being relatively unused."

"I reasoned there must be another way into this pocket dimension. How, I could not guess, but considering we rely on such a construct as our lair. We must determine how it is done."

"After you were taken, we continued down the stairs and entered the portal at the bottom of the pit. I did this long enough to take a quick snap shot of the entire pocket dimension from a specific way of looking at it.

This showed what I was looking for, there are three more portals."

I had to ask, "I thought the pocket dimensions only had one portal or connection to the real world."

"That was my understanding also, until a few hours ago. From that quick snapshot I was able to determine the locations of the three other entry points in the Earth's gravity well. We then made a quick exit up the stairs and translated back to the Compass."

Mr. Lark is relating this as we navigate quickly through the myriad corridors and tunnels that make up this place. As I look at the old man, he pauses talking while interfacing with his Oculus.

When the others use the Oculus they have to stop walking and close their eyes. Not so with Mr. Lark, he is able to operate it while keeping his eyes open and walking. Regardless you can tell his concentration is elsewhere.

His eyes come back into focus and he speaks forcefully into his microphone, "Illych, they took the bait and think we are headed for the spiral staircase portal. If we keep up this pace we will have no encounters with their security forces."

That said Mr. Lark continues with his original conversation, "One of the portals is more than one thousand meters below the surface of the South Atlantic Ocean. Another is encased in lava under an active volcano. The last one is in a hotel in London. It is surrounded by rooms that have an extra door to the space with the portal."

I interrupt at this point, "You came in from London? Wasn't there a lot of security?"

Mr. Lark frowns at my interruption and continues, "The place is a fortress with an army of security. We could not get in there."

I am starting to have a bad feeling about what was about to happen. This feeling coincides with the team entering a large square chamber with no other exits than the way we just came in. The room is damp to the point of almost being wet and really cold, just like it would be 1000 meters beneath the surface of the ocean.

Turning to look at Mr. Lark I find him smiling his Cheshire cat grin. "Here, Mr. Thomas, we separate the men from the boys."

This has to be bad.

"Without going into a long explanation about the details of how the Ouiblet operates I will tell you that with enough time I can arrange, in the future, for us to translate directly into this entry point through the ocean portal."

"Unfortunately with time pressures such as they were, in needing to rescue you, some improvisations were required."

The others have gathered closely about Mr. Lark and me.

"Entering and leaving currently requires a two-step process. The first step is we translate from this room to the ocean. For the second step each of us activates our own individual dongles to take us to the Compass."

No way, that is crazy. "The pressure at those depths will crush us instantly"

"Thomas, please give me some credit."

I see the others have all opened their helmets and are grinning maniacally at me.

"My dongle will translate a sphere of ocean 100 meters in diameter an instant before we appear nearer to top off the void. We will begin falling inside a total vacuum at approximately the same speed as the ocean rushes in around us. You will have your Compass dongle in your hand and ready. All you need to do is push the ends together and twist. An action that will take a fraction of the two seconds of time before the ocean can rush in and crush you."

That said Mr. Lark begins handing out dongles. Both sections have paracord wound through them. After I receive mine Illych takes the time to tie my wrists together so my hands cannot be separated. Then he places the dongle pieces, one in each hand and ties them to their respective hands.

Mr. Lark is going to make a void in the ocean, translate us into the void, and we need to active our own dongles to escape before the ocean rushes in and squashes us to a pulp.

I look around and the others are ready and looking at me. Glancing down at my hands and the dongle pieces in their ready positions I look back up and nod. I am as ready as anyone could be for something this crazy.

The world went black and cold and stays that way. The total vacuum I translate into painfully rips the air from my lungs. I feel the nausea of the translation, doubly so since we went from an unprepared location to another unprepared location. And now I am falling in pitch black darkness. Between the nausea, the pain in my chest, and the falling sensation a little voice in my head screams at me to push and twist.

So I do.

I swear I could feel the closeness of the ocean, like a cold wall of death, as the translation took me away. We went from standing, to falling, and now upon arriving at the Compass, everyone except Mr. Lark loses their balance and falls down on the cold stone floor. The nausea is so bad I vomit as I am counting my colleagues. In spite of the fear reaction and adrenaline after effects, I feel relief when I count four others plus Mr. Lark.

We all made it.

I stay down longer than my colleagues. Then Tank walks over to me and offers his hand. Taking it he pulls me to my feet. Without a word we walk as a group, away from the Compass towards the Citadel.

When the gates open and the clear light from inside the Citadel spread across us, I almost feel elation to be home. I am alive and not headed for the Doctor. It is time to clean up, rest, spend some time in the library, and discuss the results of the mission, and maybe a beer. I could really go for a beer right now.

Mr. Lark breaks the silence, "Get cleaned up and then four hours rest. We are then going back to finish what we started."

Bloody Hell.

Chapter 18

Four hours of exhausted bliss while asleep is ended by Illych shaking me awake. "Wake up sunshine; we have bad guys to kill." Struggling to sit up all I can think of is how the bad guys at least get a proper night's sleep. Complying with the former Green Berets instruction I dress in clean black tacticals and begin my bleary eyed shuffle to the cafeteria.

I am last to the gathering, as usual. Mike and Tank are working out the details of a knife throwing game. Except instead of throwing the knives at targets, they throw them at each other and the target tries to catch it. Sounds crazy to me but they are still working out the details.

Everyone is hungry and when breakfast starts the cafeteria is silent except for the sounds of men eating with a purpose. The excellent coffee quickly resets me to half-alive status. No sooner is breakfast ended and tidied up than Mr. Lark walks in carrying a large black duffel bag that he places on the table with a heavy sounding thump.

The five of us gather around as Mr. Lark starts talking, "It became apparent to me some time ago that conventional firearms are not sufficiently effective for the challenges we operate against. Thus I took it upon myself to explore lethal technologies that could be put into service against our foes."

"The White Fang in combination with Truestone is highly effective against individual Lesser Created. Fortunately it is rare to encounter even a single Created and almost impossible to find more than one in the same place. Unfortunately there are situations such as that Troll in the Ukraine, and the Golem Gargoyles we just fought, or massed bound and possessed such at Ehgira in Turkey that demand more effective solutions."

"Something man portable that can effortlessly penetrate the hide of a Created and has the explosive power needed to shatter statue Haemonculi. A prototype was developed and is undergoing testing. Safety issues were identified and addressed..."

Safety issues addressed? What are we about to get? Light sabres that we can accidentally chop body parts off with? How about magical dice, 1-5 you hit and kill, on a 6 it blows up in your hand. I can just picture the six of us flinging dice at monsters. We mow the bad guys down like grass but when we return to the Citadel half of us need the Doctor to replace our hands.

Mr. Lark opens the duffel bag and reaches in to pull out something long and metallic during his monologue. It is tube shaped, like a pipe, steel or metal colored. As he fully withdraws it, I realize it follows the general layout of a riot shotgun. A large diameter barrel with a full length tube underneath to hold ammunition.

Both are set in a gunmetal receiver. Instead of a butt to place against your shoulder there is a brutish looking grip sticking out at an angle instead of down like a pistol grip. The grip has an end the size of a tennis ball. My guess is the ball is so you can brace it with your body.

There was no slide under the lower tube for loading the weapon. Instead, under the receiver is a metal loop that three fingers fit into. This weapon is a lever-action like out of the old American westerns. Mr. Lark's super weapon is a lever action shotgun?

Mr. Lark continues, "...Development has been ongoing and as you can see these weapons are patterned after a lever-action riot shotgun, if such a thing exists. The barrel is heavier and has a 19mm or .75 calibre bore. The tube under the barrel holds six shells and can be reloaded from the left or right. The action is top eject and is open to allow single rounds to be fed in."

I am starting to think this man missed his calling. Instead of super-genius techno-criminal and monster-slayer, he could have been a really good gun salesman.

Mr. Lark removed both weapons fully from the duffel bag, handing one to Illych and the other to Mike.

"Both weapons are empty but you should check for yourself of course. These are the two-prototypes. I had not planned on rolling them out for delivery to the Citadel for several more months. Unfortunately, due to mission pressures I have brought them early."

Each of the team members inspects the weapons in turn. Held asks, "And the ammunition?"

"There is a problem with the ammunition." Mr. Lark said this in a way that was a little too grim.

Tank chimes in, "What kind of problem?"

Illych then speaks, "Not enough of it? Duds?"

Mr. Lark waves his hands, "No, no, the ammunition is very reliable and the prototype testing order just arrived so there is plenty of it. The problem is its level of effectiveness."

That had me jump into the conversation, "Not as effective as hoped?"

Mr. Lark is becoming visibly frustrated by all the questions we keep asking that are actually unhelpful statements, "Stop with the useless comments framed as questions. I will finish explaining. The ammunition exceeded performance expectations by a wide margin. The shells this weapon fires use a special crystalline metal explosive that binds a significant amount of energy. By unit of mass it has over one-hundred times the energy of TNT. A tungsten penetrator sits at the end of the shell to provide armor penetration."

Illych figures it out first, "This weapon is a serious hazard to the individual pulling the trigger."

"Yes, even in full body armor with siege plates, a detonation within fifty feet will be hazardous to the firer. If we load one of the weapons and accidentally fire it at our feet, we will all be very dead. Each shell produces an explosion with slightly more energy than six sticks of dynamite combined with a significantly faster combustion speed."

"That is why I chose a lever action pattern and a limited ammunition supply tube instead of magazine fed. Fully-automatic would be suicide. Semi-automatic is still too risky. Perhaps in the future I will develop less energetic shells but for now this is what we have."

Mike has a serious look when he asks, "Can we at least take these to the shooting range and run a few rounds through them?" The shooting range he is referring to is an isolated valley in the Rocky Mountains we translate to for weapons practice.

"Unfortunately no, times constraints such as they are prevents proper training. We will take both weapons with us. Illych, you will be the primary shooter. The other weapon will be carried by Tank as a backup in case the first is damaged or Illych is disabled."

That is it, we are getting an over powered wild-west boom stick that there will be no practice with.

I had to ask, "What do we call it? A boom stick?"

Mr. Lark frowns again, "Do not be ridiculous, it is a Super High Explosive Gun or SHEG for short. The word is not common and not likely to be mistaken for something else when verbalized."

The name has that bland military feel to it and it is an acronym. My colleagues will love it.

Mr. Lark ends the discussion with, "Be prepared and ready to go in thirty minutes." That is it. End of discussion, time to get ready.

With practiced ease we gear up and meet at the Citadel entryway with time to spare.

Illych still carries a KRISS and a M1911 along with the new SHEG. He also has the disassembled elephant gun in his pack. Tank decided to cut out the middle man and left his KRISS behind. Hanging from his harness is the Tommy Gun he used to cut gargoyles in half. Strapped to his pack is the backup SHEG. Mike and I are KRISS and M1911 only. Held joins us in this. The 40mm had been less effective than hoped and is outclassed by the new weapon.

Mr. Lark walks out from between a collection of buildings within the Citadel. He must be keeping things in some of them the rest of us consider unused. Dressed in his banded obsidian armor he looks as ready as we are.

While getting ready one thought had been nagging me, how were we getting back in? Down the stairs? Please God not the ocean thing again. That left molten-lava and a hotel in London. There is nothing to do now but wait and hear what Mr. Lark has planned.

Mr. Lark and Illych exchange quiet words and we are off through the opening gate with no indication of how we are getting back into the pocket dimension beneath Castle Houska. I still have the artifact for traversing the granite in my rucksack even if it will not be needed.

The exhaustion from yesterday's efforts weighs on me and I am sure the others too. The pace set on the way to the Compass is fast, more of a jog than a walk. Mr. Lark bee-lines straight into the center of the stone circle and the rest of us follow.

Mr. Lark finally announces the path of our entry. "We are going in through the ocean again. This time I have set the Ouiblet up so both stages of the translation occur automatically. It is so fast you should not even notice the vacuum bubble.

All I can think of is how wrong this approach is. An error in timing of a single second will see us all dead.

Everything goes black and the dim cold of the Compass is replaced with the dim cold and damp of the entry point at our destination. I am so amped up on anxiety and adrenaline, the translation nausea passes quicker than usual.

It had been approximately five hours since we left this place. The cold dank entry way has no guards or watchers as far as we can tell. After a silent appraisal of everyone's arrival Illych gives hand signals for us to advance with Mike as point.

We head back into the belly of the beast.

Chapter 19

Our arrival point is quiet and dark. The team is in all-
new full body armor with added siege plates and full face
helmets. Tank is also carrying a siege shield made from
ceramic ballistic plates and Kevlar. Mr. Lark is operating
his Oculus when he announces there is a lot of
interference. That can only mean a lot of supernatural
multi-dimensional activity has happened while we were
gone.

The Oculus can still see things close enough,
making it unlikely we will be surprised unless something
comes at us really fast.

Leaving the entry chamber, we quickly walk through
a combination of short passages and turns. Mr. Lark
brings us up short at one of the turns. Looking up into
the ceiling corner he waves a friendly wave at
something. Following his line of sight leads to a small
black orb not much larger than a marble high up in the
corner. A small metallic bracket holds it in place

mounted to the grey stone of the passageway. Based on Mr. Lark's uncharacteristic wave it must be some sort of camera.

Illych also observes what I had just seen. His voice growls over the ComDat, "Expect contact shortly." The sound of weapons being readied fills my ears. Tank moves to take point and sets down his siege shield with the barrel of the Tommy Gun poking out from one side. The shield consists of several layers of ceramic ballistic plating with heavy Kevlar sandwiched between. A cutout on the one side allows for Tank to rest the barrel of his weapon. I have picked the thing up in the past and it weighs a good twenty plus kilograms. A crouching man can hide his entire silhouette behind it.

The wait is short.

Mr. Lark announces the human security staff have been Bound. They are now mentally unhinged and suicidal. No sooner is his warning verbalized and the first uniformed guard runs around the corner. Controlled bursts from the veterans put him down quickly enough. Harsh lessons learned from the battle at Ehgira are put into practice.

Head shots only. It is a more difficult target to hit but one brass-jacketed .45ACP is all that is needed.

The security people start chanting. The tunnels are pretty wide but dimly lit, if at all. The chanting echoes through the dark and seems to come from every direction. I am not sure they are using a proper language or if, more likely, they are yelling out their internal emotional state and that state sounds angry.

Around the next corner the tunnel runs straight for maybe fifty feet followed by a ninety degree tee pathing left and right. Bound security, those who still have some sense, are using corners for cover, while firing their AK's at us. Tank is blocking most of it but the ricochets are murder with several impacting members of the team. They are a painful nuisance for now, not a real threat.

Illych curses over the ComDat. Looking over at him I observe him brace his SHEG while aiming down the hall. The weapon kicks hard in his hand. The tee intersection ahead of us explodes in dust and shattered rock. The dark of the tunnel flashes bright white and red for an instant and all of us are hit by debris. Nobody falls down but we now have a hell of a mess to walk on.

The opposition gunfire and chanting completely stop in the explosion and we slowly and carefully walk to the newly enlarged intersection. Pieces of security personnel are everywhere and sections of the walls now look to be partially covered in something I know is not red paint.

Mr. Lark's voice is in my ear piece, "Illych, I suggest you lead with that." No kidding, the SHEG rocks.

The chanting starts up again down the corridor ahead. Mr. Lark's voice comes over the ComDat, "More are coming and they are wearing explosive vests."

This time we use the corners of the tee intersection to our advantage. The corridors in both directions are long, dark, and filled with dust. My helmet's night vision can barely make out the charging suicide bombers. The team's weapons simultaneously bellow in rage, filling the corridor in both directions with at least a hundred rounds.

The suicide bombers, four from both directions, fall not even twenty feet into their charge.

And detonate.

The SHEG fired rounds are more powerful than six sticks of dynamite. Powerful enough to solidly destroy an automobile, for instance. The suicide bombers are wearing significantly more explosives than a handful of dynamite. The blast wave knocks all of us down and debris ricochets off of everything. Through my body armor I can feel solid impacts that would have killed an unprotected person. If not for the helmets and hearing protection we would all be deaf and bleeding from our ears.

Trying to stand is a no go. Instead I slip and fall in the dust and rocks. Visibility is reduced to not much more than arm's length. What a mess.

Out of this apocalyptic fog I can see Mr. Lark, M1911 in hand walk past me. His armor has an open face but he shows no signs of dust or grit. The disturbing chanting ends again with the explosions. I am starting to wonder if we keep tossing bombs at each other this whole place will come down on top of us.

It takes almost ten minutes for the team to climb over the dust and debris, finally making it down one of the halls. Held planted a proximity fragmentary device in case our opponents try to come at us down the other corridor. There is no way they will see it before it detonates. Not in this mess.

The explosions have blown out walls revealing chambers and other corridors nearby. The good news: unlike normal rock, like in a mine, this stuff is very homogenous and the chance of a cave in is slim. At least that is what Mr. Lark is saying as we pick our way through the carnage.

We make it to debris free level ground again and Mr. Lark consults his Oculus, updating us we have no immediate foes to contend with. It appears our enemies have congregated at the great hall where the feast in my honor was held.

A significant amount of tactical movement later puts us one long corridor from a door into the great hall. We also find more of those black marbles on the walls as we get closer. They know we are here.

Illych's voice is loud and clear as he creates a plan for breaching the great hall, "We blow that door. Then use the SHEG to clear the room. They may be bound but they are not wearing body armor, respirators or eye protection. Kill everything that comes out. After that we advance to the opening we make where that door is. Then we re-assess."

Mr. Lark's chimes in, his voice sounding small and far away, "I concur. While you do that I am going to look at something."

Held makes a choking sound and says, "What? You are leaving us?"

"You are quite capable of dealing with the situation. There are about fifty bound gunmen inside that room. I also detect three Possessed. One of them I believe is the one called Leveque that Thomas met. I suggest you be extra careful in terminating them."

That said our employer purposefully walks away down a side corridor leaving us behind.

I wanted to say something to the others but remember the Mr. Lark would hear us and I did not dare open my helmet in this nightmare situation.

Illych gives what passes for a pep talk in this crew. "Suck it up people. We have a job to do. After I blow this door we advance to hold the breach."

Tank advances about ten feet and plants his shield on the floor, bracing it by kneeling and leaning into it. Illych stands by his right shoulder and Held on his left. Mike already has a grenade in each hand, taking his place behind Tank. I check my KRISS and ready myself behind Mike.

Aiming the SHEG Illych calls out, "I am firing three shells and then we advance. Ready?"

Illych takes note of everyone's nod and pulls the trigger. The weapon bucks in his hand. I watch him snap the lever action as the first detonation sounds. The weapon bucks again. I stop looking at Illych and shift my gaze back to looking down the hall to the door. The first shell detonated just to right of the door blowing out most of the wall. The door itself is now half off its hinges. The second round impacts to the left, completely removing the door. The third round sails through the empty space the door had just occupied impacting something just inside.

We are far enough from the explosions to witness a rain of debris but not get hit by anything large enough to be concerned about. No sooner has Illych pulled the trigger for the third time and my four companions are charging down the corridor to the breach. They move so fast I am left behind. They make it halfway when a man comes running out at us through the breach. The dust and smoke swirling around his running form.

Did I say running? It was more like rocketing. Something is wrong. This man is moving faster than an Olympic sprinter, even a suicidal Bound does not move that fast. This could only mean one thing…

"Possessed!" Illych yells out as everyone's weapons roar in response.

The man does the impossible and dodges to his right. His momentum carrying him right up the wall as he continues sprinting towards us. The speed of the maneuver leaves everyone's stream of fire behind. Aim points are shifted and the gunfire continues. The man pushes off from one wall and leaps across the corridor to the other wall. Some of the rounds impact his body on the way across but the man's athletic maneuver dodges most of it. The charging man is not walking on the walls per se. His speed and momentum allow him to travel along the wall for a moment and then push off to the other side.

He is not more than twenty feet away and our weapon bolts lock open. The Possessed pushes off the wall straight at Tank driving the full length of his body into the siege shield with what has to have been bone crunching force, pushing the ex-marine backwards. The impact is so severe the big man's feet leave the ground, driving him through empty space backwards until he lands on me with both of us falling to the ground in a tangle.

I can still see the three others and the Possessed clearly. Mike leaves his empty weapon fall and with effortless agility un-sheaths his combat blade, moving to disembowel the unarmed and unarmored attacker. With speed bordering on the supernatural the Possessed kicks Mike straight in the chest armor sending him flying almost several feet backwards into the wall.

Held does something in that instant I could not have expected. He also drops his exhausted weapon and maneuvers himself close to the side of the Possessed, flinging himself at the monster.

And hugs him.

Held wraps his arms and legs around the Possessed and holds on for dear life. Our foe had not expected such an unorthodox move and struggles with superhuman strength to extricate himself from the former Green Beret. One of Held's arms bends in a direction it was never meant to go. The microphones in my helmet pick up the sounds of bones breaking.

Finally flinging Held's limp form to the ground the Possessed looks around to assess the situation only to find himself staring down the barrel of Illych's M1911. In that fraction of a second a sort of realization forms on the man's face before the weapon fires. The weapon's slide snaps back and forward and the Possessed's face implodes with a jet of organic material exiting the back of his head.

The man's body just crumples down onto the floor. Head shots, works every time.

Illych holsters his weapon and retrieves his SHEG. Quickly inserting shells, he fully reloads the weapon. Standing in the middle of the corridor, he points it into the smoke and dust filled breach.

His voice, with a dark edge to it, comes across the ComDat, "Screw this noise." Then he fires, levers in the next round, and fires again. He does this six times, reloads and repeats. He hoses the great hall down with twenty-four hi-explosive rounds before stopping.

Mike rolls away from the wall and crawls towards Held. Illych reloads the SHEG again and stands there with it pointed towards the great hall, waiting. Tank and I untangle ourselves, recover our weapons, reload them and position ourselves with Illych.

Mike removes his helmet and does the same for Held. The former Green Berets face is pale but his eyes are open and moving. He is alive. Mike does his medic thing and administers pain killers to Held. He then begins removing the injured man's armor while slowly sliding him back up the corridor away from the great hall and any potential violent activity.

We stand there, waiting for the dust to settle. Eventually a clear view into the great hall opens in the haze and we see nothing threatening. The place resembles a scene from the western front in a WW1 movie. The hall appears to have been chewed, crushed, and finally stomped into wall to wall wreckage.

The three of us walk into the breach and look closer. A few AK's are scattered about. No blood though, considering the amount of dust that makes sense.

Illych holds the SHEG in one hand and fishes an Oculus out of a pouch, closing his eyes. After a minute his eyes open and he quickly puts the Oculus away.

As he begins to back up he says, "One still alive."

A booming voice answers, "Yes, one of us is still alive."

A great slab of stone had been pulled to cover the corner of a far wall. Will a loud boom that slab is flipped away and a seven foot tall African man stands up, bloodied and obviously wounded.

Leveque.

"You have made a mess. Thomas, regardless I will make this offer once more. Join us."

Illych's and Tank's helmets make an almost imperceptible turn towards me.

"No thank you Leveque. I will stick with the sort of good guys." It is true statement, my colleagues are sort of good guys.

"There are no good guys. If only you could understand."

The big man pulls himself free from the rubble and takes two steps towards us. All three of us react by realigning our weapons at Leveque.

The stone dust contrasts with the man's dark skin when viewed through night vision optics giving the big man a ghoulish appearance.

"Where is your leader? I wish to meet Karl Lark."

I think Illych and Tank are trying to figure out what to do. Leveque is unarmed and at least fifty feet away from us. He may be possessed but there are no walls for the man to pinball off of while coming at us. Now that we know what we are up against, the tricks we had just endured in the corridor behind us probably won't be effective.

What to do?

Based on the shift in Illych's weight and the repositioning of his feet my guess is the decision making has ended and he is getting ready to put Leveque down. Even in the gloom and dust Leveque could see the change in situation. He bends his knees a bit and muscles visibly tense. Things are about to get very exciting.

"I am the one you are looking for." Mr. Lark's voice carries across the great hall as he stalks into the open space while navigating the rubble with dexterity. He does not slow his pace as he continues towards Leveque.

The big man grunts, "You wear that armor? Such arrogance for one so elderly and frail."

Mr. Lark is forty feet away, then thirty feet away, then twenty, finally stopping less than ten feet from Leveque. My throat is tight with anxiety. That Possessed in the hall almost murdered Held in just a few seconds when he got that close. He is also too close for the rest of us to shoot at Leveque.

Leveque shifts to confront Mr. Lark. "So brave to come so close, I can reach you now before they can shoot me. Does that not concern you?"

Mr. Lark's right hand makes a sweeping motion like he is slashing a sword across Leveque's chest. My night vision clearly shows the droplets from the crystal water sprinkler splash across the big man. Mr. Lark brought his magical holy water sprinkler with him and just used it on Leveque.

Honestly, I did not know what to expect. Perhaps it will melt his flesh? What if he bursts into flame? That would be different.

Then the screaming starts. It was like the screaming of several different men and women all erupting from the same open mouth, a sound neither right nor natural. I do not like it and the three of us take a few steps back.

Leveque is trying to rub off whatever landed on him. Apparently it is not working because the screaming continues with increased volume. Leveque finally gets control of himself and stops screaming. His arms hanging down at his sides, while his body continues shaking all over, he looks at Mr. Lark."

"Do you know what you have done? This causes pain. My kind has not felt pain like this since almost back

to the beginning. You dare use such a thing on me?"
Leveque bounds towards Mr. Lark, covering the distance
between them in two strides. The big man is fast but he
displays none of the amazing speed or dexterity we had
seen from the possessed in the corridor earlier.

Mr. Lark leaps into his attacker and the men begin to
wrestle while remaining standing. The old man is exactly
that, an old man. We need to get in there and help or
Leveque will tear Mr. Lark apart. I started moving
towards the fight and Illych's hand comes out to stop me.
"Wait," he says.

The big African man and Mr. Lark's armored form
are locked in combat, wrestling and trading blows but
two things are becoming obvious. Whatever was
sprinkled on Leveque has stolen his mojo and also, Mr.
Lark can fight. The big man is slower and unable to keep
up with the old man.

Finally our short leader manages to get the giant of
a man to his knees while wrapping his gauntlets around
the Possessed's throat.

Leveque continues speaking even as Mr. Lark
squeezes, "You have not won old man. When this body
is dead I take what I know to the others. This is only the
beginning and you are a weak, old, mortal man."

Mr. Lark replies in some weird language I have
never heard before. It has kind of a fast staccato to it
with some high pitched notes. Honestly I could not have
repeated even a word of it if I had wanted to.

Leveque speaks again in close to a whisper that the
helmet microphones still pick up. The big man is still
getting small amounts of air while he is slowly being
strangled. It does not look right, the large, muscular form
of Leveque losing a contest of physical strength to the

white haired old man. "You found it. After all this time it is free."

With a voice almost gone Leveque spoke his last, "Tell the Magi something for me. Tell him his brothers are gone, even Vadkeinen. I was there when Vadkeinen was thrown into the Gyre. They are all gone."

The big man finally stops moving and talking, and goes limp. Mr. Lark ghoulishly keeps strangling his opponent until he is sure the man is dead. Then he draws his M1911 and dead checks the Possessed right between the eyes with a single round.

Mr. Lark, looking none the worse for wear, turns towards us, "That is the last of them. We are now in complete control of this pocket dimension."

I thought about that. This place has four portals into it. How are we going to keep people out? I voice my concern to Mr. Lark.

"That is the reason for my diversion while you handled things here. I closed the other three portals from the inside. They are now sealed. The only way in or out until I say otherwise is through the ocean portal. Without the Ouiblet it is almost impossible to enter this place."

Illych opens his helmet, removing it to clip it to his belt. "We are alone in here now?"

Mr. Lark nods in the affirmative.

Illych calls out to Mike on the ComDat, "Get Held back to the entry point and translate Him to the Compass. This place is clear, we have no observers. Tank, go help him." Tank nods and jogs away.

Mike terse response comes back in the affirmative.

As Tank crunches across the room to the exit we look around at the carnage surrounding us.

A thought popped into my mind and I share it without thinking. Addressing Mr. Lark I said, "Why do almost all your solutions involve violence? There must be other tools in the toolbox." I regret saying it so crudely but standing in the middle of the remains of the great hall something drove me to say it. Call it temporary insanity.

"Mr. Davies, There are very, very, few examples in human history of anything of value being achieved without violence. Ending slavery, the freedom of speech, property rights, as Mao Tse Tung would say, 'All power flows from the barrel of a gun'. If recorded history tells us anything it is that humans detest change and anyone who says they will bring peaceful change is lying. This is why there are monuments to the fallen, because they had to die for meaningful change to happen. In so many ways it is a waste."

Once in a while the old man waxes philosophical.

"Now that the deeps beneath Castle Houska are secure, let us walk and take inventory of our new domain. I have been waiting to see why so much has been done to keep this place bottled up."

Chapter 20

This pocket dimension we had fought, bled and killed for is big. Big like the one the Citadel and the Compass are in. Except instead of a huge open space this place is like a multi-level mine with galleries, caverns, tunnels, rooms, corridors, and doors, lots of doors. Many are modern, having been updated in the last century. Some are hundred-plus year old affairs made of heavy plates riveted together. Others even older, huge portals made from oak or iron-wood.

The oldest are stone, either great disks that roll away to reveal the entry behind or great slabs precisely balanced on pivot points. Some places are instead sealed off with great slabs of stone work. Many have language and images chiseled into them. Regardless, Mr. Lark barely takes note as we pass by. He is apparently looking for something.

Lighting is sparse. Sometimes all there is are dim luminescence patch of rock that glows for reasons long forgotten. There are a few artifacts scattered randomly during our walk, silver cylinders the size of a large candle with white plasma guttering at the upright end, giving off a dim, soft light. As we walk closer the plasma expands upward to almost a foot in length providing a bright light illuminating everything nearby. Sometimes they are randomly placed on the floor. Others are found in their own alcove along the path of our travels. A rare few hang over our path, supported by chains.

A few times we encounter a modern caged light bulb. Mr. Lark comments that a generator is in operation for now. He does not understand why but our adversaries felt the need to bring light into certain places here in the deeps.

After more than an hour of what feels like aimless wandering we enter a fairly well-lit chamber. Several of the plasma candles are present making viewing of the space fairly straightforward. The focus of the space is a large egg shaped platform placed in the center of the room. Something huge once sat socketed into the space. The curved walls of the chamber have crystal tubes set into them along with strangely shaped sockets and what look like heavy power cables.

I am inspecting the platform when Mr. Lark speaks, startling me, and causing me to jump.

"Thomas, this is a creation engine. All the species on the Earth: birds, fishes, cows, mosquitoes, all of them, originated in one of these. This is how the ancients created life, here in one of these giant artificial wombs. Once there were hundreds of thousands of these and they played and replayed their desires out on the surface of the planet. Now they are rare. This is the first one I have found in over eight years of searching.

Unfortunately the tank that sits atop this platform has been removed rendering it less useful.

He smiles while placing his hand against the engine. His demeanor makes me feel a little creeped out. This is what Mr. Lark's has desired for so long and you can see it play out in his facial expressions and body language.

"So you can make Unicorns in this?" I feel it is a legitimate question.

Mr. Lark pulls his hand from the engine while giving me a cold look. "I could, but why not make velociraptors and find out if you can outrun one?"

Touché.

We leave the creation engine behind and keep walking. Mr. Lark is searching for something else but won't tell us what it is. Another hour of trekking through hall after hall and along many corridors and we find our goal.

The smell gives it away first. Even though I do not know what it was we are looking for or what to associate it with, I know the second that smell disturbs my senses we had arrived. It is the odor of decay. Sickly-sweet and growing stronger.

I am not surprised when Mr. Lark leads us closer to the stink through a doorway into a massive gallery. We are now standing at one of the short ends of an oval space. In the middle of the floor is a massive sarcophagus.

The smell of death is strong in this room. The lighting is barely enough to make out the perimeter of the room and the outline of the sarcophagus. As we make our way in Mr. Lark calls out for Illych to supply some light. The former Green Beret produces a high illumination lamp from his rucksack making everything in the space visible.

The creation engine was weird to look at but it was also a genius construct of sublime form. What we are looking at now was built using a less elegant methodology. It is a sarcophagus but there is a riot of cables and crystal containers piped to and from, all connected into the coffin. It looks functional but what it is for, I can only guess.

Mr. Lark's face shows no emotion as he speaks, "This is how they possess people. The machinery before you is an execution sarcophagus. A live human is placed inside and the same process that produced the stasis field we witnessed in the Ellora caves is applied. Except it does not stop at stasis, the electron probability suppression is pushed all the way and the human placed inside dies, resulting in a body lacking any sign of cause of death."

"The other part of the ritual is to guide the spirit of a greater created to connect with the deceased, joining with, and possessing it. It is a vile thing, an abomination parroting life. As much as I wish to destroy it, this thing has value."

How many have been forced into that box and killed? Did they know what was about to happen to them? I feel sick. This place has probably been in operation for a thousand years or more. Walking to the nearest wall I lean up against it.

Mr. Lark gives a nod and we keep walking.

Mike's voice rumbles over the ComDat, Held is ok. That is good news.

268   *Erik Lange*

We do not pause as we pass through the ruined great hall again. Leveque's corpse is where we had left it. Everyone is quiet. There is nothing to say really.

We walk to the ocean entry chamber and everyone fishes out their respective escape dongles.

Mr. Lark speaks just as we were about to leave, "I have some errands to deal with. We will talk again soon." And he is gone.

Then Illych is gone.

I realize I am standing alone in this awful place and a sensation of unease like some shade or wraith may come out of the walls to get me chills up my spine.

Then I push and twist and I am gone too.

Chapter 21

We brought nothing back from The Deeps, as we are now calling the pocket dimension we fought for below Castle Houska. It is a fitting name now that most of the portals have been sealed from the inside, leaving the only way in or out an impossible thousand meters beneath the ocean.

The tempo at the Citadel slowed down now that we have been back for a few days. Sleep caught up, weapons and gear cleaned and prepped for their next use. Maintenance around the Citadel is now up to date. Our next vacation is less than a week away and everyone is planning and preparing. This would be my second solo vacation since being inducted into this group of near resurrected fighting men. My destination is San Francisco, again. Although the beaches in Costa Rica, Mike's preferred destination, sound pretty nice. Maybe for my next vacation I will choose the sun.

Mr. Lark had not been around since his cryptic exit on the return from The Deeps. I have some anxiety that he is going to show up just as we are leaving for vacation. Sharing these fears with the others brought vehement denials. In the years since Mr. Lark implemented the policy of down time away from the Citadel, it had never been broken. Three inviolable months a year off: April, August, and December.

With not even three days left to vacation, the team is taking a long lunch in the cafeteria. It had been eighty-seven days since our last time off and everyone is ready to start our pursuit of what each one of us consider a good time.

Lunch is finished and the team seated at the cafeteria tables talking when Mr. Lark walks in. I cannot say any of us is surprised. He had been gone long enough that his showing up was bound to happen sooner rather than later. I was just hoping for later, like after some time off.

He is dressed in his grey suit and carrying his Oculus cane. That can only mean he is conducting himself in a professional capacity. Now we just had to wait and find out if he is coming or going.

The room has gone silent and all of us are looking and waiting to hear what the man has to say.

"Illych, Thomas, please dress appropriately. We are making a day trip to the Kharkareth. Don't fret, we will return with plenty of time to leave for your vacation."

What grown man says 'fret' in the modern age? Without a word Illych and me stand and head to our rooms. My tailored grey suits are all dry cleaned, hung up, and waiting in plastic. The suit, plus polished shoes and an M1911 in a shoulder rig later, and I am back at the cafeteria in twenty.

Mr. Lark is talking to Mike and Held about completing some mundane task as I walk in. Illych joins us shortly after and we are off.

As usual, during the short walk between the Citadel and the Compass I take advantage of the one-on-one time with my employer to ask questions.

"Have you been back to The Deeps beneath Castle Houska since the last time we were there?"

"Yes."

"Is there anything from that place that could find a home in the library here at the Citadel?"

"Yes."

"Why are you taking us with you today?"

"The information that will be shared is important to the team overall and I do not want to discuss it with you and then repeat it again to Balthazar."

"What about the other Magi Leveque spoke of, this Vadkeinen? Nothing in any of the texts in the library mentions Magi beyond Melchior, Casper, and Balthazar. And what is the Gyre?"

"Thomas, you are babbling. An immortal being called the Adversary has systematically hunted down an ancient brotherhood of superhuman Magi. One of the bad guys, as you would say, names a missing Magi, a name with no mention in any history book, and then informs us that he was apparently disposed of somewhere. This Vadkeinen is gone and all knowledge of him and his name is lost or erased, it is difficult to know which. But you are willing to talk about this; a subject great powers have gone to extraordinary lengths to hide, in casual conversation?"

"This seems like a safe place to discuss it."

"There are no safe places to discuss such things. You must learn this. In the future understand we will save such discussions for the library at the Citadel only." Apparently that is now the safe room for sensitive discussions, good to know.

After a pause he continues, "And never forget you work for me, not for Balthazar. Is this clearly understood?"

"Very clearly." I have given a lot of thought to the topic of loyalty to Mr. Lark and I am pretty sure that even the slightest hint of anything less than one-hundred percent loyal will be violently unacceptable.

After that, the journey to the Kharkareth is uneventful. We translate to a road in the middle of nowhere, followed by a short walk to a vehicle Mr. Lark had arranged to be left for us. A two hour drive along lonely roads and through virtual wilderness follows, ending at a square pillar in the middle of an open field and now we wait.

It is not long before a poorly dressed Goblin shifts into view as from the edge of my field of vision and in the voice of a young boy bids us to follow. We do so and after a short walk down the road leading to the main gates we pass into Balthazar's massive residence.

The entryway is unchanged from my last visit but who is there has. The entity, who led us into the non-Euclidean contraction Balthazar's home resides in, through the front door so to speak, is a Goblin. However, upon arriving at the Kharkareth proper we find a human male acting as the butler. In this particular case it is a man I have met before.

Hector awaits us just inside the main gates. He is wearing a navy blue suit and tie and looking quite dapper and professional. He still has an arrogant look to him and his expression gives away his less than positive opinion of my colleagues and me. This is understandable. Our arrival in Ehgira began a series of events that resulted in the massacre of half of its inhabitants. Arms-length professional is probably the best we can hope for.

Hector spoke, "Welcome to the House of Balthazar. My Master sends his greetings. Peace be upon you." The greeting is professionally delivered but feels forced. Hector better remember that Balthazar is old school and the tolerance for insolent serving staff will be very thin.

"The Master awaits you within. I will bring you to him." Our greeter turns on his heels and starts towards one of the internal doors. Mr. Lark sets off behind him. Illych and I look at each other and shrug. When in Rome…

We follow our escort down a long hall I have traveled before and it appears we are headed towards the massive library I experienced on my first visits to this place. Sure enough, we breeze through a door into a massive open space with beautiful and comfortable furnishings and towering walls of book shelves filled with books.

Inside, waiting for us, is Balthazar dressed in simple black. He rises from a chair and greets each one of us and then waves his hand for us to take a seat. Hector leaves without another word being spoken.

Balthazar begins by stating, "You have succeeded?"

Mr. Lark nods, "Yes, the influence and presence of those who forced you into exile have been removed from the pocket dimension whose gate can be found beneath Castle Houska."

Balthazar considers what Mr. Lark had just said and replies, "Was it difficult to accomplish?"

Mr. Lark smiles his Cheshire cat grin, "My organization was sufficient to the task."

Balthazar continues, "Is there anything learned you wish to share?"

"They were more talkative than I had expected." It was a simple statement that said much and Mr. Lark delivered it in his characteristic deadpan fashion.

That raised one of Balthazar's eyebrows.

Mr. Lark continues, "The head villain was a Possessed calling himself 'Leveque'. He had a pretty high opinion of himself and his organizations efforts."

"You say was, as in past tense?"

"Leveque is dead, I strangled him."

"Only the shell he occupied perished. The ancient spirit, whichever one this Leveque is, will endure. He will be back at some point," Balthazar explains.

I nodded in understanding, "He asked me to join the other team."

That gets Balthazar's attention. "That is a rare offer Thomas. You have attracted the attention of beings it is best to be unknown to." Balthazar and Mr. Lark give each other a knowing look.

I continue, "He gave what could be at best described as an alternate version of history."

Balthazar nods, "Many things can be explained in different ways. The truth is ever elusive."

The discussion experienced a long pause at this point as no one spoke for almost a full minute. The old Magi is processing the ramifications of all that had just been said.

Balthazar's eye locked mine as he asked, "And?"

"I said no. The ramifications of such a career move are beyond the pale to seriously consider."

That seems to satisfy the Magi.

"Balthazar, there were other people there, factions of loyal organizations. While I was their prisoner they held a feast to convince me to join. Representatives from every faction were required to be present but apparently they are having loyalty problems as there were obvious empty seats. One of the true believers I spoke to said some of them needed to be reminded of their loyalties."

Balthazar replies, "It is true there is much to gain from associating with ancient spirits such as this Leveque. They have immeasurable knowledge that can make a pauper into a wealthy emperor. Unfortunately, close proximity to such spirits can challenge even the most robust person. The hazards are many and a single miscommunication can prove fatal. Over time most mortals with some measure of wisdom take extreme efforts to limit their exposure."

I then relate Leveque's history lesson from my captivity to Balthazar.

The old Magi considers what was said, "In many ways his teachings are correct. I leave it to your own review to determine the truth."

"Wait? You are not going to convince me that you are correct and point out the flaws in Leveque's argument?"

"Thomas, the truth is self-evident and the first step on the path to wisdom is to truly question everything, even yourself. There are the things you know you know. Then there are the things you know you do not know. The knowledge that frightens you the most is the things you do not know you do not know. You will come to understand this over time."

How very vague and unsatisfying. You would think a Magi would be more militant in the distribution of the truth.

Mr. Lark must have come to the conclusion it was his turn to speak," Balthazar, as Leveque met his end he spoke of another Magi by name, Vadkeinen, a brother of yours?"

The Magi's face lights up, "Vadkeinen is my brother, and one of the five Magi of old. What did he say? Tell me everything." This is something Balthazar had been desperately looking for, news of his brothers.

"Leveque informed me this Vadkeinen was the last of the Magi to be dealt with. He stated Vadkeinen was sent into the Gyre. Does that have meaning to you?"

"It does not surprise me Vadkeinen was the last. He was the strongest of us, always the most prepared. But the reference to the Gyre?"

I decided to contribute, "Is a nautical reference? Something in an ocean or open sea?"

The old Magi smiled, "Neither the ocean, nor the mountains, or open desert is a threat to a prepared Magi. There is no prison on this world that could hold

Vadkeinen. Nor is he hiding in some lost pocket dimension as you call them. I would have learned of it by now."

"Since my return I have been putting my house in order and sending out spies of the least order. Only the lightest touch is being used to find evidence of my brothers. The spies that return bring nothing. This message from the Possessed is the first evidence or knowledge I have learned of what happened."

"The ancients of lower order, the ones commonly called Goblins or Faeries, and the ancients of greater orders, the Daemons, Angels, and Djinn, have been here since long, long ago. They are the remaining instruments of Those Who Came Before. These ancient beings made the Earth into what it is at their command."

"Over millions of years they made, erased, and remade their vision upon the Earth. Then a great conflict erupted and Those Who Came Before took their leave. This was the beginning of the ages of man. Civilizations have risen and fallen over and over as the Adversary pursues the end of humanity. The Magi were created to offset the Adversaries efforts."

"During the many playing and re-playing of their creations upon the Earth, Those Who Came Before found it was necessary at times to dispose of creations of a particularly durable nature. Rather than expend considerable resources deconstructing something created to be rather resilient, they used the Gyre to remove it from the Earth. Before their arrival here, Those Who Came Before originated from another world. The Gyre connects the two. The power of the Gyre was used to remove things from the Earth and send them to the other world for storage, in case it would prove useful to retrieve them in the future."

A supernatural garbage can? Connecting to another planet? With millions of years of creations deposited across its surface? That may be the most amazing thing I have ever heard of.

Mr. Lark asks the first question, "Where is this Gyre located?"

Wait? What? I find the concept of the Gyre intellectually stimulating but actually looking for it sounds like a bad idea. Prompting me to ask, "Mr. Lark, do you have an academic interest in something like the Gyre."

"I leave the academic to you Thomas. My interest is, as always, practical."

Balthazar shakes his head, "It is not anywhere. The Gyre is wildly dangerous so it was never established on this world. There is an ancient pattern by which it visits the Earth."

Mr. Lark cocks his head while looking at the old Magi, "And the pattern is determined how?"

"Mr. Lark, such knowledge has never been mine. It does appear my brother Vadkeinen was able to determine it. My guess is that in his desperation to escape the Adversary he took the road least travelled and journeyed through the Gyre."

"I do not ask you to look for him. My other three brothers are still here on this world in some form. I just need time to find the clues. Vadkeinen will be the last searched for if he truly went into the Gyre."

"What else did you find beneath Castle Houska?"

Karl Lark replies, "I found the murder sarcophagus as you said I would."

Balthazar locked eyes with Mr. Lark, "Did you destroy the abomination?"

"I did not, I wish to study it."

"As you wish. Our business is concluded for now. You have my thanks and friendship."

I took this to mean our meeting has ended.

"As I am sure you witnessed upon your arrival, mortal servants again walk the halls of the Kharkareth. It will take years but this place will flourish as it once did."

Mr. Lark stands and nods to the old Magi. Balthazar mirrors Mr. Lark. As we are leaving the library we find Hector standing right outside the door, waiting to escort us to the main gate. From there we are allowed to walk alone to the square pillar and exit this place.

Balthazar seemed happy, Mr. Lark is as happy as it appears he is capable of. Illych is not speaking much so I cannot tell if he is happy. Regardless, I know that in two days I will be in San Francisco starting thirty days of the best happiness unlimited credit can buy.

Chapter 22

Upon returning to the Citadel we did not split up with Mr. Lark disappearing as expected. Instead the three of us went to the library. "For unfinished business," as Mr. Lark put it.

The Citadel runs on United States east coast time. With no day or night cycle in the pocket dimension, everyone's circadian rhythm would be scrambled in no time, thus meal times and sleep times are rigidly adhered to. By that method of time determination it is past the middle of the night as the three of us enter the library. We are less than 48 hours from vacation.

I activate a few, low lights upon entering, keeping it dim and shadowed. It is late and I do not want bright lights waking me up too much.

Illych takes a seat in a comfortable overstuffed leather chair. Mr. Lark does the same and both of them watch me take my time to find a seat with just the right lighting.

Mr. Lark starts the discussion, "There are a few things to discuss before either of you leave for your time off."

"I have no plans to pursue this Vadkeinen at this time. Finding the Gyre has the makings of a monumental task with the potential for little return on investment. If this thing is really connected to another planet in some other solar system out in space somewhere, it does not concern me. Rescuing Balthazar, returning him home, finding the descendants of his former servants, and closing down the operations under Castle Houska was more involved than this organization is accustomed to. The compensation was excellent, no complaints there, but at several points in these most recent adventures events were driving this organization's actions beyond my interests."

Illych's eyes are closed but he is not snoring. This means he is relaxing and listening, not sleeping. At times I wish I had some of the tricks my colleagues with military backgrounds have.

Karl Lark continues, "We did recover some excellent quality artifacts from below the Ellora temple complex a few months back which made up for some of the distraction."

I never had a chance to ask Mr. Lark about those. A few months back I researched and pinpointed the location of an ancient inventory of artifacts held in stasis in caves deep underneath the Ellora temple in India. The affair had been rushed at the end and all I witnessed was Illych shoveling five small stone boxes into a duffel bag. "What were in those stone boxes? Did you ever get a chance to look into them?"

"Yes I did. One of the boxes held what in today's nomenclature is referred to as a Roman dodecahedron. Although the one we recovered is in almost perfect condition compared to the ones displayed in modern museums today."

This is interesting, I know what these are and the archaeological community has debated their purpose since they were first discovered. "I have seen these before. No one has ever figured out what they are for. There is a lot of speculation in the archeological community. They are suspected to be measuring devices or maybe even children's toys."

Mr. Lark shakes his head, "They are keys of a sort, for unlocking a very special lock. They are quite valuable should one know what they are for. That is why they are always found with other objects of importance."

"And you know what they are for?"

"Yes and I will not discuss it at this time."

So much for mysteries of the universe revealed.

"What else was in the boxes?" Maybe I can get a complete answer on something tonight.

"A short sword constructed from Damascus steel. It might have had ceremonial value in the distant past as it is just a sword with no additional properties"

"You see Thomas, Damascus steel is constructed from many, many impossibly thin layers of steel with the finest carbon layers between. The carbon gives the weapon flexibility without breaking, making such a blade remarkably flexible, durable as well as impressively sharp. No one has figured out how it was done. The ancients, whoever they were, used very thin ribbons of the highest purity iron not more than ten microns thick. Perhaps two-thousand strips are stacked upon each other with each strip is dusted with very fine carbon dust. This stack was then heated and forged to make the Damascus steel."

I do not understand everything Mr. Lark just said, so I just nod and smile like I usually do when he goes on one of his technical tirades. When he decides to get his repressed geek on, he really goes all out.

"What about the other boxes, what was in them?"

"Yes they contained items of value but we will discuss those at a later date. Instead let's discuss the offer Leveque made."

"I did not accept the offer."

"No you did not and your honor is intact. He also mentioned my name during your discussion. My reasoned conclusion: his curiosity comes from researching our names and finding our real world footprint diminished. Both of us had lives in the real world at one time. Since then our presence is noticeably absent for those with resources that know how to look. They have our photos and locating our old lives and histories would require little effort. Most likely Leveque's goal was to get someone on the inside to report on the anomaly that is our organization."

Mr. Lark had a life before becoming a criminal overlord? "So Karl Lark is your real birth name?"

"Yes Thomas, I have a real mother and father and was once as young and obnoxious as you are."

Who calls a full grown man in his early forties young?

He continues, "It was bound to happen sometime, this organization appearing on someone's radar.

Without thinking I spoke, "Why couldn't it appear on people's radars before I got stuck here?"

That got a humorous snort from a now very awake Illych.

"No Thomas, you would be here, bound to me just the same. Only more people would be looking for me, some with genuine interest, others just looking for the payout on a bounty. Of course I would not have had the need to kidnap and question you either and I could have left you to their attentions."

Note to self: quit giving Mr. Lark reasons to dispose of me.

Illych spoke, "The confirmation from those thugs at the airport that someone out there is looking for us is useful intel."

Mr. Lark nods, "Yes it is. Not only did you show up on facial recognition but we left a hangar full of dead bodies to show we do not appreciate such interest."

He sits back in his chair and is silent for at least a minute, "I see no reason to change the vacation protocols at this time. The others are still unknown to whoever is searching. Only you and Thomas were recorded. Illych, it is unlikely you will be identified during your time off due the remote nature of the location."

Illych smiles and comments, "And if they locate Thomas it would only lead us to whomever is showing interest."

I thought about that for a moment, "Wait, what, I am bait?"

Mr. Lark replies, "Hardly, and in the event something happens we are more than capable of recovering you. Should you be taken into custody just relax and wait for us to arrive. Perhaps it will give you additional incentive to keep a low profile while out and about on your own?" Now Mr. Lark is smiling his Cheshire cat grin again.

That denial of my status as bait sounded a lot more like an affirmative. During my vacation I need to stay away from networked cameras. I also need to start thinking of a place to vacation that is not as technologically connected as San Francisco.

Apparently our meeting is over because Mr. Lark stands up and without further words starts walking towards the door. Illych and I look at each other and shrug. Our employer leaving means it is time to go to sleep. Less than two days and I am out of this place.

Chapter 23

I sleep in late that morning. There are no
outstanding tasks assigned to me and I quite honestly
have nothing to work on outside of the library. After
stopping by the cafeteria, finding it eerily empty, I eat a
quick breakfast and pour myself a coffee to go, and head
for the library.

Mr. Lark is always sending me new artifacts to
review, confirm, catalog, and evaluate. This is the most
fun, never ending, job I could have hoped for. I once
calculated the approximate value of the artifacts
contained within the stone walls of this library. It is truly a
princely sum, not including s the rare, one of a kind,
previously unseen, items.

So there I was, sitting in my library at the Citadel. I
had started calling it my library. After-all, the only
possessions I retain from my life before Mr. Lark are all
contained in this one place, all my books and notebooks.
Adding to that is the considerable body of materials in

the never ending stream of papers, texts, grimoires, folios, and books Mr. Lark keep sending. I firmly believe the man has a giant warehouse somewhere filled with dusty book shelves and wooden crates.

Weirdly, I fantasize about him going there, pulling things from boxes and removing more things from shelves and making a pile on the floor. Once the pile is big enough he declares, "That will keep Thomas busy." A day or two later boxes of stuff show up at the Citadel.

It is a dream come true, a never ending supply of old paper and velum. The smell of it alone brings a smile to my face. Other than tending to the biological necessities of being human, I would never leave this place.

"That will not do Thomas." I turn in my chair to see a grey suited Mr. Lark leaning with both hands on the Oculus of his cane. "As your employer it is disconcerting to enter your work area and find you sitting, open mouthed, looking up at the ceiling with a vacant expression and a silly half-smile upon your face."

"I beg your pardon but I was thinking. Thinking is part of what I do."

"A famous sculptor created a statue of what a man looks like when he is thinking. It does not resemble whatever you were doing."

"Yes, of course, is there a task I might complete for you?" Maybe I could redirect his tirade into something constructive.

"Yes Mr. Davies, you can go to your personal quarters and change into a grey suit. We are going out."

I stood and started for the door. Last night I had hoped would be my last interaction with my employer prior to vacation.

Apparently that is not to be.

Mr. Lark interrupts me half-way to the exit, "You are not curious as to where or whom?"

I shake my head side to side and reply, "Why ruin the surprise?" and keep walking.

A half-an hour later I am at the gates to the Citadel in a tailored grey suit, my black shoes polished, and a large caliber handgun under my left armpit. A quick bite at the cafeteria on the way here was in order as who knows how long whatever this is, could go on for.

Mr. Lark and Illych walk into view from between two of what pass for buildings in the Citadel. Mr. Lark is still wearing his grey suit but Illych is in standard black tactical dress. That's odd, if Illych is coming with us he would be dressed the same. But he isn't, meaning he would not be going with us. My reasoning sounds childish even to me but that is how things work.

Illych is always part of the group if anyone accompanies Mr. Lark.

That means it will just be me and Karl Lark alone together.

I must have had a deer in the head lights look on my face causing Illych to comment as they approach. "Relax Thomas, there are other things planned for you in the future. I am sure you will be coming back. Well, at least I am reasonably sure you will be." Then he smiles.

The gates open and Mr. Lark starts out. This is my cue and I fall in next to him. The pace is quick and Mr. Lark says nothing the entire way to the Compass. We are two quiet grey ghosts passing through the cold and gloom. After recent events I am not in a talking mood so I pass on the opportunity to quiz my employer.

We translate from the Compass to a luxury hotel room suite. Mr. Lark takes a seat in a comfortable chair. I do the same and we wait in silence. It is very difficult but my employer is obviously thinking and does not wish to be disturbed.

Zoning out into my own thoughts I regularly consult the giant watch on my left wrist to the point I had to consciously stop myself checking the time every few minutes.

Better than two hours pass in silence.

When Mr. Lark speaks it startles me, my head moving suddenly in surprise. "I have brought you for a reason. As you are aware the operation of the organization you are part of is funded by activities largely brought to my attention by some individuals whom, for a lack of a better description, I call the brokers."

"The brokers contacted me and I have been offered an unusual contract. The escaped children from the Bright Child Genetic Initiative would like to talk and are willing to pay for the privilege. "

"This is an unusual contract. Usually we just move something or interrogate something or kill something. This contract purchases the client up to two hours of continuous, uninterrupted time to talk to me. I am not required to answer questions and the contract explicitly states I can sit silently for the entire meeting. It also explicitly requires I listen the whole time. The reason for your accompanying me on this contract is my understanding of human emotion and conversational subtlety is lacking. While the children we are meeting with may be similarly impaired, I need someone to watch the discussion and intervene if I am failing to understand context."

Mr. Lark looks directly at me, "Do you understand your role."

I nod, "Yes, I understand." This is serious and I must behave accordingly.

Mr. Lark stands, "It is time."

We leave the hotel room. I do not know for sure where we are from a geography standpoint, other than being in Europe. This is determined from the electrical outlets on the walls. Every window we encounter in our short walk is covered.

Our path leads to an underground garage. Waiting for us is a Mercedes limousine. The door to the backseats is open and the car running. No other person is in sight. Without a word Mr. Lark enters the vehicle and I follow, closing the door. The windows are tinted completely black and there is a divider between us and the driver, preventing us from seeing the driver and anything outside the vehicle.

Mr. Lark is never one much for emotions and he is difficult to read most of the time. But now the man's face is an expressionless rock. I do my best to follow his lead and keep quiet during the drive.

When we stop, my watch tells me some twenty minutes of driving passed. The vehicles door opens and we exit out into a small windowless garage. Now I see our driver. A big barrel chested man in a suit, drivers cap, and wearing sunglasses stands holding the car doors handle.

Following my employer through a large, ornate wooden door we walk down a short hall to a room with a conference table and chairs in one half and a circle of comfortable chairs and a sofa in the other.

After we enter, the doors close behind us, leaving the two of us standing alone.

Or so I thought.

Two figures of similar height, lean and well dressed, are standing side by side within the circle of comfortable chairs. They are male and female, teenagers at that awkward age when girls reach their almost full adult height and have developed and boys have yet to sprout up.

At least a minute passes with the four of us staring at each other. Then the girl speaks, "Thank you Mr. Lark for meeting with us."

"My actions are purely mercenary. A contract was offered and I have accepted. No thanks necessary. Before the discussions advance further introductions must occur."

"A mistake on our part," The boy says. "My companion is Yael and I am Heiko."

Mr. Lark waves to me, "This is my employee Thomas and you already know my name."

He continues, "Before I begin I will clarify our contract. In exchange for the agreed upon financial consideration this discussion will last for 2 hours. That is 120 minutes. At minute 119 I will stand and begin leaving. When the time is up I leave through the door I entered."

At this point, after listening to him talk to these children I was wondering if there was a point to him sounding like such a jerk. They are kids for crying out loud.

Heiko nods, "Yes Mr. Lark, the terms of the contract are clear."

My employer walks into the circle of chairs and takes a seat facing the pair of children. I soon follow and the children sit opposite us.

Heiko begins, "We funded this meeting to discuss your actions while working for the Bright Child Genetic Initiative. You tracked our escape to the pond and collected a significant bounty for that achievement. How did you do this?"

Mr. Lark remains expressionless and says nothing.

Heiko observes Mr. Lark's lack of response for a moment and speaks again, "Yes, I have recently learned this expression. A magician never explains his magic."

The boy continues, "You tracked a splinter group of the survivors to Miami. My sources have told me you had already concluded the contract with the Bright Child Genetic Initiative before then. Why did you continue the search?"

It occurs to me this kid is the one who ordered me beaten to a pulp while Illych and I were being questioned. My guess is beating the crap out of Heiko is somehow forbidden by the same contract that brought us here. I would not really beat a teenage boy to a pulp, but the rubber hose treatment back in Miami made me consider it for a moment.

Mr. Lark again sits there unresponsive. I have had enough of this and speak up. "This is not working. He is not going to tell you anything. My guess is if you offer information in return you might get what you are looking for." I turn to see Mr. Lark looking at me with a raised left eyebrow.

Heiko nods, "This is acceptable. An exchange of value Mr. Lark?"

Karl Lark nods in acceptance.

"What can we tell you Mr. Lark?"

"What is the Bright Child Genetic Initiative?"

"About 25 years ago a group of wealthy individuals came to the conclusion that a specially trained group of highly intelligent people could accelerate technological discoveries. If the cabal could engineer such an accomplishment they could gain a tremendous amount of wealth and power from this advantage."

"They scoured the globe sourcing reproductive materials from the best and brightest. In vitro fertilization based on careful selection and matching, combined with cutting edge genetic engineering to enhance the desired traits."

"The result is us." Heiko stops here and waits.

Mr. Lark replies, "During the tour of the research facility I was able to determine the staff had been murdered, most likely by the children themselves. In the laboratories we briefly toured I observed the high energy physics experiments. Then I understood the vehicle used to escape and the danger of such methods. Such a device leaves background signatures that are detectable for some time. When I found the signature it led to the pool you arrived at. Now continue about the Initiative"

"The embryos were implanted over four years at 250 per year. The 250 surrogate mothers were well cared for and closely monitored. The oldest of us are sixteen and each cohort is one year apart. Each year saw 125 males and 125 females implanted."

Mr. Lark interjects at this point, "Why females? The intelligence distribution reaches much higher in males."

"Yes, but a large of group of males with no females present would be extremely violent and difficult to manage. Research has demonstrated this. A compromise was made to make the genders equal in order to help keep the group more manageable."

"The genetic engineering used was not proven science and the miscarriage rate was much higher than expected. As each child was born it was inspected. Any physical deformity saw them excluded from the program."

'Excluded from the program', I knew what that meant. Just another nice way to say they were most likely killed. Whoever this cabal is, they are awful people.

"The result was approximately seven hundred healthy boys and girls with the ratio skewed slightly in the girls favor. Then the education regime followed by testing began. In simple terms the low end cutoff was an IQ of 145. If you tested below that you were retested the next day. A second failure saw your removal from the program."

Mr. Lark takes his cue to continue, "Upon finding the corpses of your fellow test subjects I had technically completed the contract. The number of corpses present guaranteed a significant bounty. Although I suspected some of you had survived, the numbers were small compared to the level of effort that would probably be needed to hunt down the stragglers. I chose to omit that survivors were possible and bring the contract to a close."

That made no sense. He stopped the search because it was not worth it to hunt down the stragglers. But then he continued the search again anyway?

I had to ask, "You stopped the contract search because continuing would not be worth it. But then you continue the search? Why?

Mr. Lark replies, "The financial incentive was insufficient in the first case. In the second case my curiosity was sufficient."

"Does that answer your question?"

This time Yael answers, "Yes."

Her voice was higher pitched but soft and pleasant to listen to. "Will you continue to pursue us?"

Another question for Mr. Lark, more is needed from the children before he will speak again. Taking the initiative I speak again, "Please continue about the experiment so he can answer."

Yael continues where Heiko had left off. "By the time the fourth cohort was born the first cohort's children were three years old. New challenges manifested. The children could all read and write by two years of age and curiosity had been one of the selection drivers for the genetic contributors. The result was hundreds of high energy genius children tearing the place apart."

Mr. Lark chuckled, "They did not expect this?"

Mr. Lark had just expressed humor. That is weird.

"No they did not. This was coupled with other side effects of the genetic engineering produced unexpected challenges. Highly intelligence often correlates with low empathy and the selection and engineering process had actively sacrificed this characteristic in the pursuit of maximum achievement in the desired areas. This resulted in a crisis. The level of psychopathy was well beyond human norm. The children began experimenting on each other and the staff. Some became straightforward serial killers."

"The Initiative was forced to test the children for psychopathic characteristics and remove those who failed the test from the program. This testing was applied continuously from age one onwards. When the first cohort reached eight years the original seven hundred accepted live births had reduced our numbers to less than three-hundred and fifty.

"The testing had ended the crisis but it was still a dangerous place and the children and staff knew this."

"Your turn Mr. Lark."

"You can expect no pursuit or action that would be construed as negative or malevolent from me or my organization. I will however be checking on you from time to time. Make of it what you will."

He continues, "I request you continue. Consider this to be a question in the bank so to speak."

Yael continued, "Very well Mr. Lark."

"Heiko and I are first cohort. Unbeknownst to the staff we had developed a soundless language that allowed us to communicate without anyone else knowing. Over the next seven years we learned what we could. The Initiative began having us work on projects. In the beginning it was simple stuff, more a learning opportunity than making a contribution to science."

"Then they pushed us into high energy physics. We began cutting edge research and had a number of successes. Our pace was slower than they expected and the encouragement turned to pushing which in turn became threats. They people running the Initiative had not produced the results as quickly as the cabal wanted."

"We played into this and announced a discovery in fusion and materials manufacture. The prototype worked well. The whole thing was a ruse however. We had found a way to escape. The first part of the plan was to get five of us out a year ahead of time to help prepare for the rest of us. An industrial accident covered their escape. Only Heiko survived the first escape attempt."

"A year later, at the proscribed moment, we killed every staff member within a two minute window and affected our escape. We knew the survival rate would be low but we wanted out and we accepted the risk. The fatality level was higher than expected but for those of who live, it was worth it."

I looked over at Mr. Lark. He is smiling. Not the big Cheshire cat grin, just a simple upturn of the mouth. I am unsure but I think the story made him happy.

He stands and began walking for the door. Realizing our time must be up I follow.

As we pass through the doors I look at my watch.

The two hours had ended fifteen minutes ago.

Chapter 24

Dr. Chatzas looked at the clock on her desk. Mid-afternoon and she has been waiting all day for this moment. Mr. Lark gave specific instructions on how and when to contact him. A phone call at a particular time and no details, just a mundane statement, "I would like the lilies, not the daisies." What a strange little man. Did he create that message just because she is a woman?

Contacting him is not optional, especially not when considering what she had found. The statue is in perfect condition and something Mr. Lark would be interested in. Not contacting him first would leave her vulnerable. The techs confirmed it is original and could not have been sculpted by hand. The report they generated states it was manufactured using some form of advanced 3D printing. Having gone to look at it firsthand, she immediately understood its unique nature. Appearing as the bust of a woman wearing an impossibly elaborate head dress, its value not obvious to the casual observer.

Discovered during the ongoing investigations in the labyrinth of tunnels and storage rooms beneath the British Museum, it had been carefully packed and packaged in materials dating to late 17th century or early 18th. Just another treasure scooped up by the ever expanding British Empire and carefully stored away.

A similar bust is on display in Spain in Madrid, The Lady of Elche. In relatively poor condition compared to the one currently held in the high security vault beneath her feet. This bust is just as complex and x-ray reveals it to be hollow also, with something technical in appearance contained within. Of course, this find will never be put on display nor featured in any archaeological discussion.

During his last visit to the British Museum Mr. Lark had not been a tourist. He had come as a thief. In addition to violating the high security vaults integrity and making a mockery of its unique form of protection, he had left with my unconscious body draped over one of his goons. Not only did he steal from the national treasure that is the British museum, Mr. Lark left with the prize he sought. For extra insult, he kidnapped and interrogated Dr. Chatzas.

She still has a hard time with elevator doors opening. Sometimes breaking out in a cold sweat and shakes upon hearing the elevator bells unique sound.

None of it mattered in the end. Lord Halluk paid her the honor of visiting her home. She had honestly and completely explained her experience with Mr. Lark and his thugs. Somehow that opportunist Thomas Davies is part of what they are doing.

The ancient Djinn explained such things happen and confidence in her service is still intact. What is to be done now is this Karl Lark must be convinced of the error of his actions. This will take time, but Dr. Elisabeth Chatzas, will play a key role.

Dr. Chatzas does just as Mr. Lark instructed. After the old man is notified she is to leave a message for Lord Halluk. The plan is for her to assist Mr. Lark, should he request it, and not concern herself with the Djinn's counter efforts.

After leaving that ridiculous message as required, she waits a few minutes and then calls a lawyer contact. The lawyer will relay the message to the Lord Halluk. Everything is set in motion.

Games within games, plans within plans, it is the way of the immortals.

www.ingramcontent.com/pod-product-compliance
Lightning Source LLC
Chambersburg PA
CBHW052025240626
47153CB00006B/1952